RECIPE FOR LOVE

Emma had not had a man in her life in so long that she had almost forgotten the pleasure of surrendering herself to one. She slowly began to relax and fuse her body to his. The beating of their two hearts thundered in her ears.

Looking deeply into her eyes, Jordan whispered, "I've been attracted to you since the first day I met you. I think I've been in love with you since the Las Vegas trip. I know that tonight I felt myself being drawn to you in a way that I did not know was possible. I love you, Emma, and I want you in my life forever."

Emma tried to express her feelings about him and the evening. "Jordan, I'm a very deliberate person. I enjoy your company, your smile, and your energy, but I have to take it slowly."

"I won't rush you," Jordan replied as he pulled her closer and nuzzled her neck. "I'll simply use all of my powers of persuasion to convince you that you should think the same way that I do. I'll convince you that marriage to me would be far more interesting than anything you've ever known. I want us to share a life with all of its strings and commitment."

BOOK YOUR PLACE ON OUR WEBSITE AND MAKE THE ARABESQUE ROMANCE CONNECTION!

We've created a customized website just for our very special Arabesque readers, where you can get the inside scoop on everything that's going on with Arabesque romance novels.

When you come online, you'll have the exciting opportunity to:

- View covers of upcoming books

- Learn about our future publishing schedule (listed by publication month and author)

- Find out when your favorite authors will be visiting a city near you

- Search for and order backlist books

- Check out author bios and background information

- Send e-mail to your favorite authors

- Join us in weekly chats with authors, readers and other guests

- Get writing guidelines

- AND MUCH MORE!

Visit our website at
http://www.arabesquebooks.com

RECIPE FOR LOVE

Courtni Wright

ARABESQUE
BET
BOOKS

BET Publications, LLC
www.bet.com
www.arabesquebooks.com

ARABESQUE BOOKS are published by

BET Publications, LLC
c/o BET BOOKS
One BET Plaza
1900 W Place NE
Washington, D.C. 20018-1211

All Kensington Titles, Imprints, and Distributed Lines are available at special quantity discounts for bulk purchases for sales promotions, premiums, fund-raising, and educational or institutional use. Special book excerpts or customized printings can also be created to fit specific needs. For details, write or phone the office of the Kensington special sales manager: Kensington Publishing Corp., 850 Third Avenue, New York, NY 10022, attn: Special Sales Department, Phone: 1-800-221-2647.

BET Books is a trademark of Black Entertainment Television, Inc. ARABESQUE, the ARABESQUE logo, and the BET BOOKS logo are trademarks and registered trademarks.

First Printing: July 2001
10 9 8 7 6 5 4 3 2 1

Printed in the United States of America

One

The summer sun streamed through the stained-glass windows and cast gold, blue, red, and orange ribbons across the glistening dark oak floor. Paintings of cottages in New England, covered bridges in Pennsylvania, the snow-covered mountains of West Virginia, and the St. Michael's on the Chesapeake Bay in Maryland peppered the deep rose-colored walls. Family photographs of happy people gathered for a graduation, a wedding, and a grand opening added a personal touch to the professional atmosphere of the office. Certificates from the Cordon Bleu mingled with framed letters of appreciation from satisfied customers.

Golden binders filled with menus from celebrations ranging from simple barbecues to elaborate dinner parties lined the top of the cherry credenza. Each entrée, salad, beverage, or dessert received personal attention from highly skilled chefs who labored to produce gastronomical perfection. Nothing was too good for the clients of EJ's.

Fresh flowers in shades of mauve, rust, and rose punctuated with blue and white filled sparkling crystal vases atop every table. The blue-and-white-striped awning over the front door bore the initials of the establishment's owner in gold letters. Everyone in the

Washington, D.C., metropolitan area knew that at EJ's only the best ingredients served with loving care combined to create delights for the palate. No one ever walked away unsatisfied from an affair catered by EJ's.

Emma Jones sat behind an oversize cherry desk, her fingers playing in her deep brown, short-cropped hair. Her dark brown eyes twinkled with barely contained laughter as she listened to her friend Bonnie Booker describe the newest member of the law firm where her husband was a partner. From the animated way in which she spoke, to the agitation of her long, expressive hands, and the emphatic widening of her carefully made-up eyes, a casual observer would have thought that Bonnie had fallen in love despite her being happily married for ten years, but Emma knew differently. Bonnie was engaged in one of her favorite activities—matchmaking.

"He's just to die for, Emma. George is tall, handsome, and forty-five. He works out and has a great build. His gray eyes have those sexy heavy lids, and his lips are just perfect for kissing. He's a great conversationalist, plays tennis and golf, and has an MBA in international commerce as well as his JD. He's just wonderful. I can't think of anything missing from his profile. Oh, and he's divorced without children, so there are no strings attached to him," Bonnie gushed as she alternately paced the office and perched on the edge of her chair. She had burst in unannounced as she often did when she had business of a romantic nature to discuss.

"He sounds perfect. I'm sure you won't have any trouble finding someone to escort him around town," Emma replied as she glanced at her appointment calendar. She only had a few minutes in which to hurry her best friend from her office before her new client arrived.

"That's what I've been trying to tell you. When can I arrange the meeting between you two? Are you free this Saturday? I could arrange a little informal cook-out to welcome George to town, and you could just happen to be there," Bonnie suggested as she studied her friend's face for the rejection she instinctively knew she would receive.

"I'd love to meet him but not now. This is a very busy time for me, and I just can't get involved right now. I hardly have time for myself. I haven't been able to schedule a manicure in weeks. I certainly don't need the weight of showing someone around town," Emma replied as she cast a long look at her watch and lightly tapped the crystal with her nail.

Frustrated, Bonnie stated, "You never have time, and it's always your busy season. If it isn't wedding season, it's the holidays. Then there are the birthday bashes for this town's celebrities and the never-ending political receptions and galas. During the reelection cycle, I hardly ever see you. I should just give up on you. This guy is perfect for you in every way, and you won't even meet him."

"You know that I don't like blind dates or setups. They never work out. Besides, I don't want any attorneys in my life ever again. Your husband, Steve, is the only nice one I've ever known. Anyway, do you remember the author you introduced me to last year? What was his name . . . Philip Laser? He said that he wanted to research the catering business for a book he was writing. The man had more hands than an octopus has tentacles. Every time I turned around, he was grabbing me. The only thing he wanted to study was my body. No, thank you. I don't have time for that. I love you, and you're my best friend, but I'm through with your matchmaking," Emma responded with a negative shake of her head.

With a huff Bonnie conceded, "Philip did come on a little strong, but George is different. He's more laid-back and conservative. You'd like him."

"That's what you said about John Bailey, Peter Francis, Anthony Pastors . . ." Emma interjected quickly before Bonnie could launch another assault.

"All right, I get the point," Bonnie said with irritation, and picked up her purse. "You don't have to beat this dead horse. I'm only trying to keep you from spending the rest of your life without love and companionship. But if you'd rather go it alone, who am I to stop you?"

Rising, Emma escorted her friend to the door and said, "You know I appreciate all you try to do for me. I'm just not interested in having a man in my life right now. I'm completely content to devote myself to my business. I'm happier now than I've ever been. I'll let you know when I want companionship. In the meantime, I enjoy spending my free time with you and your family and our other friends."

"By the time you finally realize how miserably unhappy you are, you'll be so old that I won't be able to find anyone for you. I'll have to look for a man who puts his teeth to soak in a glass overnight, too. I give up for now. I'll bring over those linen samples later today. I'm on your calendar for three o'clock." Bonnie sulked as she waved good-bye and exited through the customer-filled anteroom.

As the supplier of the linens, silver, crystal, and china for EJ's, Bonnie had to admit that Emma's business was indeed thriving. The five consultants on the payroll stayed busy coordinating wedding receptions, bar and bat mitzvahs, and all kinds of parties, which left Emma free to attend conferences, supervise the chefs, study new techniques of management and cooking, and market her catering business to large corporate and political accounts.

Closing the door with a merry chuckle, Emma returned to her desk. In the five free minutes before her next client, she reflected on the life she had built since her divorce four years ago. Emma had completely immersed herself in her catering business and given herself little time to think about feeling lonely or bitter. She seldom spoke of her ex-husband, who'd left her for the arms of another woman, and she considered his departure a blessing now that she was a successful businesswoman rather than the ornament on his arm that he had required, the shadow he had wanted her to be. When Emma thought about him at all, it was with a sweet sadness that he was not around to see the person she had become. She stood tall on her own now and never looked back at the old days when he expected her to be the complement for a powerful attorney rather than her own person.

Her business, financed by the hefty divorce settlement, had quickly become one of the most highly respected catering operations in town. Her town house, situated in the historic section of Alexandria, Virginia, was often featured in architectural magazines, and her red convertible BMW was the current model. Her closets contained the latest fashions. Her tennis and golf games were the envy of all her friends and impressed many clients. As she rushed from one business or social engagement to the other, Emma was confident that the divorce was the best thing that could have happened to her. She did not need a man to complement her and make her feel complete. The happiest day of her life had been when she'd reclaimed her maiden name and tossed her wedding band into the toilet. Knowing it vanished into the Po-

tomac River had filled her with a profound and almost unspeakable joy. Now she had herself, her
friends, her work, and her very happy life.

"Ms. Jones, Mr. and Mrs. Russell have arrived for
their ten o'clock appointment," announced the voice
of her secretary, Pasha Hughes.

"Thanks, Pasha. Show them in," Emma replied as
she straightened the already neat desk and advanced
toward the door.

As was her habit, she greeted all of her guests as
they entered her office in the hopes of making them
feel welcome and comfortable. Her secretary had
standing orders to hold all of her calls. From the
moment the Russells entered, until the time they'd
leave, they would receive Emma's undivided attention.

Claudia and Frank Russell were one of the most
prominent African-American couples in town. Everyone vied for invitations to their parties because only
the smartest, most successful people attended their
soirees. Emma knew that she would be the envy of
all the caterers for having arranged the christening
of their firstborn son.

Emma watched as Claudia Russell eased into her seat
and folded her long, slim legs primly at the ankles
around which sparkled matching delicate diamond-
studded bracelets. On her feet, Claudia wore incredibly
soft calfskin leather shoes in the richest mahogany that
matched the color of her silk suit to perfection. Her
carefully laced, delicate fingers looked burdened by the
weight of the enormous round-cut diamond surrounded by equally impressive baguettes that radiated
vibrant colors. Considering that their child was only two
months old, Claudia had quickly regained her figure
and was the envy of every new mother.

Claudia Russell appeared unaware of the impres-

sion she made as she waited patiently for her husband
to join her on the sofa. Her eyes glistened with love
and the effects of undisturbed sleep. Emma had
heard that the Russells employed a full-time nanny.
Otherwise, Claudia would have looked as exhausted
as all the other new mothers who employed her to
cater their baby's christenings.

Studying Frank Russell as he lowered himself onto
the sofa, Emma saw that he was as elegantly and simply dressed as his wife. Emma could tell that one of
the most famous menswear designers had constructed
Frank's suit of the softest black wool and silk blend.
The fabric clung to his muscular body without being
either too tight or too loose. The tailor's efforts had
been impeccable, as was the shine on his loafers and
his freshly manicured nails. Her own home-manicured
nails looked dreadful by comparison.

Taking her seat opposite them, Emma could understand the envy that would soon fill the hearts of her
competitors. The Russells were definitely people with
money to spare. They would want only the best and
the most elaborate for Frank, Jr., who as yet was unaware of the silver spoon that would feed him his
morning cereal. Emma could hear the happy clinking
of coins as she pulled her chair closer.

Resting the pad of paper in its gold leather case
delicately on her knees and uncapping her pen,
Emma leaned forward and said, "I hope you've had
time to review my sketches for floral arrangements
and the menu I've suggested. I think you'll find that
for an evening affair of this nature, quail eggs in
aspic with caviar, spring pea soup, lobster thermidor
with duchess potatoes, tournedos of beef with mo-
rels, asparagus hollandaise, quails with cherries, and
fresh fruit salad will please even the most discerning
among your guests."

The Russells inclined their heads in unison as
Emma passed the menu to them for the required initials. As they made their marks, she stepped toward
her desk and buzzed one of her consultants. When
the door silently opened, Emma made the introductions and watched as Judy Remington escorted Mr.
and Mrs. Russell to her office at the end of the hall.
Judy would spend the next couple of hours putting
the finishing touches on Emma's creative genius.

The rest of Emma's day passed quickly with the
Abram bat mitzvah plans moving along smoothly.
They had wanted a simple affair and had invited only
two hundred of their closest friends. The Abrams had
favored a menu filled with dishes reminiscent of the
old days when people had time to linger over a meal
and relish its flavors. After consulting many reference
books, Emma had created a meal that would have
made Moroccan kings salivate.

Having introduced both families to the consultants
who would coordinate the reception with the church
and synagogue, arrange for the delivery of the flowers, and supervise the chefs and wait staff, Emma was
free to spend her time planning ways to expand her
already successful business. After the initial meeting
with each family during which she helped them select
the menu that best fit their budgets, Emma gave the
final preparation responsibilities to her wonderfully
talented staff. She would see her clients again when
it was time for her to make a personal appearance at
their affair. She trusted her staff completely and allowed them the creative freedom they required.
Emma's respect for their abilities had earned her the
reputation of being a fair employer and a highly com-
petent businesswoman.

In much the same way, Emma had forged her relationship with Bonnie. When Emma first opened her

catering company, she wanted to use as many African-American businesses as possible as her suppliers. Bonnie Booker, the owner of a highly successful linen supply company, responded to Emma's call for support with elegant damask tablecloths and matching napkins in a myriad of colors and patterns, including many that were Afrocentric in design. In addition, Bonnie had provided Emma with crystal, china, and flatware for all occasions. The professional union was exactly what Emma had hoped to find, and so was the friendship that grew between the two business-women. From their first meeting, Emma and Bonnie were inseparable.

However, as is the nature of all friendships, there were tensions. In the case of Emma and Bonnie, the topic of matchmaking caused the most friction since they never argued about work. Each gave the other professional distance and respected the other's expertise. Unfortunately, Bonnie could not take the same approach to her desire to manage Emma's social life. Even now, several years into their association, that topic of dating and finding a match for Emma could cause an immediate but easily repaired rift between them.

That afternoon, during Bonnie's three o'clock appointment, they discussed linen and crystal orders for the summer months as Emma poured Bonnie a glass of mint tea. Behind Bonnie's professional demeanor, Emma could almost hear Bonnie plotting her next move. Emma knew that her friend would not stop her scheming regardless of how much she objected to the usually misdirected efforts.

"You'll never guess who I ran into today," Bonnie chirped as she sipped her tea and munched a simple late snack of a roast turkey sandwich with endive, sprouts, and light mayonnaise from EJ's carryout.

"Who?" Emma asked skeptically although she knew that Bonnie would tell her without any encouragement.

"I just happened to drop by my husband's office today after I finished my calls this morning. I was very put out by your lack of appreciation for my efforts, I want you to know, and wanted to tell Steve that you were not interested in meeting the new partner." Bonnie pouted in her good-natured way. "Anyway, he took me to lunch at the new rib place around the corner. I've been wanting to meet the owner for quite some time and, since we arrived before the noon crunch, I found her at the front desk. I might not be able to sell you on meeting men, but I do a wonderful job of marketing my company. She signed a contract on the spot. It turns out that she wasn't satisfied with the quality of the service she's been getting with her supplier and was looking for someone to provide the linens for her business.

"To make a long story short, while I was eating the most wonderful shrimp gumbo, an old college friend walked into the restaurant. I hadn't seen him since I was a freshman representative to the honor board, and he was the captain of the football team. He was every woman's ideal catch while he was in medical school."

Interrupting, Emma demanded, "Why are you telling me all this? It sounds like you're leading up to another matchmaking attempt. You know I'm not at all interested."

Shrugging her shoulders and sighing deeply, Bonnie replied, "I'm only telling you about my day. Give me a break. I heard you say that I'm to back off. I simply wanted to share my experience with you. You are my best friend, you know."

"I'm your prime target, you mean. All right, continue your story. Just remember when you come to the end of it, I don't want to hear that you've arranged a blind date of any kind," Emma remarked as she settled into the smooth leather of the sofa.

Bonnie continued with a roll of her eyes and said, "Well, Jordan Everett has certainly aged well. He has this wonderful streak of white cutting into his thick, black hair over his left eye. And, Emma, the gaze from his gray eyes is just as penetrating and direct as it was when he captained the football team. His tall, trim body still moves with the litheness of a tiger. The only difference is that his voice has deepened and mellowed with the years like the finest of wine. He's a hunk! I could see Steve trying to suck in that little gut of his at the sight of Jordan's muscular body. I won't have any trouble getting Steve to work out after this."

Laughing at the vision of Bonnie's comfortably chubby husband trying to look thin, Emma said, "You shouldn't pick on Steve. He's a good husband and father. He can't help it if he's gained a few pounds in the ten years you two have been married."

With a wave of her hand Bonnie retorted, "I'm not picking on him. I'm simply relaying what I saw. I'm just surprised that Steve's eyeballs didn't go into orbit from the effort of pulling in his stomach, that's all. Anyway, Jordan has just moved from New York to Washington to work on a special task force at the invitation of the president of the United States, of all people. It seems that Jordan's some kind of big-shot specialist on the treatment of drug addiction, especially in teenagers. The president has asked Jordan and a group of other specialists and advertising bigwigs to design television campaigns targeted at young people. The president hopes to start educating teenagers on the dangers of mixing alcohol with drugs and automobiles, pretty much the same way as the ads against doing drugs. Anyway, he appointed Jordan to be his special assistant on this matter."

"He sounds as if he'll have his hands busy. What happened to his practice?" Emma asked as she carefully studied her friend's face. She had a gut feeling that there was more to this story of rekindled friendships than met the eye.

"Jordan said something about his partners taking care of things in his absence," Bonnie replied offhandedly as she continued with her story. "Anyway, he asked me if I knew the name of a reliable caterer because he has to host his first quasisocial gathering next week. Of course, I gave him your name and your card. He lives in one of those fabulous apartments at the Watergate. You've catered functions there thousands of times. He promised to call you today. I know it's short notice, but I hope you can fit him into your schedule. Think of the contacts you'd make from this job. See, I'm always thinking of you, and I didn't mention a blind date even once."

"Well, I must say that I'm relieved. Thanks for sending a little business my way and for not arranging anything personal," Emma responded with a wary smile. She still expected the other shoe to fall despite Bonnie's denial of any romantic dealings. She could feel something lurking over the horizon.

Rising to leave, Bonnie said, "If you two should happen to hit it off, I won't be in the least surprised."

"Now, Bonnie, you promised!" Emma scolded as she shook her head.

"I'm not going to interfere. I'll just watch while the fireworks go off as I know they will," Bonnie retorted with her hand on the doorknob.

Before Emma could say another word, her secretary's voice interrupted over the intercom, "You have a call on line one. It's a Dr. Everett. He says that Bonnie referred him to you."

"Thanks, Pasha, I'll take it," Emma replied as she slid behind her desk and opened the binder in which she always took copious notes as she consulted with her clients. She waved good-bye to Bonnie and lifted her brows in a repeated warning.

Bonnie took that opportunity to slip out the door. She wore a large smile on her face as she left. Already she could hear the birds singing sweet love songs for her friend and Jordan Everett.

Two

Jordan Everett's little gathering turned out to be one of the most discussed social events of the summer. His guest list came directly from the blue book of Washington society and the White House social register. As a member of a presidential committee, he invited everyone with whom he worked, from whom he wished to gain favor, and to whom their work was indebted for success. Hollywood was well represented, also, because the stars were big supporters of the campaign against drinking and driving. Many of them had volunteered their services for commercials that were already airing to favorable reception on television, and many more had sent word through their agents that they would like to join the effort. Their presence almost dwarfed Jordan's large Watergate condo as they swept through the door in their tuxedos, gowns, and diamonds.

The dining room opened onto the expansive balcony, creating the perfect large space for entertaining on a summer evening while providing the feeling of intimacy. Emma had arranged for a local florist to deliver potted ferns that she had lit from underneath to create appealing shadows. To add to the feeling of a lush garden, she had ordered flowers of every de-

scription and color and a lit fountain gurgling and
flowing happily over a mound of rocks.

Emma had replaced the mahogany table, which
only sat twelve, to make way for the round tables provided by Bonnie's company. Emma's staff had covered
each one of them, as well as the chairs, in the best
mauve damask cloths in subdued Afrocentric patterns
Bonnie could provide. Glistening ornate china, crystal, and silverware, also from BB Inc., sparkled in the
light of the freshly cleaned chandelier. Multiple floral
arrangements in individual little baskets clustered in
the center of each table were available for the guests
to take home as a memento when the evening ended.

Emma arrived after the guests had been seated and
the first course served by her staff, dressed in mauve
jackets and black trousers for the occasion. She
slipped silently into the kitchen to check on the food
preparation, knowing that her attention was not really
needed. The chef, wait staff, and bartenders were the
best in Washington. Emma would not have hired
them if their credentials had not been of the highest
caliber.

"Any difficulties this evening, Albert?" Emma asked
as she accepted a taste of the pâté de foie gras on
which the guests were currently munching and eyed
the chateaubriand that would be the entrée. The succulent aromas swirled around her head as she stood
in the center of yet another kitchen that evening. She
was so busy these days that it was only the change in
menus that told her where she was at any given time.

Barely stopping his work, Albert replied as the perspiration glistened on his ebony forehead, "No,
Emma, everything's going just great. This kitchen is
a dream to work in, unlike some of our other jobs.
It has plenty of counter space, the newest appliances,
and every gadget my greedy little heart could want.

That butler pantry is a helpful addition, too. We won't have to fight for space while clearing the table between courses. This should be one of our easiest jobs. We'll make EJ's look really good. You should get a lot of referrals from this gig."

"The guest list is certainly high profile," Emma agreed as she read through it one more time. "I don't think I've ever seen so many celebrities in one room except for a fancy charity gala. Dr. Everett certainly runs with an impressive crowd. It would be lovely if some of his business came our way."

Albert only nodded absently; he was too occupied with creating roses from radishes and lemons to carry on further conversation. The time for conversation would have to wait until they could sit down and share a postmortem of the evening.

Emma stood to the side as her army of waiters and waitresses hurried into the kitchen carrying empty plates. They smiled and nodded as they picked up the heavy trays laden with the next course. From the dining room, Emma could hear the contented murmur of animated dinner conversation and the subdued sounds of a string quartet. The musical accompaniment was one of Emma's trademarks. Regardless of the affair, she always interested the client in a little light music to create the atmosphere.

Seeing that her assistance was not needed, Emma turned to Albert and said, "I'm going to the Epps' party. I'll return shortly. I'm only in the way here. If you need me, you have my pager number."

"See you later," Albert replied as he uncorked the muscat to accompany the apple crepes glazed in Calvados for dessert. He hardly noticed as Emma slipped through the back door of the condo.

All of the guests had left by the time Emma returned a few hours later with Bonnie at her side. Albert and the staff of EJ's had just put the finishing touches on their clean-up efforts to return the kitchen and dining room to normal. As Emma looked around the condo she could see nothing that would indicate that a very important dinner party had occurred here only a short while ago. Not even a napkin lay forgotten on the coffee table. The only remnants of the evening—plastic crates bearing her EJ's monogram and overflowing with cooking utensils—stood in the hall waiting to be loaded onto the trucks at the service entrance. Beside them rested laundry hampers containing soiled table linens and crates of china and crystal bearing the BB Inc. name.

Jordan Everett greeted Emma with a big smile and a hearty handshake as she entered. In a white dinner jacket, he was even more handsome than he had been the first time Emma met him in her office. His professionalism had been striking then; whereas his broad shoulders and deep, resonant voice almost took her breath away now. Yet, beyond the handsome, sophisticated, professional physician demeanor, Jordan exuded a truly interesting personality. He was a man who enjoyed being with people.

"My first dinner party in Washington was a great success thanks to your chef's magic in the kitchen and your staff's very professional attention to my guests. I couldn't have pulled off this evening without you," Jordan remarked as he handed Emma a sealed envelope bearing the check for the evening's services.

"You could have managed without me but not as well. I'm happy that you found my company's service to your liking, Dr. Everett," Emma replied with a chuckle and humble inclination of her head.

"The name's Jordan, and if you're free on Wednesday, I'd like to take you to lunch to show my appreciation," Jordan suggested as he studied Emma's face in the low light of the living room. He had been quite taken by her gentle beauty when he had first met her, but now, in the glow of the evening, Jordan had difficulty pulling his eyes from her face.

Smiling graciously as she moved toward the door, Emma replied, "Thank you, Dr. Everett, but I'm leaving for a conference on an early flight on Monday. Besides, I have a policy of never allowing my business and personal lives to intermingle."

Entering the foyer from the kitchen at that moment, Bonnie interjected helpfully, "You could fly out a day late. You know that those conferences are all alike. Most of the first day is spent registering and attending silly dinner parties anyway."

Shooting her friend a look that could kill, Emma turned to Jordan and said with a smile, "Unfortunately, that's not a possibility this year. You see, I'm hosting one of those 'silly' dinner parties myself on the first night. Thank you for the opportunity to cater your party this evening and for the invitation to lunch."

Stepping aside for Emma's men to carry out the last of the crates, Jordan replied, "There will be other opportunities for us to become better acquainted. We'll meet under purely social circumstances soon, I'm sure."

"Perhaps, but I'm usually so busy with my work that I have little free time. Thank you again for making EJ's your caterer of choice," Emma responded gently but firmly as she guided Bonnie from the room. She tactfully ignored the confident smile on Jordan's handsome face and the glowering expression on Bonnie's irritated one.

"What's wrong with you?" Bonnie snarled as soon as they stepped into the empty elevator. "You could have offered him another day since you'll be out of town this week. You didn't have to turn him down like that. Jordan Everett is a very eligible bachelor. You'd better act fast before someone else snaps him up."

"You know I'm not in the least bit interested in a romance. I'm perfectly happy with my life as it is. I don't want any entanglement. I hope you didn't tell him that I was available," Emma replied as she studied Bonnie's face for signs of meddling.

"No, I didn't suggest anything. I simply answered his question when he asked me if you were unattached," Bonnie confessed guiltily.

"When did Dr. Everett see us together before our first meeting about tonight's dinner? You told me that he was an old college friend that you ran into. What's up? Did you stage this meeting to trap a man for me?" Emma demanded as she began to smell the stench of her friend's scheming.

"Jordan is an old friend, and I did meet him accidentally," Bonnie said with a huff. "However, I did leave out one small detail. Between the time I saw him again and I introduced you to him, he saw us eating lunch at Classic's. I tried to make the introductions then, but you refused to cooperate if I remember correctly. A few days later, I ran into him again downtown. We were standing on the same street corner, so naturally we chatted while waiting for the light to change. He asked me about you then. It seems to me that I told him all your vitals including the part about your business. That's when he said he'd like to meet you on a purely social occasion. I suggested that he use the party tonight as a way of making the connection. I didn't know about this new policy of yours. I didn't suggest anything. This meeting was all his idea. You can't accuse me of matchmaking this time. Anyway, that's how it happened. You can be mad at me if you want, but I meant well."

Trying not to be irritated with her best friend, Emma replied, "I appreciate the business referral, but I certainly wish you would stay out of my personal life. I'm very capable of meeting men without your help."

As the elevator door opened, Bonnie retorted, "Maybe you are, but you never do. You'd sit alone in that house of yours every evening if I didn't arrange for you to meet people. You'd turn into a hermit if I didn't force you to come out."

"What's wrong with being alone? I'm with people all day and most evenings. I don't see why you won't allow me to have a few minutes by myself," Emma rejoined, refusing to allow Bonnie to boss her around.

"There's nothing wrong with being alone as long as you're not in hiding, which is exactly what I think you're doing," Bonnie said. "You're afraid to let yourself care about anyone after that dreadful marriage of yours. You've convinced yourself that you don't need the responsibility and closeness that comes with a relationship. You're just scared, that's all. You think that all men are as creepy as your ex-husband. Besides, Emma, you always have a good time with the men to whom I introduce you."

"I'll admit that they are nice men—well educated, gainfully employed, extremely pleasant, good conversationalists, and capable dancers—but I'm not looking for a man. That's what you won't accept. I don't want to become involved with anyone. You know how nasty the last year of my marriage to Marvin was. The divorce looked like a party compared to that period of my life. Every day finding another clue of his infidelity until I finally caught him in bed with not his secretary but mine. I don't ever want to go through that again. It's hard enough divorcing a worthless husband, but it's even more difficult to find a good secretary," Emma replied with a chuckle laced with sarcasm.

"Not all marriages go bad. Steve and I have been married for ten wonderful years. Besides, Jordan is divorced, too. He knows about pain. He told me that his wife, the woman he met while doing his internship, left him for a celebrity. He learned about the affair from the gossip section of the newspaper. He might not want more than a good, steady relationship. You should give him a chance." Bonnie persisted as she watched her crew load the last of the BB Inc. crates into the truck.

"There isn't much difference between a committed relationship and marriage from where I sit," Emma concluded as she climbed into her new sports car and listened to the purr of its powerful engine. "In either one, you grow to trust the guy, look forward to seeing him, and overlook his negative traits because of the positive ones only to find that he has clay feet. No, thank you. I'm content with my own shortcomings. I don't need someone else's weighing me down."

Leaning through the open window, Bonnie quipped, "You're too negative. You should try looking on the positive side for a change. Jordan might be just the right man for you. Instead of welcoming the possibility of a future with him, you're turning your back on the opportunity of a lifetime because your former husband was such a louse."

"I am being positive. I'm positive that I don't want to become involved with anyone right now. Good night, Bonnie. I'm going home. I'll see you tomorrow," Emma waved with a laugh, then tooted her horn.

"Humph!" Bonnie replied as she watched Emma

disappear around the corner. With a shrug, she climbed into her car and drove away.

The next day, the style section of the newspaper contained details of Jordan Everett's dinner party, including the name of the caterer. Emma's phone did not stop ringing as she got one booking after another. Suddenly, Emma was not only one of the busiest caterers in Washington, she was also among the most famous.

Walk-in traffic was brisk as all kinds of people stopped by to make arrangements for Emma to cater their next barbecue, birthday party, wedding reception, or family reunion. Every available date and time slot quickly filled. Before the office closed for the day, Emma had to turn away disappointed customers who asked to be added to the newly created waiting list in case someone canceled. EJ's was booked for an entire year with the exception of the dates that Emma held open for her repeat customers.

Even the little café that she operated next door to the office was crowded all day. When she had first opened it, Emma had hoped that the lunch and dinner foot traffic would help publicize her business. By the end of its first year, she had a steady take-out clientele that formed the basis for her repeat customers who hired her catering business. As her reputation spread, the revenue volume for the catering arm of EJ's outpaced that of the café, but out of loyalty to her initial business venture, Emma did not close the doors. Besides, the café was highly successful in its own right since the menu contained several of the catering business's favorites and many specialties unique to the smaller establishment.

That day, however, there was no difference in the two establishments in the minds of the customers. People lined up from morning until late into the evening as they ordered sinfully delicious sticky buns and specialty coffees, croissants filled with creamy salads, thick aromatic soups, and pastas in rich, cream-laced sauces. By the time the exhausted chefs closed the doors, not a single pastry remained on the shelf. Even all of EJ's homemade ice cream in fourteen sumptuous flavors had sold out.

"Stick with me, kid, and I'll make you a millionaire." Bonnie grinned when she stopped by the office to congratulate Emma on her day of glory and of being in the limelight.

"I don't see you exactly going hungry. What's good for this goose is good for her friend. Don't forget that I serve every meal, every cracker, every canapé on a BB Inc. plate," Emma said, laughing as she turned off her computer for the evening. She had missed her usual exercise session and was a bit stiff from sitting all day. However, she could not leave Pasha to handle the calls, do the scheduling, and greet the clients alone. Overnight, EJ's needed a bevy of secretaries and other support staff.

"I'm not complaining," Bonnie commented as she inspected her nails. "I'm simply trying to point out that my little referral to Jordan Everett has paid off quite handsomely. You're the talk of the town, and I'm proud to be the supplier of your table linens and china. If you'd only cooperate, you'd discover that I've made a good selection in men for you, too."

The day had been hectic for both of them. Bonnie had been so busy coordinating her schedule with Emma's for the next year that she had missed her exercise and manicure session. Bonnie had even canceled her usual lunch with Steve to be available in her office. If this fame continued, she would have to settle down and actually work for a living rather than play as she did with her very financially successful business.

Locking the door behind them, Emma replied, "I thought we agreed that you would give me a break for a while. I appreciate your sisterly efforts on my part, but I'm not interested. Case closed."

"Fine. I won't bring it up again. I was just trying to suggest that you're missing the opportunity to avail yourself of my services in matters of the heart as well as of the bottom line. End of discussion," Bonnie agreed as she slipped her arm through Emma's.

"That's the fastest you've ever agreed with me on this subject. What are you planning? I'm very suspicious," Emma commented as she studied the Cheshire cat smile on Bonnie's face.

"Not a thing. I'm completely innocent," Bonnie smirked with a wicked glint in her eye.

"We'll see about that!" Emma replied as they walked together toward the garage.

The smile never left Bonnie's face as they worked their way through the crowds heading for the theater or for one of Washington's fashionable nightclubs.

That night, as Emma packed for the trip to Las Vegas and the caterers' association conference, she wondered what Bonnie had up her sleeve this time. They had been friends too long for Emma not to suspect that Bonnie was planning something that dealt with a man and a "chance" meeting. She hoped that Bonnie did not have matchmaking on her mind again, although she had to admit that her finances had taken a wonderful upturn because of her friend's efforts. Meeting Jordan Everett might have done nothing for her personal life, but the sudden recognition by his associates certainly made her business sing.

Three

The glitter of the Las Vegas strip rushed up to meet them as the plane landed on the runway. The town, nestled in the thick dust of the valley, spread out on all sides from its central lane of activity. The bright sun sparkled off the massive structures and played along the majesty of golden lions, sprawling scenes of Venice, landscapes of Manhattan, and replicas of ancient pyramids. Amid the barren desert lay a city whose energy and excitement invited visitors from all over the world to come and play.

The airport itself was a thriving casino that beckoned travelers to empty their pockets of spare change or newly minted bills. Slot machines stood in clusters in the central waiting areas and lined the walkways leading to the baggage claim section. Only the rest rooms offered a respite from the opportunity to win the cost of a vacation or a new car.

The organizers of the conference had selected the most prestigious of all the hotels in which to hold the meeting of caterers and suppliers from around the country. The blazing sun reflected off the marble façade as the cab pulled in front of the legendary casino. The marble statues of Roman centurions seemed to snap to attention as Emma and Bonnie collected their bags and stepped upon the moving walkway that would carry them into the depths of the glistening structure. They could almost hear the cheering crowds in the amphitheater and see Caesar himself standing at the door to welcome them.

Overhead, the melodic tones of the concierge invited the newly arrived guests to dine on sumptuous fare, attend performances by legendary entertainers, wander through the shopping arcade, and take a chance that Lady Luck would smile down on them in the massive yet intimate casino. Holograms played on strategically placed screens, depicting happy revelers feeding slot machines, celebrities entertaining smiling patrons, and people mingling in the central shopping plaza.

Inside, the heat of the day disappeared and the noise of the garish Las Vegas strip receded into memory. The reception area throbbed with life as gamblers, families, newlyweds, and conference attendees mingled. In the distance, the sound of ringing slot machines beckoned everyone to enter the world of gambling in which it was always night and the chance of going home rich was ever-present.

"Wow! I think we'll have a good time here," Bonnie gushed as she gazed at the richness of the gold and marble.

"No wonder the accommodations were so pricey. This is certainly the best of Las Vegas. Let's hope that the agenda is as dazzling as the surroundings," Emma commented.

"For the moment, this is the best, but did you see the new casino they're building next door? The replica of the Via Rialto is breathtaking. We'll have to make a return trip when it opens," Bonnie suggested softly as she accepted her keycard to their room from the smiling desk clerk.

"Shush, don't say that too loudly. For years this has

been the casino of choice for the rich and famous or the wanna-be rich," Emma advised as they followed the bellhop toward the elevator that would take them to their rooms on the eleventh floor.

"As if they didn't already know that catch-up will soon be the name of their game," Bonnie remarked as the elevator door opened to the expanse of freshly laid gold carpet and shimmering white-and-gold walls.

The thickness of the carpet muffled their steps as they walked down corridors lined with paintings depicting scenes of Ancient Rome and busts of long-dead emperors. As the bellhop opened the door to their room, Emma and Bonnie were almost blinded by the sun bouncing off the heavy gold drapes at the wall of windows and the matching bedspreads lying across the two queen-size beds. Tipping him generously, they sent the bellhop on his way so that they could unpack and explore the hotel and the strip before queuing up for registration and the beginning of the evening's first session.

"This is much larger than our hotel room last year in New York. There's plenty of room for us to get out of each other's way. Maybe this time your snoring won't keep me awake," Emma commented as she shook out her suits and hung them in the armoire.

"I don't snore!" announced Bonnie with her hands placed indignantly on her hips.

"Oh, really? Maybe you should ask your long-suffering husband about that," Emma said, chuckling as she disappeared into the bathroom with her bag of cosmetics.

"For your information, Steve says that I sputter daintily," Bonnie called as she stashed her lingerie in the massive dresser.

"That's love talking. Take my word for it. You snore," Emma rebutted, refusing to be drawn into further discussion of the nocturnal vocalizing of her best friend.

"We'll ask Steve when we return home. He'll defend me," Bonnie insisted as she continued her inspection of the room.

Emma commented as she stuck her head around the corner, "You should see this bathroom! We shouldn't have any trouble getting dressed on time with two of everything except the shower. One of us could take a tub bath if we were in a real rush."

Sticking her head inside, Bonnie commented, "This is certainly the most unflattering mirror I've ever seen. Do I really look like that? I didn't realize that the flight took so much out of me. Look at those wrinkles. While we're out here, I should fly to L.A. for a face-lift by one of the cosmetic surgeons to the stars."

"You look fine. It's probably these make-up lights," Emma said as she searched for the switch. "If I adjust them for daylight instead of evening, you look great as usual. Now, let's go. I want to explore a bit before the sessions start."

"Maybe, but I still say that a trip to Hollywood isn't a bad idea," Bonnie simpered as she followed Emma down the hall.

Emma and Bonnie blinked despite their sunglasses as they stepped into the heat and blinding sun of the strip. Everywhere they looked they saw people walking from one casino to the other. Many carried bottles of water, some toted purchases, and still others licked rapidly melting ice cream cones. Everyone, regardless of their age or build, wore shorts, sandals, and loose-fitting clothes against the oppressive desert heat.

The two women wandered from one opulent hotel casino to the other. Despite the lavish New York skyline, the enchanted castles, the looming pyramid and talking camels, the elegance of Monaco, and the emerald-green backdrop to the glistening lion, their hotel, they decided, reigned supreme among the establishments.

As they plotted their course to reach the next casino barely a half block away, Emma and Bonnie blended into the crowd of people. By the time they reached the corner, they were already hot and thirsty despite the low humidity. Pointing toward the sign of a famous San Francisco chocolate and ice-cream vendor, they ducked inside for sinfully delicious creations.

"Let's come here tomorrow, too," Bonnie enthused as she licked the sticky raspberry and chocolate sauces from her spoon.

"If we do, we'll have to fly in the cargo bay on the way home. We won't be able to fit into our seats," Emma said, laughing as she scooped up yet another spoonful of rocky road, chocolate chip, and double-dark chocolate ice creams.

"Ladies, enjoy your day," crooned a familiar voice as a man with thick black sideburns and dressed in a flowing white cape walked past their table. Over his shoulder, he carried his guitar as he licked hungrily at his ice cream cone and stepped into the street. The sun bounced off his gold-studded suit as he waved good-bye.

Looking up from her sundae in astonishment, Bonnie exclaimed, "An Elvis impersonator! They really do exist."

Pushing aside her empty dish, Emma replied, "That's probably not the only one we'll see. I read that there are thousands of them in Las Vegas. Just like the slot machines that they have in every convenience store, there's an Elvis on every corner."

Returning to their hotel, Emma and Bonnie strolled through the shopping plaza and gazed at the stunning displays by world-famous couturiers as well as the smaller, more intimate shops run by local Las Vegas vendors. At every intersection of the avenue-lined shopping arcade, they found yet another shop bursting with unique items for them to carry home. From Western wear to larger sizes, from impressive names in jewelry to art galleries, the casino's shopping concessions offered something for everyone.

Darting into one of the smaller jewelry shops, Bonnie quickly purchased a thin rope chain and a slot machine charm for herself and dice cuff links for Steve. Smiling happily at Emma, she said, "This place is a shopper's delight. Take me away from here before I spend all my money on the first day."

"Considering the way money runs through your fingers, it's a good thing your business is so profitable. However, as one of your major clients, I can't help but wonder how much of your extravagant taste I'm supporting," Emma teased as she linked her arm through Bonnie's and led her toward the main lobby and the bank of elevators.

Smiling innocently, Bonnie replied as she fingered the new charm that nestled among the others at her throat, "You'll never know."

They quickly showered and changed from shorts into the business suits that were the required attire for the evening. Passing through the casino on their way to the conference rooms, Emma dropped a quarter into the nearest slot machine for her first-ever pull of the arm. The dial spun and landed on three cherries.

As the coins fell into the trough, Bonnie exclaimed, "If only I could get you to take a chance on men. See how lucky you are!"

"I'm lucky with a quarter, but my love life has been much less rewarding. Listen, we're here to have a good time, learn a few new catering techniques, and enjoy ourselves. Let's just keep it at that, shall we? No matchmaking of any kind. Okay?" Emma replied as she traded in her cup of coins for dollar bills.

"You're putting a damper on my enjoyment of the trip, but if I must, I suppose I can restrain myself for one week," Bonnie reluctantly agreed as they collected their conference information packets and pinned on their name tags.

The two friends spent the rest of the evening listening to association officers as they outlined the week's activities and set the tone for the conference. After dinner, the keynote speaker talked enthusiastically of the changes in the catering business, the opportunities for success and financial reward, and the new wave of advertising available on the Internet. From the roar of the applause, Emma and Bonnie could tell that their fellow conferees were excited about the future of the catering business and about being in Las Vegas.

By the time the evening session and dinner had ended, Emma and Bonnie were so exhausted that they could barely pry themselves from their seats. The steady flow of wine had not helped their condition one bit. The time difference had finally caught up with them. As the other conferees chatted about their plans for spending the night casino hopping, Emma and Bonnie looked skeptically at each other and tried to slip away unnoticed.

"We're going to check out the show at the casino at the south end of the strip. Would you like to go with us?" asked Karen Jet, who owned a business in Los Angeles. She and two friends were ready to take in some nightlife.

"No, thanks," Emma replied after casting a quick peek at Bonnie's barely open eyes. "We've been on

the go since six this morning and, unfortunately, our
bodies think it's two A.M. We'll see you in the morning
session."

"No problem. Maybe tomorrow night," Karen replied as she almost sprinted out the door and into
the Las Vegas night illuminated with the light of millions of glowing bulbs.

Watching Karen's vanishing back, Emma and Bonnie joined the crowd in the lobby. As they got into
an elevator, Emma thought she saw a familiar face at
one of the distant dollar slot machines. Unfortunately,
the flow of bodies into the elevator blocked her view
before she could be certain. When Emma looked
again, the person she thought she had seen had disappeared into the depths of the crowded casino.

The next day, the sessions began to blur as Emma
and Bonnie moved from one information-packed
meeting to the other. They ate a breakfast of eggs
Benedict and sweet cantaloupe halves filled with ripe,
red strawberries, while a speaker shared his experiences of using the standard direct-mail and magazine
approach to advertising. As the waitress poured another cup of rich tea, he encouraged all of them to
give a usually unused strategy the opportunity to reap
profitable results for their business.

Over a delicious salad of endive and fresh succulent
mushrooms with a light dusting of crispy bacon, they
listened as a woman from the West Coast extolled the
benefits of making contact with the consumer first
rather than waiting for the client to come to the caterer's establishment. She encouraged the rapt listen-
ers to participate in their city's block parties, to serve
samples from their menus, and to offer their services
gratis to the holiday bazaars of the various religious
organizations.

Emma, Bonnie, and the others in attendance rel-

ished savory lamb chops in mint sauce while listening
to an advertising executive from New York spell out
the benefits of combining the Internet with print ads.
He suggested not only the usual discount to online
shoppers but the inclusion of a sample recipe on the
page. From his studies, the gentleman had discovered
that customers enjoyed trying the caterer's fare in the
privacy of their own homes and turned to the generous professionals for larger affairs.

Waiters in white jackets trimmed in gold served dinner culinary masterpieces as a representative from a
world-famous cooking school delivered a slide show
and demonstration on the latest techniques for incor-
porating the pressure cooker into the large quantities
of foods that were processed by a catering establishment. He labored to show them how to reduce
food preparation time while still producing the gas-
tronomic delights for which the most successful caterers are famous. Emma and Bonnie were so busy
savoring the samples that they found paying attention
a particularly difficult task.

By dessert, Emma had sat and listened long
enough. From the way Bonnie fidgeted at her side,
she could tell that her friend was tired of sitting also.
Their ears, rumps, and waistlines could only take so
much.

Leaning over as she pretended to pick up her
dropped napkin, Emma whispered, "Are you ready to
go? I think we can slip out while he changes cassettes.
I don't think our clients are ready for this. I can't
imagine serving pot roast and trying to convince our
clients that it's chateaubriand."

"I thought you'd never ask. D.C. is too savvy for
this charade. We'd get drummed out of town as flim-
flam artists for sure if we tried this," Bonnie replied
through barely moving lips as she dabbed the last

crumb of the delectable chocolate cake from the corner of her mouth. Placing her napkin beside her plate, she palmed her small purse and waited.

When Jim Baxter paused in his presentation, Emma and Bonnie carefully eased from their table near the door and slipped into the silent hallway. The conference facilities were located on the second floor, away from the noise and temptation of the casinos. Walking quickly, they rounded the corner and rushed down the long staircase that led to the main floor. With every step they felt more liberated and guilty for leaving the meeting and the others.

"I can't believe we did that. I've never done anything like this before. We're always the goody-goodies in a group. No matter how boring a presenter is, we stick it out," Emma breathed as they entered the casino.

"I don't know why we didn't do it sooner. I would have suggested it before dessert, but I thought you were really involved in what the presenter was saying," Bonnie replied as she lost her second crisp dollar bill in a nearby slot machine.

"I was ready to leave when he showed the slide of the colorless stew. I'm sure it looked more palatable than that, but his slide was dreadful," Emma commented as she fished out the ten dollars she won on the first pull of the one-armed bandit.

Looking at her sideways, Bonnie sulked. "If I had known that you'd show me up so badly at the slots, I wouldn't have suggested that we leave."

"You didn't suggest it, I did. Beside, I don't have any more control over this machine than you do over that one. It's just time for a payout, that's all," Emma responded as she won a hundred-dollar jackpot. The loud chiming of the slot machine caused everyone to gather around them and watch as the coins fell into the trough.

"If you could bear to tear yourself away from these one-arm bandits, let's play a little blackjack. Maybe my luck will change at the tables," Bonnie requested as she beckoned toward the closest table with two empty seats.

"All right, but I'm not very good at card games. The slots are more my speed. I don't have to think as I feed in my coins and pull the handle. It doesn't take any brainpower or cause any anxiety. When I'm on vacation, I like no-brainer activities," Emma replied as she settled into the chair on the end beside Bonnie. The green felt of the tabletop beckoned her to come and deposit her cash.

"Don't worry, you'll get the hang of it in no time," Bonnie said encouragingly as they anted up their chips. "I'm not really much of a gambler, either, but I want a person on the other side of my money when I lose. There's something about shoveling coins into the slots that just leaves me cold. I know I can't win against a casino, but I would rather lose to someone who smiles graciously as she takes my money rather than a machine that simply clanks and blinks."

"Well, it won't take me long to lose the twenty dollars I brought to gamble. After that, I'll watch you. I don't intend to waste any of my winnings," Emma replied as she watched the dealer place the cards in front of her.

"Possible twenty-one," the dealer announced as she dealt the second card faceup.

"You're doing okay . . . better than I am," Bonnie said, snorting as she looked at the three of spades showing in her hand. When it was her turn, she would definitely ask for another card.

Emma sat quietly until the dealer looked in her

direction. As their eyes met, they smiled as Emma flipped over her hole card. "Blackjack," she whispered as Bonnie looked on incredulously.

"I thought you weren't any good at this game," Bonnie commented, remembering the three cards she had to draw to bring her hand total to nineteen but not enough to beat the dealer's twenty.

"Beginner's luck," Emma replied as she added the chips to her growing pile.

Bonnie's only reply was a very loud, unrefined "Humph!"

The dealer chuckled at their friendly bickering and dealt the next cards from the shoe. This time, Emma won with eighteen when the dealer busted. Bonnie, sadly, joined him in the loser's pool. Emma did not dare to look in Bonnie's direction. She could feel her friend's frustration as she lost yet another bet.

"The odds seem to be in your favor tonight," commented a familiar voice from the crowd that had assembled to watch Emma's good fortune.

Emma turned from the table quickly to gaze into the face of Jordan Everett. Smiling, she gathered her chips and slid off the chair. "Yes, and I think I'll quit while I'm ahead. What brings you to Las Vegas?"

Jordan replied as he gently touched Emma's elbow, "I had an unexpected trip to Stanford University for a brief meeting. Rather than return to Washington immediately, I stopped in Las Vegas for an overnight. I remembered that you said that you would be attending a conference here, and thought that I might be able to find you."

"We're very happy that you did. Aren't we, Emma?" Bonnie added as she joined them for the walk to the cashier's cage.

"Yes, it's very nice seeing you again. I hope your stay here will be as pleasant as ours has been," Emma replied graciously, already sensing Bonnie's not-too-subtle involvement in the coincidental meeting.

"I'll only be here one night. Might I treat you ladies to a nightcap?" Jordan offered. When he smiled, the deep dimples played at the corners of his mouth while the light danced in his big, frank eyes.

Responding quickly as she backed away, Bonnie said, "That's so sweet of you, Jordan, but this run of bad luck has turned me into a grouch. I think I'll just go up to our room now. You two go off and enjoy yourselves. I'll lick my wounded pride and read a book instead. I wouldn't be good company at all."

Ignoring the pressure of her friend's hand on the small of her back, Emma replied, "I really should call it a night, too. The sessions start at eight o'clock, I'm afraid."

"Don't worry about that," Bonnie chirped with a big smile. "I'll take copious notes. You can sleep in. You're not on the schedule until later. Remember? They rescheduled your talk for later in the day."

Bonnie vanished into the crowd before Emma could object. Now that she was alone with Jordan in a room filled with strangers, she would have to think of something to say or the evening would turn into the longest one of her life. Emma decided that she would have a serious talk with Bonnie when she returned to their room.

Emma turned and said, "Well, I guess that leaves us to fend for ourselves. I think I would like to have that drink, Jordan."

"Wonderful. I was beginning to think that both of you would turn me down. I hate drinking alone. Gambling is a solitary activity, but having a drink in a quiet bar demands company," Jordan responded as he took Emma's elbow and guided her toward a secluded corner of the darkened cocktail lounge. The singer had already taken center stage by the time they arrived.

Easing into the soft dark blue leather, Emma relaxed as the singer's luscious alto filled the room. She had not taken much time for herself in years and was constantly on the go. She spent her only spare time in the shower and that was often interrupted by the ringing of the telephone. More than once Emma had dashed into her bedroom dripping water along the way. Everyone knew that Emma believed in keeping her fingers in the pie of her business. As the lyrics washed over her, Emma closed her eyes and breathed deeply.

Jordan smiled as he watched Emma sway to the rhythm of the soulful tune. He could tell from the way her eyelids fluttered and a smile played at the corner of her kissable lips that she was totally engrossed in the music and had completely forgotten his existence. Rather than feel insulted, Jordan found her independence refreshing. He had discovered in his professional dealings with people that few of them were sufficiently comfortable with themselves that they could enjoy their own company while with someone else. Emma appeared to be one of those rare people who felt so confident in herself that she did not rely on someone else to show her a good time.

As he studied Emma's smooth brown skin and watched her sway to the music, Jordan broke the silence. "She is good. Too bad more people won't get to hear her. She should be a headliner, not just a filler in the bar."

Unable to keep his voice from penetrating the velvet of the moment, Emma replied with a tranquil smile on her face, "She's fabulous. It's so seldom that I have a chance to chill out. I'm afraid that I allowed the music to carry me away."

"What do you do when you're not working?" Jordan asked, unable to drag his eyes from Emma's lips.

Chuckling softly, Emma replied, "I'm never not working. My company absorbs all of my time. I'm not complaining, because I enjoy the life I'm living, but it leaves me with precious little time of my own. My friends had learned to accept my absences and plan around my seasonal lulls, which are coming less often now."

"I've often wondered about the life of a caterer. What do you do all day? It seems pretty glamorous to me," Jordan commented as the waitress left his rum and Coke and Emma's gin and tonic.

"When I'm not in the office, I'm planning menus, supervising arrangements, meeting old clients and making new ones, talking with suppliers, and running my business. I have a highly capable staff of chefs and waiters who make each engagement appear unique despite the number of affairs we cater in a day. My incredibly reliable bookkeeper handles all the invoices and payroll for me. My secretary keeps my calendar to perfection. However, it's on me to make the contacts and do the follow-up. EJ's is my business. I don't have partners, and I'm not backed by corporate money. The majority of my business comes from referrals or newspaper coverage of celebrity events that I cater. The rest I have to win on my own. I'm a chef in my own right, so I give cooking demonstrations at country clubs, department stores, and churches. I've written two cookbooks, and, when I have time, I do book signings. I'm always busy."

Shaking his head incredulously, Jordan asked, "You didn't mention a social life. Is there someone special in your life?"

"No, I've been divorced for several years, and during that time I've been too busy building and maintaining my business to take time out for romance," Emma replied. "I learned from a very labor-intensive marriage that being involved with someone is a full-time job unto itself. My ex-husband was very high maintenance. He's a very successful attorney who expected me to be available at a moment's notice to accompany him. Often I would have to cancel my plans, leaving friends and family shaking their heads at yet another missed appointment. It's a life I don't ever want again. I'm perfectly happy with the way things are right now."

Smiling, Jordan commented, "Not all relationships are unhappy ones. Some of them actually nurture the partners. You might want to give another one a try."

"I seem to remember that Bonnie, in her attempt to foster our association, mentioned that you've only just moved to Washington. I take it that you didn't find the right person, either, otherwise you wouldn't have sacrificed the relationship for this new position of yours," Emma responded with a raised brow.

"Touché," Jordan conceded. "However, my marriage was doomed from the start, I think. We married too young and grew apart. She couldn't understand my almost obsessive devotion to my work. I spent more time in the lab than I did with her. One day when I came home, I found a note on the refrigerator door. She had left me."

"What is it that makes you such a proponent of marriage? Your track record isn't any better than mine," Emma said as she sipped her drink and gave Jordan her full attention.

"Since my divorce, I've gotten my priorities straightened out, I think. I know the importance of having someone special in my life. I have all the notoriety that I need, and, frankly, I find it poor company," Jordan replied with confidence but without a trace of arrogance. "I'm considered by many to be an authority in my field. I've certainly devoted enough time to researching the effects of alcohol and drugs on adolescent behavior. I felt quite honored when the president selected me to be on the commission that would design the media ads aimed at educating the youth of America on the dangers of mixing alcohol and drugs with driving. In the last few years, I've felt as if I were missing something. Dating isn't enough. I need someone special in my life. I realize that simply being honest about the mistakes I've made and realizing that I need the company of one special person doesn't make me an authority on remarriage, but it certainly enables me to know what I want to do with my life."

Shifting slightly, Emma pointed out, "I suppose that one day I'll come to the same conclusion, but for now I have to continue on my set course. I could use a little more professional publicity but not personal exposure. My divorce settlement gave me the freedom to open the business, advertise it and stock the kitchens properly, and offer competitive salaries to talented chefs. My contacts in Washington provided me with a very sound client base. However, I'm not a household name yet and don't want to become one because of scandal. Despite Bonnie's efforts to sing my praises at every opportunity, there are still two catering companies that outpace mine in terms of revenue. As long as I'm number three, I'll have to work harder. Until I'm number one in Washington, I simply don't have time to divert my energy to building a relationship."

"Being that busy and working that hard can lead to a lonely life. Take it from a man who knows," Jordan interjected between sips.

"True, but it's the life that I choose right now. I'm still young enough to feel that the future's ahead of me, not behind. There's plenty of time for me to think about settling down again. Right now, my business has to come first," Emma concluded as she placed her empty glass on the table and picked up her purse.

Taking the cue, Jordan signaled to the waiter who appeared immediately with the bar tab. Signing the slip, Jordan said with a touch of resignation in his voice, "I suppose that means that Bonnie was mistaken. She led me to believe that you might be interested in meeting a gentleman of means and reputation who is looking for a woman with whom to build his life. From her description of you and from what I've seen so far of your efficiency in running your business, I thought that you might be that woman for me. I guess I was misinformed, and I regret if I have in any way forced my attentions on you."

With a smile Emma replied, "Your attentions toward me have not in any way been intrusive. However, Bonnie is my dearest friend, and, like most people who care about me, she wants only what's best for my welfare. Being a happily married woman, she thinks that marriage to the right man would be to my advantage. She thinks that I'm missing something in my life and refuses to see that I am perfectly happy with all facets of my life. I'm sorry if she led you to believe that the possibility might exist for something more to develop between us, but I'm afraid that at the moment my focus is entirely on work."

Touching Emma's elbow lightly as he guided her from the bar, Jordan asked, "Does this mean then that you are not available for occasional evenings at the theater and dinner?"

"Jordan, I have enjoyed your company, but, as I've said, I really have very little opportunity to socialize," Emma replied as they approached the bank of elevators. She smiled warmly in an effort to show him that her rejection of his suggestion was in no way personal.

Bowing slightly, Jordan commented, "Then it will be my task to convince you that you should schedule an evening with me just as you would plan to oversee a reception. I'll be in touch very soon. Good night, Emma."

Looking into the depths of his eyes, Emma saw genuine warmth and interest. Extending her hand, she replied, "Good night, Jordan. Thank you for the company. However, I won't make any promises that I can't keep."

After the elevator closed between them, Emma thought about the handsome man she had left on the main floor. Jordan certainly had not forced his attention on her although he had firmly stated his intention of pursuing her acquaintance. He was polite yet determined in making his desires known. Smiling, she wondered if he would call and, if maybe this time, Bonnie's meddling had produced positive results.

Bonnie! Marching down the silent hall with only the hum of the ice machine as company, Emma mentally prepared the words she would speak to her well-intentioned, albeit irritating, best friend. Emma had to make Bonnie understand once and for all that when she was ready to date again, she would make her own connections. She did not need the help of a matchmaker.

Opening the door, Emma entered their room to find Bonnie propped up on a pile of pillows, watching television. She wore a cream-and-black striped nightgown and robe with matching slippers that sat on the floor next to the bed. Beside her lay an abandoned copy of the latest romance.

Turning, Bonnie bubbled, "Tell me all about it. How was your first social meeting with Jordan? Isn't he just about the most charming man you've ever met?"

Slowly Emma placed her purse on the table while carefully formulating her words. Although she was irritated by Bonnie's meddling, she did not want to hurt her friend's feelings. She knew that Bonnie only had her best interest at heart.

Through lips tightly closed in a show that was more pretend than reality, Emma replied, "Jordan appears to be a lovely person. I just wish you hadn't tried to arrange something between us. I've told you a thousand times that I'm not interested in romantic entanglements right now. I really don't want to be thrust in the position of having to hurt people's feelings."

"I'm only trying to help. I don't want you waking up one morning old and wizen with regret for company," Bonnie retorted as she picked up her book to take refuge from her friend's piercing stare.

"We'll worry about that when the time comes. Right now I want you to promise me that you will never again interfere in my personal life. You've created a situation here with Jordan that I'm stuck trying to undo. You simply must stop. When I'm ready to date again, I'll let you know. Until then, butt out!" Emma stated firmly.

"By the time you decide that you want a man in your life, all the best ones will either be dead or married," Bonnie replied with a snort of disdain and a loud rustle of the newspaper that also lay untouched on her bed.

"I'll have to take my chances. Considering some of the men you've selected for me, I'd rather be alone. Do you remember Ben Newton, the guy with the thick glasses and the thinning hair? And how about Frank Plum, whom we discovered later had a wife in Boston," Emma remarked with a chuckle.

"I'm not perfect. I only try hard. Besides, Jordan looks like a winner to me. Not many jerks get appointments like that," Bonnie quipped without looking up from the book in which she feigned interest.

"Maybe, but I'm not interested in finding out. I'll talk to you more about it in the morning," Emma said with a shake of her head as she disappeared into the bathroom to remove her makeup and slip into her subdued lime-green nightgown.

"Humph. You'll thank me one of these days. I can't remain unappreciated forever," Bonnie replied.

Emma never really became angry with her friend over her matchmaking efforts. In fact, she often found them humorous. However, she had grown tired of Bonnie's unsuccessful attempts to organize her life. The next time Emma wanted male companionship, she would find it herself. For the remainder of the conference, she intended to focus on work and nothing else.

Four

Clients crowded the waiting room and offices of EJ's when Emma returned to work filled with a wealth of knowledge gained at the conference. The chatter of happy customers as they munched samples of the cuisine that had made EJ's famous obscured the soft jazz in the background that played constantly, lending an atmosphere of serenity to the establishment on less hectic days. Socialites with carefully coiffed hair and wearing the latest in haute couture sat beside denim-clad teens and their harried mothers as they waited for their turn with one of the consultants who would arrange an evening that they would long remember.

Handing her a stack of callback slips, Pasha said with a happy smile, "I'm certainly glad to see you. The phone has been ringing off the hook. Everyone who hadn't heard about the function we catered for Jordan Everett before you left for Las Vegas has heard about it now. We're swamped with appointments. The consultants are up to their ears in meetings. I'm turning people away in droves. We could double or triple our business if we could find enough cooks to keep up with the orders. The lines to the carryout have been around the corner for days."

"I'm sure we could, but we would forfeit most of our personality if we did. We'd become just like our competitors. Our food would taste every bit as institutional as theirs. I think we'll stay as we are despite this opportunity to charge ahead. I decided when I first opened this business that I'd keep the personal touch regardless of the degree of success," Emma responded as she flipped through the stack of pink papers.

"But think of all the money you'd make. You'd be rich. You'd be able to give me a raise," Pasha quipped with a broad smile, knowing that Emma was a very generous boss.

"If I paid you any more, I'd have to work for you," Emma retorted as she left Pasha laughing in her wake. They both knew that Pasha was the best secretary in the business. More than one competitor had tried to woo her away from Emma.

Dropping her attaché case on her desk, Emma sorted the messages according to urgency. To her delight, she discovered that the majority of them were congratulatory calls from satisfied customers who wanted to express their appreciation for the professionalism of Emma's staff and the superior quality of the cuisine. The few that required immediate attention were from anxious clients who only needed her personal reassurance that everything was progressing according to schedule. The vast majority were new clients.

Smiling, Emma tossed the congratulatory messages into the out box for Pasha to file, and gave her attention to the others. Among them were calls from two new clients who wanted her to visit their homes to assist them personally with their selections. Emma enjoyed those visits and felt that they gave her tremendous insights into the personality of the people and the manner in which her menus and presentation could complement their planned celebration. From the addresses of the callers, she could tell that visits to these mansions on Massachusetts Avenue would make for delightful afternoon outings.

While she instructed Pasha on making the appointments for her, Emma read the last two messages. The one from Bonnie would keep until the excitement of the day died down a bit although she was sure that her friend must have a delightful tidbit to share, considering she seldom left her bed before ten. Emma often wondered how Bonnie's business could be so well run with a boss who spent so few hours in the office, but she never voiced her concern. After all, because of her husband's thriving law practice, her position at the country club, and her dedication to her church, Bonnie knew everyone in town who might have a need to rent table linens, crystal, and china. Obviously, her sales force did a fabulous job without her.

Fleetingly, Emma wondered if she would one day be able to slow down and give herself a social life and a little time to herself. Maybe Jordan had been correct. Maybe it was time for Emma to start thinking of herself instead of the business. Maybe she could begin to live a little.

However, Emma quickly pushed that thought from her mind knowing that it was not in her nature to sit idly by while others worked for her. Despite constant urging from Bonnie, Emma had resisted the idea of employing a housekeeper, saying that no one could clean her house as well as she could. The truth was that Emma would not know what to do with her free time if she did not have furniture to dust and floors to mop.

The last message was from Jordan Everett, inviting her to lunch with him tomorrow. Fingering it slowly as a frown played across her usually unlined brow,

Emma decided against returning his call. As the intercom crackled, she absentmindedly folded the slip of pink paper into a tiny square that she placed on the edge of her desk and flicked over the side with her manicured nail. As the paper football fell into the trash can, Emma smiled victoriously. She had decided that Jordan wanted more than she could offer. She could tell that a relationship of any kind with him would only lead to complications that she did not need in her life. Reaching that resolve and scoring an imaginary touchdown made Emma feel that her day was off to a good start.

Picking up the morning newspaper, Emma scanned the front page before turning to the style section. The usual litany of crimes and scandals in the nation's capital caught her eye. The last article at the lower left held her attention for a moment as she read that a local church had begun an outreach program designed at teaching high school students valuable trade skills not learned in the classroom. Quickly writing herself a note, Emma decided that she would have to investigate the possibility of becoming involved in that effort. Her business was a financial success, and she was always on the lookout for ways to give back to the community. If she could interest young people in the catering business, Emma knew that they would find the independence of self-employment very rewarding.

When Emma turned to the style section, she discovered a large photograph of Jordan Everett smiling from the middle of the page. Scanning the article, Emma saw that he had been appointed to yet another special government health committee. He had only returned to Washington from Las Vegas a few days ago and already he was big news. However, his latest political accomplishment was not what grabbed

Emma's interest; she found the discussion of his personal exploits more enlightening. Considering that Jordan had only recently tried to convince her of his genuine interest in developing a relationship with her, Emma found the paragraphs about the women in the available bachelor's life very informative. As she had expected despite Bonnie's efforts to convince her otherwise, there was more to Jordan Everett than he let on.

"Well, he certainly doesn't waste any time," Emma muttered to herself as she placed her cup of tea on the desk. The Wedgwood china in the Osborne pattern clicked slightly with the force of her effort.

"Who doesn't?" Bonnie demanded as she strode into Emma's office with her usual flair and without being announced. A cloud of Poême by Lancôme surrounded her as she entered.

"Jordan Everett. He's all over the style section. What brings you here so early? I've never known you to start work before noon," Emma said as she handed Bonnie the newspaper.

"Girl, I have to call on two clients before lunch," Bonnie replied as she scanned the article about Jordan. "I'll be exhausted before two o'clock if this pace keeps up. Your new success is killing me! Once your competition found out that I supply all of your linens, china, and crystal, my phone wouldn't stop ringing. I'll need that appointment at the salon in order to restore my beauty. Why the interest in Jordan? I thought you didn't care about him."

"I don't, at least not in the way you mean. I just find it interesting that a man who was doing his best to hit on me is the center of attention two days later surrounded by a bevy of beautiful women. That's all," Emma responded as she turned her attention to the pile of correspondence on her desk.

"If you're thinking that he's a player, don't. That's just publicity stuff. You know that men in this town have to keep up appearances," Bonnie said as she sank into one of the overstuffed chairs in the conversation section of Emma's office.

"Well, he's the least of my concerns at the moment. Did you read this article about the outreach program at the church in town? I'd like to see what I can do to help out," Emma said as she showed Bonnie the article.

"Great. We can do something together. Oops, gotta run. Call me on my cell phone if I need to meet you somewhere. I'll talk to you tonight," Bonnie commented as she sprang from the chair and bolted toward the door. As was her pattern, she would arrive a little late for her appointment. Regardless of her best intentions, Bonnie never managed to be on time for anything. In others, tardiness was insulting. In Bonnie, it only added to her charm.

Shaking her head at her friend's hasty retreat, Emma dialed the number of St. Timothy's Church. Almost immediately, a cheery voice answered, and informed her that her participation in the new program would be greatly appreciated. Emma immediately signed up for that night's open six o'clock slot. With a quick smile, she volunteered Bonnie's expertise in decorating as another course option.

Leaving a short message on Bonnie's voice mail, Emma turned her attention to the pile of work on her desk. She soon forgot all about the questionable attentions of the smiling Dr. Jordan Everett. The running of EJ's was much too important, and she had too many clients in need of attention to allow Jordan to distract her attention from her work. As she pressed the intercom button, Emma cleared all thoughts not related to her work.

The hours passed quickly as Emma met with new clients and conferred with suppliers. She did not break for lunch but instead munched a delectable sandwich from her own carryout next door. The shrimp salad on croissant fairly melted in her mouth and the succulent peaches and mango topped with shaved nuts with a wash of honey and balsamic vinegar was a treat sent from heaven.

By the time she cleared her in box and arranged her calendar, Emma was exhausted. Gathering her things, she remembered that she had volunteered to teach a cooking class at the church that night. Rushing to the carryout next door, she filled a basket with the ingredients she would need for the demonstration. Not knowing the condition of the kitchen, she threw a mixing bowl and a frying pan into a shopping bag along with a whisk and some herbs, and placed it in a box along with the rest of the ingredients.

Waving good night to Benny who managed the carryout, Emma took the supplies out to her car, slipped behind the wheel, and headed into the heart of the city. As she drove, she listened to the sounds of cool jazz on the radio. Although she had purchased a CD player for her car, Emma loved the selections of the local deejay so much that she could not bring herself to switch from her usual habit of listening to him. Tonight, the selection was especially relaxing as Emma turned her red practical sports utility into the crowded parking lot of the church.

All of her friends had called her "Trucking Mama" when she'd first purchased the vehicle, but Emma hadn't cared. In her line of work, she could never tell when she would have to haul supplies and crates of produce to a client's home. After struggling to force her tiny sports car to accommodate the necessities of her profession, Emma relegated it to a pleasure-only vehicle. For work, she preferred a larger vehicle, never regretting the decision for a minute. The sports utility offered her the visibility she loved over stalled traffic and the cargo capacity she needed in her business.

Pressing the remote lock, Emma balanced the box of supplies carefully as she slipped the strap of her bag over her shoulder. This was a rough neighborhood and one that she would not ordinarily visit at night. However, Emma felt reasonably safe. The local homeless man on the far corner did not seem to notice her as she entered the church.

"Ms. Jones?" a female voice called as Emma stepped from the darkness into the bright lights of the parish hall.

"Hi. Yes, I'm Emma Jones," Emma introduced herself as she gingerly set the box on the table. It was not heavy although its size and the fragile contents made it unwieldy. Although Emma had wrapped everything with care, it was still possible for one of the items to shift and cause damage to the more delicate contents. She did not want to have the ingredients spoiled through her carelessness, and disappoint the students who expected a cooking demonstration.

"I'm Doris Johnson, the parish secretary. Let me help you carry that. Your class is waiting." A small, gray-haired woman with a tight bun and sensible shoes greeted her with outstretched arms.

Following Mrs. Johnson to the kitchen of the parish hall, Emma marveled at the mixture of austerity and elegance in the old house. The massive exposed pine beams in the ceilings, the ornate but worn oriental carpets on the floors, and the huge oil paintings that lined the walls gave the ancient building a feeling of permanence. The pale yellow glow of wall sconces illuminated the gallery of photos of past popes and bishops that lined the dark-paneled walls.

To Emma's delight, the kitchen was anything but tiny. As a matter of fact, it served as the refectory for the priests as well as the cooking area. A massive pine table with three sets of six-foot benches lining the sides and four chairs at each end separated the dining area from the work space. The latest commercial quality range, dishwasher, and refrigerator stood in waiting. A huge microwave and dual wall ovens along with a double china closet filled the opposite wall. Stainless-steel and copper pots and pans of every size and description hung on hooks from the ceiling.

Beaming with pride, Mrs. Johnson said as she watched Emma's obvious pleasure, "I hope our modest kitchen will meet with your approval."

"I'm delighted. It's much more than I had expected. I guess I won't be needing these," Emma replied as she began to unload her supplies, leaving the frying pan, mixing bowl, and whisk in the shopping bag.

With a chuckle Mrs. Johnson responded as she left to usher in the students, "No, I don't think you will. We're rather state-of-the-art here."

Alone in the cavernous kitchen, Emma surveyed her surroundings as she awaited the arrival of her students. She knew that in its earlier history, St. Timothy's had been a thriving, yet small monastery. As church attendance dwindled, the friars had moved away, and St. Timothy's had become a parish church complete with Sunday school, bingo games, and even a teen basketball team. The size of the kitchen served as a reminder of its former life.

Emma did not have long to marvel at the majestic stone walls of the former monastery's refectory. The boisterous members of her class entered and quickly took their seats, holding in their hands napkins folded in the shape of giraffes and flowers. Smiling, Emma knew that they had just left Bonnie's class on table setting and napkin folding.

"Well, everyone," Emma began gleefully, "let's crack an egg!"

In no time at all, Emma had the mixed group of men and women eating out of her hand. She expertly cracked eggs with one hand and whipped the whites with sugar until glistening and stiff before folding them into the creamy yokes for an omelet. She grated orange peel without getting any of the bitter white into the mixture for the French toast. She dusted some ripe, red strawberries with powdered sugar and dipped others in melted milk chocolate before arranging both on a crystal platter. None of the students moved during the demonstration as they waited eagerly to taste the simple, yet elegant breakfast treats.

When the hour-long session ended, Emma gathered her few belongings and left a satisfied class merrily munching on the fruits of her labor. Much to her satisfaction, she had convinced them that breakfast could be both nourishing and fun. As she exited the refectory, they muttered their appreciation and waved fingers sticky with sugar and syrup.

Backing into the hallway, and bumping into a body, Emma turned with a startled cry. "Oh, sorry, I didn't see you!" she apologized as she picked up the purse she'd dropped.

"No damage done," the familiar voice replied.

"Jordan! I'm surprised to find you at an evening of domestic demonstrations. I thought that medicine was your primary interest," Emma commented as she repositioned her bags and continued down the hall.

"It is, and that's why I'm here. I conducted a session on the treatment of alcoholism and its impact on the family. I authored a paper on this subject not long before I accepted the appointment to the president's committee," Jordan answered as he took the bag with the heavy frying pan from Emma's arms. "Someday, I might want to open a little practice and leave the rat race behind me. Besides, I like to give something back to the community. This church offers many programs like this one. I'm just doing my share. How'd you happen to hear about it?"

Strolling toward the entrance, Emma replied, "I read about it in the paper. So Bonnie and I decided to volunteer."

"Bonnie told me about it. Small world," Jordan remarked with a chuckle as they reached the door.

"Not so small," Emma responded with a shake of her head as a smiling Bonnie joined them.

"Wasn't this a wonderful evening?" Bonnie gushed as she rushed to meet them with a huge tote bag hanging over her shoulder and a briefcase in her hand. Emma knew that Bonnie carried table linens in one and silverware in the other as was her habit whenever she visited clients. Bonnie did not go far without samples of her wares. Tonight, she had used them as instructional tools.

"Wonderful!" Emma replied before whispering, "Imagine meeting Jordan here."

Ignoring her hidden meaning, Bonnie chattered contentedly. "It makes me feel so good to do something for someone other than my family and friends for a change. Not that knowing how to set a table will change the course of anyone's life, but at least I shared something a little different with my students. For a moment, they weren't thinking of their bills."

Jordan chuckled at Bonnie's innocent but self-centered observations, then joined the conversation. "True, they were trying to figure out how to turn a damask napkin into a giraffe."

With a delicate shrug of her shoulders, Bonnie countered, "I know when I'm being ridiculed, so I'll leave you now. Emma, I'll see you tomorrow. Jordan, I might forgive you in the near future, at least by next Saturday when you've promised to attend my dinner party. Good night to both of you."

Standing together on the dark sidewalk, they watched as Bonnie sped away in her little convertible. Emma was glad that Jordan could not see her expression. Once again, her best friend had contrived to bring them together.

As Jordan finished loading Emma's belongings into the cargo section of her truck, he slipped his arm through hers and said, "There's an ice-cream shop at the corner. I promised myself a scoop when the session ended. Let's go."

"Jordan, I have so much paperwork to do. I'll have to take a rain check," Emma sputtered as he led her across the street.

"Not this time, Emma. Every time I've wanted to take you to dinner, to the theater, or to the movies, you've had something else to do. Not tonight. Tonight you're eating ice cream with me. And I won't take no for an answer," Jordan replied with a laugh as he held open the door to the cute little parlor.

"OK, but only one scoop of chocolate raspberry truffle in a cup," Emma agreed as she pointed to the sinfully rich ice cream and took her seat at a table for two.

As she waited for the ice cream to arrive, Emma looked around the shop. Instead of being the typical, commercial ice-cream establishment, Antonio's carefully reflected the days of the ice-cream parlor with a long soda fountain area where the clerks made specialty creations and individual tables for the patrons. Overhead, fans circled lazily, creating a gentle breeze that rustled the napkins in the metal holders. Photographs of the founders dotted the clean, white walls and reminded the patrons of the days in which ice cream was a novelty and not a staple available at every grocery store. Emma felt wonderfully at home and comfortable as she leaned her elbow on the cool, white-and-gray-speckled marble top of the little bistro table. As a matter of fact, she forgot to be in a hurry to return home and began to enjoy herself in this quaint place where no one paid any attention as they enjoyed their ice cream.

"This was a great idea. This place is right out of the 1890s. It's wonderful!"

Licking the sticky chocolate syrup from his fingers, Jordan replied, "There's one just like it in San Francisco, only more famous and crowded. This one offers the same selection of fabulous creations but with shorter waits."

"A place like this is a real treasure and an asset to the neighborhood. I hope it has enough business to stay open," Emma commented, greedily licking the ice cream that stuck to her spoon.

"I understand that it does a very brisk business all the time, even in the dead of winter. People do like their ice cream. I stop in here every chance I get. The neighborhood isn't the greatest, but this shop draws people from all walks of life," Jordan responded between spoonfuls of luscious chocolate and freshly whipped cream.

"I've never heard of it, and I try to keep abreast of all food establishments, especially since I offer homemade ice cream at my shop, too. Are you going to eat all of that?" Emma said as she scooped up the last of her ice cream.

Chuckling, Jordan pushed his overflowing glass closer to Emma and replied, "I bought the biggest one they made, thinking that you'd want to join me in this decadence. I'm not surprised that you didn't know about Antonio's since it's not the usual high-brow establishment to which you're accustomed. I bet you'll return now that you've had a taste of what it has to offer."

Wiping the strawberry syrup from her lips, Emma responded, "I certainly want to thank you for introducing me to Antonio's. I don't think I'll be a stranger after this evening. I just hope I'll be able to fit into my clothes after tonight. I don't know when I've tasted better ice cream or had a more enjoyable time."

Laughing at the joy of having distracted Emma from work and introduced her to the pleasures of Antonio's, Jordan said as he gazed earnestly into her eyes, "There are so many other wonderful places I can show you, if you'd let me. This is only the beginning."

"Jordan, I really—"

"I know. You don't want to become involved. You're too busy. Your work is your life. You've had one bad experience, and you don't want another. There's no time in your life for involvement. You've already told me all that, and I'm not buying. This time, I'm not taking no for an answer," Jordan responded as he guided Emma to the door and out into the warm night and to her vehicle.

"All right, Jordan, I do have to admit that you know how to show a girl a good time. I really do have a commitment tomorrow, but I'm free on Sunday," Emma agreed as she buckled her seat belt and put the key into the ignition.

"Great! I'll pick you up around two. Wear jeans and tennis shoes because we'll spend a lot of time outdoors." Jordan beamed as he patted Emma's hand fondly.

Pulling away from the curb, Emma smiled and said, "I'll see you then."

On the drive home, Emma could not keep her mind off Jordan, the ice-cream parlor, and their up-coming outing. She would have to go shopping before Sunday for a pair of jeans and tennis shoes since she had not owned either since her college days. In her line of work, Emma was always dressed to the nines even when casually attired in silk slacks and shirts.

More compelling than her concern about what to wear was her worry about making a good impression. Although Emma had known Jordan professionally and had shared a pleasant evening over delicious ice-cream treats, she had spent little time alone with him. After years of being unattached, she was concerned that she had lost the knack for small talk. First dates had always frightened her, and this one was no exception.

As Emma pulled into her driveway, she could feel the beginning of a true anxiety attack. Her chin even tingled as if a pimple were threatening to erupt—something that had not happened to her since her wedding day years ago. Despite the complexity of her menus, the notoriety of clientele, or the number of engagements on her plate, Emma had not felt this nervous in years. She always took the bumps and snags of catering in stride and was hardly ever fazed by the need to make last-minute changes. The prospects of going on a date with Jordan had already set her head to spinning in a way that catering the wedding for the daughter of the ambassador of Egypt had not.

Later, slipping under the covers in her room illuminated by the full moon, Emma wondered if she would survive until Sunday. The usual paranoid stream of questions filled her mind. She wondered what she would do if she and Jordan did not get along during a lengthy drive into the country. There was always the possibility that their date would take them for a hike in the woods that would produce absolute silence. She might not be able to think of anything to say during the long hours of walking among the flora and fauna. She might trip and turn her ankle, forcing Jordan to have to carry her back to the car. The next day a wicked poison ivy rash might break out all over her skin.

Pushing the bewildering array of possibilities from her mind, Emma closed her eyes. She consoled herself with the thought that Jordan was one of the most famous physicians in the country even if he rarely saw a patient these days. If something happened, he would be able to provide care. Besides, there were worse things than silence.

Five

Sunday morning dawned sunny and pleasantly
warm. After a quick shower, Emma pulled on her
freshly washed new jeans and slightly scuffed new
tennis shoes. She had carefully rubbed a little soil
into the toe of each shoe so that it would not look
as if they were new. She had washed the jeans to
remove the brand-new feel and stiffness. Although
the label said that they were prewashed, she did not
want to look as if she were wearing new clothes. Slipping into an equally new and freshly washed white
cotton T-shirt, she quickly surveyed her image in the
mirror before rushing downstairs to pack the picnic
basket.

When Jordan had called to confirm their date, they
had agreed that Emma would provide the lunch as
long as she kept it simple. Immediately, she had decided on pâté and crackers, fruit and cheese, and a
light, hard-to-find dessert wine that was among her
favorites. She carefully packed these delicacies inside
a linen-lined wicker basket into which she added
plates, napkins, wineglasses, and several ice packs.

Rushing to the door on the first ring, Emma smiled
happily as she gazed into the beaming face of Dr.
Jordan Everett, who did not, in any way, resemble a
noted physician while in his present attire. Jordan,

although strikingly handsome, wore an old, faded, thin cotton plaid shirt opened to expose a muscular chest covered in thick dark hair. On his feet, he wore scuffed tennis shoes with tiny holes at the toe. His jeans were so worn at the knees that the fabric had frayed. Next to him, Emma's carefully aged clothing screamed newly purchased.

"Ready?" Jordan asked as he took the basket from her.

"Where exactly are we going?" Emma asked as she allowed Jordan to propel her down the driveway toward his waiting car.

"We're going to Solomons Island on the Eastern Shore of Maryland. It's a quaint little fishing town. You'll like it," Jordan replied as he eased into the light Sunday-morning traffic.

"We're going fishing?" Emma almost gulped. She was not the outdoorsy type and was not convinced that she wanted to modify her behavior.

"Not fishing, crabbing. You'll love it, or at least you'll enjoy the fruits of your labor!" Jordan responded with glee as they headed out of town and away from the life that Emma knew and loved.

"Okay," Emma replied without conviction.

Emma had grown up in Washington where, every summer, the residents would break open millions of the famous Chesapeake blue crabs. They would spice them until it was hard to tell what caused the shells to turn bright red—the steaming or the seasoning. Then they would spread old newspaper or cut-open grocery stores bags on the tabletops, butter a few ears of corn, grab mallets and nutcrackers, and have a wonderful time extracting the firm, succulent flesh from the shells.

At least, others enjoyed the experience. Emma had never learned to relish the taste of the celebrated crustaceans. They were filthy, bottom-dwelling scavengers whose blue shells were often covered in sludge and bits of seaweed before being rinsed and tossed into the steaming pot. They snapped fiercely in an attempt to avoid the inevitable trip to the plate. They smelled up the kitchen, alive or cooked. The stench of the wharf lingered for days and clung to curtains, clothing, and fingers. The saltiness of the seasoning also hung around for days and mingled with the stench of vinegar that permeated the water, the air, and her hair.

Although Emma prepared blue crabs fried in the soft-shell stage, in crab cakes, and in soup for her clients, she had never learned to enjoy the taste of crabs. Now, as the car sped along Route 50, she tried to think of a way to avoid eating them. Unlike many, she could not hide behind an allergy to them to save her from the pending unpleasantness. She could think of no way around it; today she would dine on Maryland's precious catch of the day.

The drive to the Eastern Shore was delightful. Trees lined the quiet road that ran perpendicular to the busy highways. Fields of corn dotted the horizon. The weather was warm but not humid as Jordan's pearl-gray convertible sliced through the traffic. Emma relaxed against the soft, gray leather upholstery and listened to the hum of the engine. They rode in silence with the top down and the CD playing soulful music.

"We're here," Jordan announced two hours later as he stopped the car in front of a cute Cape Cod house with a great front yard view of the Bay.

"I didn't know that we would be visiting anyone," Emma commented as Jordan led her up the flagstone walk.

"We're not. This is my getaway house," Jordan replied as he swung open the front door. "Do you like it?"

Stepping inside, Emma was awestruck by the splendid view of the Bay that greeted her. Looking past the tastefully selected furnishings, she could see the lazy water dotted with sails from the expanse of windows in the living room. The sun sparkled off the surface of the water as the waves lapped against the shore. Everywhere she looked, the grandeur of Chesapeake Bay met her eyes. Seagulls flapped their wings and dipped into the water. Children ran along the sandy beach with their parents following behind them. Lovers strolled, holding hands in the warm sunshine.

"Do you like it?" Jordan repeated, standing alongside her in front of the window.

"It's incredible. I've never seen anything so beautiful."

"That's a mild reaction to the one I had. I was bowled over when the Realtor showed me this place. I wanted a quiet, weekend getaway . . . not too far from the city, away from the politics and the noise. This place was just perfect. Bonnie introduced me to a decorator who picked out just the right combination of comfort and formality to suit me. Let me show you around the place. If you think this view is impressive, just wait until you see the one from the master bedroom, but I'll save that for last," Jordan replied as he led Emma first toward the dining room, then the kitchen, and his office complete with computer. Each room had a wonderful view of the Bay although none could match the one from the living room.

"I thought you said this was your getaway house," Emma commented, pointing to the computer on the massive cherry desk.

"It is, but I don't want to be completely isolated

from the world while I'm here. I make it a rule never to do any work while I'm here, but I enjoy reading the newspapers online. Let me show you the rest of the house. The best is yet to come," Jordan responded as he continued the tour.

Stepping aside at the door to the last of three bedrooms, Jordan pressed a button that caused the curtains along the side wall to part. As they did, the most breathtaking panorama came into view. Emma watched as the full expanse of the Bay filled the room. Sparkling sand, fluttering gulls, and lapping waves seemed to fill the space as the curtains separated to expose a wall of windows and an unobstructed view to Chesapeake Bay.

"Imagine falling asleep to the moon shining on the water. The first morning I woke up to this view, I felt as if I were in heaven," Jordan whispered from her right.

"I don't know how I'd sleep knowing that I might miss a minute if I closed my eyes," Emma replied breathlessly. She had never experienced the Bay as an integral part of someone's home. Its presence filled the room to overflowing and left her in awe.

"Well, I won't say that you'd get used to it, because I haven't yet. Let's go for a swim. The water might be a little cool yet, but at least there aren't any jellyfish," Jordan instructed as he linked his arm through hers and walked into the hall.

Looking shocked, Emma replied, "I didn't bring a suit. You didn't tell me to come prepared for a beach outing."

"Don't worry. You'll find everything you'll need in the room next door. I took the liberty of buying a suit for you. I'll meet you in the living room in ten minutes," Jordan said with a smile as he watched Emma's incredulous expression.

"Okay," Emma replied with raised brows. "You certainly are a man of many surprises."

Closing the door behind her, Emma leaned against the frame as she scanned the room. She saw nothing on the bed that might hint at the presence of a bathing suit. Walking to the cherry triple dresser, she opened the top drawer to find a conservative black maillot with matching shorts and cover. Holding the suit to her body, Emma was impressed to see that Jordan had selected the correct size without asking her. The size ten would fit her trim figure perfectly. Jordan had even purchased black beach shoes in a size eight, suntan lotion, and lip gloss.

After putting on the beachwear, Emma smiled as she took in her reflection in the full-length mirror. The suit showed off her figure to perfection. The hours on the treadmill and at the weight machines had paid off. Slipping her feet into the shoes and adjusting the waist of the shorts, she felt pride in her appearance. She was proof that even a busy executive could find the time to exercise.

Jordan was waiting for her when Emma appeared in the living room with her bag as the grandfather clock in the hall chimed the hour. True to her word, she had used only ten minutes to change, hang up her clothing, and admire her reflection. Jordan was impressed that Emma was not only fabulous to look at, but punctual, too.

"I'm glad to see that everything fits, and nicely, too, I might add," he said with a smile.

Blushing at the attention and the appreciation of her long hours of hard work at the gym, Emma smiled and asked, "Are we ready? The water is calling my name."

"Follow me. I've already set out the umbrella and

the chairs." Jordan grinned like a small boy who was about to show his friend a prized toy.

Taking her hand, Jordan led the way through the immaculately clean kitchen to the mudroom and the beach beyond. The sun shone brightly as they stepped onto the deck that surrounded the house on three sides and provided a place for leisurely dining and for basking in the beauty of Chesapeake Bay. Gulls flapped their wings and called happily as Jordan threw scraps of bread into the air for them to catch. Emma laughed as an especially brave bird swooped down and took the offering from her fingers.

Walking beside Jordan with her fingers laced through his, Emma felt completely happy and at ease. She had been reluctant to take their relationship to the next level, but now she was glad that she had. He made her feel as if she belonged in his life. The easy tone of their conversation relaxed and reassured her as she matched her strides to his. She could not remember a time when she had enjoyed someone's company so completely.

Emma had expected to see the towels and umbrella flapping in the gentle breeze as they rounded the clump of marsh grass that served as the separation between Jordan's backyard and the Bay. However, she was greatly surprised by the sight of a cabana complete with roof for shade, his-and-hers changing rooms, and an oversize shower facility.

"May I offer you a soda? Perhaps you'd prefer something stronger?" Jordan asked with a bow.

"Oh, no thanks. I'm already drunk on the view, but a soda would taste great. So this is the Bay that everyone raves about. All my life I've lived within driving distance of heaven and never saw it in all its beauty," Emma said as she watched the white sailboats drifting along as if without a care in the world. An occasional speedboat whipped up the tranquil lapping of the water against the shore and the piers.

Sinking into the offered chair, she did not even notice as Jordan eased from her side to return quickly with two tall glasses of soda. Absently sipping the cold, refreshing liquid, Emma could not tear her eyes away from the water. She had never been a water baby and preferred the hustle and bustle of the big city. However, as yet another sail disappeared on the horizon, Emma could understand the pull that the Bay and the Atlantic Ocean beyond had on the lives of men and women.

Emma remembered the visits to Annapolis when she was a child and the stunning views of the Severn River waterfront from the restaurants. Her father had brought them to the historic town for the seafood, but Emma had come for the entertainment. She loved to watch the gulls as they soared happily overhead and begged for food from the tourists who stood on the dock. She had laughed at their hilarious antics.

As she grew older, the midshipmen of the U.S. Naval Academy became the major attraction in Annapolis. Emma and her friends had made numerous trips to the Yard to watch the mids walk down the tree-lined lanes in their summer-white uniforms. Although she had found many of them handsome and great conversationalists, Emma had decided that a life without roots was not for her. However, her best friend had married one of them as soon as they'd graduated from college.

"A penny for your thoughts," Jordan offered as he sank into the chair at her side.

"I wasn't thinking anything special, just remembering other visits to the Bay. It's lovely here," Emma replied without turning her attention away from the peaceful water and the gently gliding boats.

"I love it here, too. I can't wait another minute for that swim. Will you join me?" Jordan asked as he pulled off his T-shirt to expose a well-defined chest.

"Maybe in a little bit. I'm not much for cold-water swimming. Come back for me if the water's eighty degrees," Emma said, laughing as she waved him away.

"Suit yourself. After my swim, let's eat that lunch you packed," Jordan replied as he kicked off his sandals and started across the warm sand to the water. "Later, we'll go crabbing for our dinner. See you in a little bit."

"Sooner than that if the water's cold," Emma shouted over the roar of the tide.

Laughing, Jordan waved, turned, and trotted toward the shoreline. Without hesitating, he walked into the water up to his waist and then dove under the foaming waves. When he reappeared, he wrapped his arms around his body, shivered, waved, and slipped under again.

Deciding that Jordan must enjoy cool water, Emma pulled out the paperback that she carried in her bag. Propping it on her knees, she quickly became absorbed in the story. With only the lapping of the waves and the calling of the gulls as her companions, she was perfectly at peace.

"Is lunch ready?" Jordan asked as he dripped water onto the sand.

"Oh, I guess I lost track of time. It's so lovely here. Dry off while I get it ready," Emma replied as she quickly set the table with the delectable dishes she had prepared.

As they munched the light repast, they chatted like old friends. There was none of the tension between them that often interferes with a new relationship or a first real date. They were comfortable together and at ease on the little strip of beach that they had claimed as their own.

"So, you've never gone crabbing. You'll like it. It's really very easy. At least the way I do it is simple," Jordan pointed out as he finished the last of the Merlot and licked the last remnants of the pâté from his fingers.

"Never," Emma replied. "I've seen plenty of news footage about the shortage of good waterways, the premature harvesting of crabs, and the difficulties the men experience as they try to make a living on the Bay, but I've never caught any myself."

"You eat crabs, don't you?" Jordan asked as he studied her face closely.

"Well, I've never actually eaten any. I've prepared many dishes with them, but I've never sat down to a meal of crabs. All that cracking and picking seems like a lot of work to me for so little meat," Emma confessed as she returned the empty containers to the basket and tidied up the cabana.

"I'll just have to be the man to introduce you to the wonders of the Maryland blue crab. But first, let's go for a little swim," Jordan replied as he took Emma's hand firmly in his grasp.

"Isn't the water cold? You looked chilled. I can wait until next time," Emma suggested as she pulled toward the shore. The water was so close that she could feel the spray on her face.

"I was only joking. It's wonderfully refreshing with only the slightest chill. Let's go!" Jordan shouted as he broke into a run, taking Emma with him.

As soon as her toes touched the pleasantly warm water of the Bay, Emma forgot all of her hesitation. Diving into the surf beside Jordan, she glided through the water as if born to it. She felt wonderfully at home and alive as the current caressed her body and moved her in its embrace.

When they finally returned to the cabana, Emma felt relaxed and exhilarated at the same time. Her skin tingled from the stinging water, her muscles twitched from the exertion of swimming against the currents, and her heart pumped from the exertion. She was tired in a wonderful way.

"Did you have a good time?" Jordan asked as he toweled off and wrapped the towel around his waist.

"Better than you can ever imagine. Thanks for not letting me stay on shore," Emma replied with a smile as she slipped into the terry-cloth coverup.

"Great! Now, let's change and go crabbing. I can't wait to introduce you to one of my favorite foods," Jordan said as he picked up the basket and led the way into the house.

"What are your other favorites? Will we have to catch them, too?" Emma shouted over the calls of the gulls.

"No, they're much simpler. One is thick, chocolate cake, and the other is . . . well, I'll tell you about that one some other time," Jordan replied with a wicked grin as he held the door open.

"Okay . . . I won't pry. I know when to leave well enough alone. I'll meet you here in twenty minutes. I need to shower off some of this salt and sand," Emma said as she vanished into the bedroom that Jordan had prepared for her.

"Let me know if you need any help," Jordan replied almost under his breath.

"I heard that, and I can take care of myself just fine. I'll see you in a bit," Emma said, laughing as she shut the door between them.

"Just my luck. The woman's not only beautiful, but she has great hearing," Jordan whispered to himself as he peeked around the corner at the closed door. He almost expected Emma to reappear. Shrugging his broad shoulders, Jordan gave up and walked to the other bathroom and a much-needed shower.

As the warm water washed away the smell of the Bay, Emma wondered how different a shower with Jordan would be from the solitary one that she was enjoying. She had almost decided to call his bluff when she overheard his offer of assistance but decided against it. She was not ready yet to let down her guard to him completely. She was enjoying every minute of their time together, but she still needed to know him better before allowing the relationship to move to another level. She knew that too many seemingly perfect matches made in the heat of the sun quickly turned to nothing special in the cool of the evening. In the meantime, Emma would make herself content with a soapy loofah sponge.

Jordan was not as resigned to his state of loneliness. He had planned the day very carefully and had trusted the sun and surf to take care of washing away the last of Emma's resistance to him. He could see the wall that she had built between them slowly cracking, but it was not ready to crumble. Rinsing the burning shampoo from his eyes, Jordan wondered how much longer he would have to wait for Emma to realize that they were meant for each other if she would only give their relationship a chance.

Six

Crabbing with Jordan was nothing like what Emma had imagined. She had pictured them sitting on the end of the pier with their crab pots resting on the sandy bottom while a leisurely sunset glowed around them. She had pictured them holding a can of soda or beer as the crab willingly climbed into the pot in search of the waiting bait.

The reality was a bobbing, almost flat-bottomed, boat captained by a smelly, crusty old seaman whose idea of entertaining his paying customers was to spit tobacco juice in a well-aimed stream in the direction of the cracked spittoon. Some city folks might have found his behavior quaint, but Emma thought him disgusting. The sight of the brown spittle clinging to his yellow-gray beard, the smell of diesel fuel, and the rocking of the sorry excuse for a boat almost made her sick.

"Isn't this fun!" Jordan shouted over the coughing and sputtering of the motor as he checked his empty crab pot.

"Wonderful," Emma replied as she stepped aside in time to avoid having a misguided stream hit her new tennis shoe.

"I'm so glad I decided to hire him rather than taking out my little boat. This is so much more enjoyable. I don't have to steer and can just enjoy myself," Jordan chirped as he tossed the rusted cage overboard again.

"I can't imagine preferring the leather upholstery and the wood-trimmed elegance of your boat to this cracked seat," Emma muttered under her breath as she tried to enjoy herself despite the bile rising in her throat.

"What did you say?" Jordan asked as he transferred the snapping blue crab from his second pot into the half-full bushel basket.

"Nothing important. I was just wondering how many more you plan to catch. How many can we eat? Remember, I'm not really a crab fancier," Emma replied, burping delicately.

"I can easily put away two dozen plus corn. Once you get the knack of cracking them, you'll probably eat a dozen yourself. They're kind of small, anyway. We'll try to fill the basket. The leftovers will keep in the refrigerator for tomorrow," Jordan explained as he counted the contents.

"Oh," Emma muttered as she turned her attention to the shore. The beach looked so far away. She wondered if she could swim the distance or if the tide were too strong. If the rocking of the boat did not stop soon, she decided that she would give it a try.

Slipping onto the seat beside her, Jordan continued to babble about the joys of cooking and eating crabs. Emma barely listened as she tried to think of a way to end the torture of the crabbing experience and retreat to the safety of the city. She did not want to endure an evening of cracking the red, spice-covered claws, wiping the sticky "mustard" from her hands, and avoiding the "dead man's fingers" in her search of a morsel to eat. Jordan might look with relish on the experience, but she wanted to go home. Fighting with the electric opener for the contents of a can of tuna was more to her taste. Sighing deeply, she regretted not having driven herself to Jordan's retreat.

If Jordan noticed Emma's boredom and discomfort, he did not let on as he expertly shared his personal tips on the eating of hard-shell crabs. Between his vivid descriptions, the rocking of the boat, and the smell of the skipper, Emma was turning a decided shade of green. If she did not escape soon, she would certainly lose her composure and her lunch.

Just as Emma thought that she would jump overboard and try to swim to shore, the bells on the end of the twelve trot lines started to jingle furiously. Rushing from one to the other, Jordan carefully lifted each heavy crab pot out of the water. Placing it on the deck, he quickly emptied the contents and turned his attention to another. By the time he had emptied each one, the basket was full. Emma was finally free to return to land . . . and the crab dinner.

The aroma of the sea and the squirming crustaceans filled the car as they drove back to Jordan's house. Although Emma's stomach had settled now that she was no longer captive on the rocking boat, her nose had not been liberated from the unique smell of crabs. Even with the windows open, she knew that eau de crab clung to her hair, clothing, and skin.

Although Emma had developed many dishes in which crabmeat played a starring role, she was not prepared for the experience of cooking them. She watched attentively as Jordan set the huge steaming pot on the stove and seasoned the water with vinegar, beer, and peppers from a well-used red can. Opening the lid of the basket, he gingerly extracted the crabs and tossed them into the steam as they clung together in a long, wiggling, snapping blue line.

"Doesn't this smell great? You'll love them. They're

ready as soon as they turn completely red," Jordan commented over his shoulder as he pushed the last recalcitrant crab into the pot. He did not wait for her response as he started tossing more crabs into the second pot.

Emma stared horrified as the crabs inside the pot wrestled with one another as they tried to escape. It looked to her as if the pot rocked with their violent efforts. Finally, their struggling slowed and stopped. However, the smell changed from the old disgusting one to something akin to sewer stench as the crabs cooked.

Suddenly Jordan's dog let out a yelp. One of the crabs had escaped from the basket and had skittered toward the young dog. Thinking that it was a new toy, Buster had playfully patted it with his front paw. The crab, already agitated by the captivity of the basket, snapped its fierce claw tightly around the dog's paw. Buster now stood shaking his injured paw and looking helplessly from Jordan to Emma for rescue.

Lifting the top of the pots for a quick peek, Jordan turned to her with satisfaction on his sweating face. Water and seasoning spots dotted his clothing. An abandoned claw stuck to the heavy glove that had protected his hands from attack. He looked very pleased with himself, almost like the caveman hunters who returned triumphantly with food for their family across their back.

"Jordan, look at Buster. A crab got him," Emma shouted over the sound of scratching crabs and clanging utensils.

"He should know better than to play with them. Last year, one of them pinched his nose while we were down here visiting friends. Come here, Buster, so I can remove that monster. That's a good boy," Jordan said as he skillfully extracted the dog's paw from the crustacean's grasp.

"Let's set the table on the deck. The first batch will be ready in just a few minutes. There's newspaper in the corner, paper plates in the cupboard, and nut picks and mallets in that drawer," Jordan instructed as he pointed in the different directions from which Emma could retrieve the necessary items.

Barely able to stand the smell of the crab-scented steam any longer, Emma nodded and moved in the direction in which he had pointed with his gloved hand. She quickly gathered the items as the claw attached to the glove dangled helplessly in the air. Standing on the deck, she breathed heavily of the fresh Bay air, only too happy to be free from the odor of the kitchen.

The setting sun sparkled on the water, turning it shades of purple, blue, and crimson. The comforting sound of the waves lapping at the shore greeted her ears. In the distance, Emma could see the glow of cookouts and hear the laughter of children as they played on the beach.

"Dinner's ready. I hope you're hungry," Jordan announced as he brought the tray of bright red crabs to the brown-paper covered table. The Silver Queen corn glistened with butter.

"Great!" Emma replied as she tried to be a good sport and not ruin his dinner.

"Let me show you how to open them. First you pop off the claws and legs. Then you insert the blade of your knife here at the tab. Lift up and pull back. Now stick your fingers inside the shell and pull to separate the top from the underside. Remove the dead man's fingers and the mustard if you don't want to eat it. Pick out the meat with one of these nut picks or with your fingers. It's sweet and delicious. You'll love it."

"I'm sure I will," Emma said as she gripped the spice-covered crustacean and pulled off the legs. Fishy water and excess spice splattered her clothes. The salt burned the tiny cut in her cuticle.

"The bibs! I forgot them. Just a minute," Jordan announced as he rose from the table and vanished into the house.

Alone again on the deck, Emma examined the meal more closely. The salad and corn looked very inviting, but the main course of steaming crabs did nothing for her. She could have endured crab cakes and a thick bowl of soup, but the idea of picking the meat from them after dissecting them left her cold. To be polite, she would eat one. After that, Emma decided that she would satisfy her hunger with the corn.

Jordan carefully tied the huge plastic bib around her neck and spread the fabric over her clothing. Taking his seat opposite her, he watched with anticipation as Emma returned to the task of extracting the morsels of meat from the hard shell. He smiled at her success and turned his attention to the large male crab on his plate. For a while they did not speak as music from the living room drifted onto the deck.

After what seemed to Emma like hours of silence, Jordan looked up from the pile of crab carcasses on his plate. He looked surprised to see only the one on hers. He had been so engrossed with his own pleasure at picking the delectable treats, that he had forgotten Emma's possible discomfort.

Finally Jordan asked, "Aren't you hungry? I would have thought the salt air would have increased your appetite. It always makes me eat like crazy."

"I'm not a big eater. One crab was enough for me. I'll just sit here and watch you," Emma replied with a gracious smile.

Already Emma was counting the minutes before

they would return home. As lovely as she found the
Bay, she had experienced enough of the joy of crab
eating and could not understand people's desire to
spend exorbitant amounts of money for a bushel of
them. To her, a crab dinner was greatly overrated.

The ringing of the telephone interrupted their dinner. As Jordan rushed into the living room, he wiped
his hands on the red-stained bib that covered his
shirt. The pile of shells and the discarded corncobs
lay forgotten on his littered plate. From the serious
tone in his voice, Emma could tell that their evening
had come to a close.

Scooping up the plates, Jordan said, "That was the
president. We'll have to return to D.C. I'm sorry to
have to end our evening so early."

Rolling the spice-spotted paper into a neat package,
Emma tried to sound disappointed as she replied,
"Don't worry, Jordan, we can always come here again
sometime."

Following him into the kitchen, Emma forced the
corners of her mouth not to smile. She was more
than ready to leave the smell of Maryland's fabled
delicacy. Returning to D.C. would not pose a hard-
ship. If she never saw a crab in anything other than
soup or cakes, she would be only too happy.

Emma listened attentively on the drive home to
every detail of Jordan's responsibilities on the president's task force. She was impressed by his self-effacing
demeanor in light of the significance of his work and
would have understood if he had been conceited about
being so close to the source of world power. However,
he very simply told her stories of his experiences without embellishing the facts or painting himself in a glo-
rified role. Despite his culinary preferences, Jordan's
modesty was quite becoming.

The streetlights were flickering in the summer evening heat as they pulled to a stop in front of Emma's home. Although Jordan was an interesting man, she was not ready for the relationship that he clearly wanted to begin.

Walking her to the door, Jordan carefully grasped Emma's hand in his and said, "I had hoped to be able to talk you into staying longer with me at the beach. I hadn't counted on this interruption. Maybe we could try again next week?"

"I really can't, Jordan. My calendar is filled for the next few weeks. This was the last free weekend for some time. You'll have to give me a rain check until after Labor Day," Emma replied, happy that she did not have to lie. Her business obligations really would keep her out of contact with her friends until September.

"That long? Well, in that case, this will have to last me for a while," Jordan said as he pulled Emma into his arms and placed a warm kiss on her upturned lips.

Emma's surprise at finding herself in Jordan's arms quickly changed to acceptance as the nearness of him seeped into her body. Relaxing a bit, she found that she enjoyed the feel of his strong yet gentle closeness. She almost abandoned her reasons for not wanting to pursue a relationship with Jordan until the lingering smell of crabs reached her nose. The cloying odor of the salt and the seaweed mixed with the peppery seasoning clung to the gentle fingers that softly brushed her cheek, bringing with it the sudden return to the hopelessness of their relationship.

"Jordan, let me be perfectly honest with you about any possibility for a relationship between us," Emma began as she disentangled herself from the comfort of his arms. "Yes, my schedule is tight, but that's not the only reason that I can't see you. I just don't think that we're compatible. You enjoy activities that I don't. You're an outdoor person, and I'm definitely not. We're of an age that we shouldn't have to give up our pastimes to be with someone. I wouldn't think of asking you to stop enjoying crabbing, but I don't want to do it. The smell and the sight of them turn me off. I can't help it, and I can't pretend to enjoy your hobby."

Looking at her in the moonlight, Jordan replied, "Emma, this is really just a small part of my life. I can go crabbing without you if you're really that against it. If you'd said something today, we wouldn't have had them for dinner. I wouldn't feel deprived by not being able to eat them. I want a chance to know you better and to have you in my life. That's what's important right now."

"It's not just the crabs, Jordan," Emma retorted, shaking her head. "It's more than that. It's your high profile, your demanding job, and your lifestyle. When I become involved with a man again, I want to know that I come first with him. That's not possible with you. We can't even have dinner without you receiving a call from the White House. No, Jordan, it won't work."

Looking dejected, Jordan stated, "I know you'll find this difficult to believe after tonight, but I usually have more control over my life than this. True, I work late evenings, but you probably do also. It'll only take co-ordinating our schedules to make our relationship work. Tonight's an anomaly. I'm usually at home evenings after eight without anyone calling me."

"You're right," Emma said as she unlocked the door and stepped inside. "I do find it difficult to believe considering the number of times that I've seen your name on the guest lists for functions I've catered. No, Jordan, we're better off ending this before it gets started. Neither of us needs to be disappointed at this stage of our lives."

Throwing his hands wide, Jordan replied, "I guess I'll just have to prove it to you, Emma. I won't take no for an answer. I'll call you next week. We'll have dinner without the interference of the telephone. You'll see."

Shaking her head at his persistence, yet smiling at his determination, Emma commented, "You're facing an uphill battle. Good night, Jordan."

As the door closed on the weekend, Jordan noticed the brightness of the moon. He loved the relative quiet and laziness of the summer. His work usually slowed down a bit during the hot months, giving him time to relax at the beach. He could already tell that this summer would be different. Between the constant demands of the White House and Emma's reluctance to see him, he would certainly have his work cut out for him.

Giving Emma's house one last look as light flickered behind the sheers at the front windows, Jordan shrugged and folded his tall frame into his car. He had encountered difficult situations in his climb up the professional ladder. He would simply have to figure out a way to manage these two important forces in his life. He wanted both with equal determination.

As he drove down the silent street, Jordan promised himself that he would sacrifice neither for the other. In many ways, Emma's shell would be more difficult to crack than a crab's. Smiling, Jordan knew that he was ready for the challenge. He already knew that Emma was a treasure that he would not allow to drift from his life.

Seven

Emma's desk contained the usual clutter of partially planned menus, correspondence, bills, phone messages, and contracts. The recent surge of publicity had increased the EJ's cash flow by a staggering amount. She had already budgeted a raise for all of her employees and, at this rate, would be able to offer another in six months.

The only thing that would make the success sweeter would be an invitation to dinner at the White House. Like all caterers of the rich, famous, and powerful, Emma wanted just once to enjoy their lifestyle without being among the staff providing it. She wanted to be served in the style to which she had enabled so many to become accustomed.

"Good morning!" Bonnie chirped as she bounded into the room in her usual unannounced fashion.

"Don't you ever knock? I could have been involved in amorous pursuits," Emma scolded lightly as she smiled at her friend.

"That'll be the day," Bonnie retorted with a chuckle as she perched on the nearest chair. As always, she did not sit back and relax. She was always ready to rush off at a moment's notice.

"Stranger things have happened. I'll get invited to the White House for dinner one day, too," Emma said as she pushed aside her work. She had learned from their long association that concentration would be impossible until after Bonnie left.

"Well, then, this is your lucky day. Not only do you have the honor of my company, but I come bearing gifts. Take a look at this," Bonnie replied as she tossed a thick, gold-embossed, off-white envelope onto Emma's desk.

"You're kidding!" Emma commented in disbelief as she fingered the seal in the upper left corner. "Is this really for me?"

"No, it's for another Emma Jones. I delivered it to the wrong person," Bonnie quipped. "Of course, it's for you. I intercepted Bob, your mail carrier, on my way in. He is one handsome man. I had never noticed the depth of his hazel eyes until today. There's something about a brother with light eyes that sets my heart on fire."

"Bonnie! I'm surprised you ever got married. I've never seen you in the company of a brother who didn't make you go limp at the knees," Emma replied as she carefully slipped the blade of the letter opener under the flap.

"I have a deep and sincere appreciation for men, that's all. Being married doesn't stop me from looking and enjoying God's handiwork. I'm especially fond of his greatest accomplishments. I certainly hope you get that open before the next century," Bonnie pointed out as she watched Emma's painfully slow progress.

"Don't rush me. I'm savoring every minute. It's not every day that I receive an invitation like this. I've dreamed of this moment ever since I opened the business," Emma answered as she gently extracted the matching response card and invitation.

"You're the slowest person I've ever met. Consider-

ing you never do anything except work, I'd say from
the way that you're approaching this task that you
never get invited to anything. Hurry up! Neither of
us is getting any younger," Bonnie snarled as she tried
to peek over Emma's shoulder. Her hands itched to
snatch the paper from her friend and read the contents for herself.

"Oh, my!" Emma sighed as she held the invitation
for Bonnie to read. "I've been invited to a White
House dinner in honor of the arts. Can you imagine
it? Me, a simple caterer lifting my pinkie with the best
of them."

"Would you please stop! You've making me sick to
my stomach. Take off the robe of humility. It's about
time that your light shone from under that bushel
basket of yours. You're the best caterer in the Washington Metro area," Bonnie scolded with a laugh as
she gazed at the elegantly composed letter.

"All kidding aside, I am thrilled. What should I
wear? How should I act? You said it yourself. I'm not
exactly the most socially mobile person," Emma replied as she propped the invitation against the photo
depicting the front of the shop, which she kept on
her desk.

"I wouldn't worry if I were you. The place will be
packed," Bonnie commented as she returned to her
seat. "Besides, everyone knows that you're the most
artistic and talented caterer in the area. It's about
time you received the recognition that you're due. I'll
be the proudest person there. Everyone will be waiting to hear your reaction to the food. Being invited
to this dinner means that you've arrived. I've very
proud of you."

"I wouldn't dare criticize the White House chefs.
I'll be on my best behavior all evening," Emma as-
sured her friend as she marked the date on her cal-

endar. "Considering that the White House employs some of the best chefs in the country, it shouldn't be too difficult to give the meal and its presentation a five-star review."

"Still, I'm glad I'll be there to see your moment of glory," Bonnie replied as she puffed up her chest and raised her head proudly.

"Wonderful! I bet they invited you because of the success of your business, too," Emma said with genuine pleasure at having Bonnie share the evening with her.

"No, I'm the Mrs. on the envelope," Bonnie responded with a shake of her heard. "Don't forget that my husband is with an influential firm. This is one of those payback deals. His firm must have contributed a large sum to the reelection effort and now we've been invited to dinner at the White House."

"We'll just have to make sure that everyone understands that you're a successful businesswoman and should have been invited because of your contributions to the arts. After all, you're the one who finds all the organizations that we support," Emma stated, her irritation with the continuing double standard showing.

Before Bonnie could respond, the jingling of the telephone interrupted their conversation. Knowing that her secretary was at lunch, Emma picked up on the second ring.

"EJ's, Emma Jones speaking," she answered briskly in her most professional voice and reached for a notepad. As always, Emma was prepared to take notes.

"Hello, lady. Did you receive your invitation yet?" Jordan's deep, sexy voice greeted her ear, making her wish that she could find his company to her liking.

Feeling the color rise in her cheeks despite her determination to keep Jordan out of her life, Emma smiled and replied, "Yes, but how did you know that I'd been invited? I suppose we're seated at the same table, too."

Chuckling, he stated, "As a matter of fact, we are."

"How did you arrange that?" Emma asked incredulously, although she already sensed the answer.

"The president owes me a few favors for late nights and lost weekends. If I remember correctly, the most recent one directly affected you," Jordan replied with a deep chuckle that made Emma feel warm and soft all over.

Before she continued the banter, Emma ran through the mental list of reasons for not liking Jordan. She did not want her reaction to his sex appeal to misrepresent her feelings for him. In her mind, their relationship had no present or future and only a shaky, very forgettable past. She would have to remain true to her convictions despite his obvious determination to win her affections.

"He's a very accommodating boss if he'll allow you to invite a nobody to one of his famous dinners," Emma replied, feeling the wind flow from the sails of her elation at being invited.

"I didn't have much to do. Your name was already on the list," Jordan responded with a little less than his usual confidence at her tone. "My secretary remembered the professional connection between us and asked if I wanted us to be dinner companions. She winked and implied that she thought that something more might come between us than simply salad. It seems that she thinks of herself as a matchmaker. Anyway, I quickly agreed. I hope you don't mind."

"I'm thrilled to have been invited. Your company will be an extra bonus," Emma replied, trying not to sound either too standoffish or too inviting.

"Great! I know you're busy so I won't keep you any

longer. I'll see you at dinner," Jordan concluded with restored vigor.

"Yes, Jordan. I'll see you there," Emma replied quickly.

Sighing, Emma hung up and explained the gist of the conversation to the waiting Bonnie. Although she found Jordan's attention flattering, Emma did not want to start something that she had no intention of continuing. She had never given a man the wrong impression of her feelings toward him and did not plan to start now.

"Look at it this way, Emma," Bonnie counseled. "You won't have to eat dinner alone with him or suffer through any more crabs."

"You're right. It could be worse. But I still don't have anything to wear," Emma agreed.

"We'll solve that problem later. I know just the place. We'll whip through there tomorrow at lunch. You'll look so wonderful that all of the single men, including Jordan, will have a hard time keeping their eyes off you," Bonnie said as she gathered her things and walked to the door.

"Let's not overdo it. I'd like to present the 'sophisticated businesswoman not looking for a man' look," Emma replied with a wave and chuckle as Bonnie closed the door behind her.

As the silence filled the office, Emma again picked up the invitation. She did not care if she would have to share a table with Jordan, a man that she could not like because of their differences but that she found decidedly attractive. She, the owner of EJ's, was on her way to a White House dinner.

But Jordan would be there and they would share a table. Walking to the window, Emma allowed the thought of being with him again after the disastrous crab dinner to play through her mind. She could not deny that Jordan was an exciting man. The sound of his voice over the phone almost made her dismiss her resolve to remain unattached. His wit and charm almost compensated for his love of crabbing and obsessive dedication to work.

Returning to her desk, Emma decided that Jordan did not really possess any serious flaws. He simply was not the man for her at this time in her life. Tomorrow she might look at her future and Jordan differently, but today she would remain firm in her decision to keep him at arm's length.

Emma accomplished a remarkable amount of work despite the constant interruptions from phone calls. As soon as the article with the list of attendees appeared in the paper, everyone she knew called to congratulate her on the invitation, and bookings increased threefold. Scratching her head, she calculated the increased income and salaries from this notoriety. This free advertising had certainly made a difference in her cash flow.

The calls continued for the next few days. Old friends with whom she had not spoken in years suddenly remembered her number. Even her former husband called to say that he had seen the article and was proud of her accomplishments. Emma doubted that she would ever stand in anyone's shadow again.

With Bonnie's help, Emma purchased the perfect black evening gown. The tight bodice accentuated her waist as the bustier clung to her firm bust. The matching gold metallic-thread embroidered shawl draped perfectly around her shoulders. She had found the perfect pair of gold-and-black evening sandals that clung to her feet with the tiniest of straps that crisscrossed across the top of the foot and accentuated her slim ankles.

Watching Emma turn to view her reflection in her bedroom mirror, Bonnie commented, "Now, that's a dress! It's professional and alluring at the same time. I hope the other women have good psychiatrists. They'll need them for ego repair after they see you in that outfit."

"You exaggerate, but I appreciate the thought. It is a drop-dead-gorgeous gown. And it does look good on me!" Emma laughed as she accepted the compliment. She had been floating on a cloud of happiness since the invitation arrived and did not plan to stop now.

"I'm just glad I'm happily married," Bonnie chirped as she gathered her purchases and headed toward the door. "I'd better get home before I find a Dear Jane letter on my plate. Don't come downstairs. I'll let myself out."

"Thanks for the help. I couldn't have done it without you," Emma replied as she embraced her dear friend.

"You could have but not as well. See you later," Bonnie stated as she eased from the room and down the circular staircase. Emma listened as Bonnie quickly activated the security system and closed the front door.

"I feel like Cinderella on the way to the ball," Emma whispered as she stepped out of the dress and hung it in the closet. It had been a long day, and she was tired. Knowing that the next day would be longer and even more demanding, she slipped into her favorite sleep shirt. She would read for a while and then go to bed early although she doubted that she would sleep.

As the clock in the hall struck eleven, Emma put down her book, crawled between the sheets, and turned out the light. Her friends had stopped calling with their congratulations. The silence of the last hour had been perfect, and she promptly fell asleep.

A huge bouquet of dendrobium and baby's breath arrived before Emma could leave for work the next morning. Accompanying it was a card that read, "Until tonight." Despite her best efforts, Emma could not disregard Jordan's determination. It had been a long time since a man had cared enough to pursue her with this energy. The longevity of the flower selection did not escape Emma's attention.

As a matter of fact, her ex-husband was the last man to spend this level of energy on her behalf, Emma realized as she made her way to the office. He had showered her with gifts, taken her on long rides in the country, and spent a fortune on theater tickets. Unfortunately, as soon as the ink had dried on their license, he had turned to his work for excitement and later to her secretary, leaving her to her own resources.

If it had not been for Bonnie, Emma would have spent many lonely nights with nothing to do. Bonnie had taken Emma under her wing and included her in all of her family's plans. Even when Emma had felt like the third wheel, Bonnie had insisted that she accompany them. It was during that period of loneliness that Emma had learned to depend on Bonnie, and they had become the best of friends. They always knew when to help and when to give space.

Now it looked as if Jordan wanted to make a place for himself in her life. Emma found the prospects intriguing and unsettling. As Emma sorted through her in box, she wondered if she could accept the change that Jordan's presence would make in her level of independence. She would keep an open mind. The dinner at the White House would prove very insightful.

Eight

The White House looked like a fairy-tale with small
white lights twinkling in the trees, mirrors and crystal
reflecting hundreds of candles and thousands of
chandelier lights, and tropical flowers flowing from
vases both large and small. Waiters with fresh linen
folded over their arms anticipated the desires of the
guests. Before a glass became empty, wine or brandy
from a crystal decanter appeared and refilled it. Plates
of unspeakable eye appeal held indescribable gastronomical treats. Wine of only the most celebrated vin-
tage flowed as freely as the rose-scented water of
fountains in each corner of the massive dining room.

Not to be outdone, the ladies wore custom-made
gowns from the most famous couturiers. Their jewels
had come from the depths of their safe-deposit boxes
for the occasion or had been borrowed from willing
jewelers who realized the benefit of having their name
mentioned in such well-heeled company. Their hair
had been manipulated into styles bordering on creative art.

Even the men had been infected with the feeling
of festivity. On an evening like this, only the best tailored tuxedo from the leading men's clothing de-
signer would be appropriate. The lapels could not be

too wide or narrow, and the color had to be conservative but not stodgy.

Many guests had opted for rented limousines and drivers.

Emma stepped out of her limousine with the assistance of a gloved dressmess-attired Marine. The red and gold of his uniform gave a festive air to the front portico. Thanking him, she eased into the line of guests who drifted into the White House on the mingled fragrances of expensive perfumes and roses. Chandeliers glittered overhead on the famous portico as the White House staff in freshly pressed tuxedos greeted each guest.

Not all of the stars glittered in the sky that night. Movie and theater celebrities rubbed elbows with foreign dignitaries and high government officials as they wandered through the public rooms of the White House. Most of them were tastefully dressed in stylish but not flashy gowns, although a few had donned the flamboyant fashions of Hollywood that exposed more flesh than was customary at White House dinners. After all, this was an evening dedicated to the celebration of the arts in all of its many forms.

Sweet strains of music from a string quintet greeted Emma as she joined the receiving line. The president was famous for greeting each guest prior to ushering them into the dining room. According to what the newspaper explained, he wanted each one to feel as if the White House was truly the peoples' house. From the length of each conversation, Emma could tell that he was quite successful in lavishing each guest with charm.

Standing in line, Emma scanned the magnificent East Room with its stunning tapestries and glorious silk rugs. She marveled at the splendor of a room that only hours before had received curious guests in shorts and T-shirts. She could understand the pull of the White House and its famous occupants. She had taken the tour many times herself when entertaining out-of-town guests, and never grew tired of seeing the magnificent house.

Emma's head felt light with excitement, and the air seemed to have taken on a thinner quality. The chandeliers twinkled more intensely than any she had ever seen. The colors of the flowers that adorned every table and vase were more vibrant than those of the Botanical Garden only a few blocks away. She stood among the rich and famous of the world, something she had only dreamed that she would do. She felt like Cinderella as she waited for the prince to notice her.

And he did. Jordan had arrived early and had been searching the faces for Emma's. Finally finding her, he had smiled broadly and rushed to her side. He turned many heads as he took the most direct route across the expanse of the room rather than walking around the outskirts as many others did. Jordan was so focused on Emma that he did not notice as the admiring glances followed him.

"Good evening," Jordan said as he stepped closer and lightly touched Emma's arm.

"Jordan, I'm so glad to see you. Bonnie hasn't arrived, and I was beginning to wonder if I'd ever see a familiar face. You look quite dashing in your tux," Emma replied, grateful at having someone to chat with while waiting to shake the president's hand.

"I've been watching for you. You look terrific," Jordan commented as he stepped close enough to smell her perfume. He added, "And you smell great."

Feeling her cheeks color, Emma responded, "Thanks. Just a little something Bonnie helped me pick out. Is it always this packed at these dinner parties?"

"Always. I don't think I've ever attended a small gathering of less than a few hundred close friends of the president. I guess it can be overwhelming at first," Jordan agreed as he surveyed the crowd.

"It's more than a little overwhelming. My head is spinning. I've never seen so many people trying to appear confident and unimpressed in my life. I wonder if their knees are knocking as hard as mine," Emma commented as she looked at the clusters of people who appeared inured to the glitter and pomp of an evening at the White House.

Laughing, Jordan replied, "That's why they're talking so fast and so furiously. They think that no one will hear their knees knocking if they say lots of forgettable things. Don't worry, you're doing fine."

"How long did it take you to get used to all of this?" Emma asked as she inched closer to the president. She could see the top of his head from where she stood.

"Who says I'm used to it? Each time I'm invited to one of these, I have to gird my loins against the possibility of attack. I never know what kind of piranha will come out with the stars. I'm always nervous at these affairs," Jordan replied with a confident air that belied his words.

"But surely not tonight. This is an arts evening," Emma pointed out with a fleeting frown that darted across her brow.

"Tonight I'm more nervous than I've been in a long time," Jordan replied as he stepped a bit closer so that they would not have to shout over the din.

"Why?"

"Because you're here," Jordan stated simply as he looked deep into Emma's eyes.

"You needn't worry about me. I'm definitely not as threatening as Orrin Hatch or Ted Kennedy," Emma replied softly. She felt both flattered and startled by his direct approach.

"You are in your own way. I care more about your opinion of me than theirs. I can always heal my reputation. Feelings are harder to mend," Jordan whispered. The touch of his hand on her arm and the closeness of his face created a safe place where they could be alone in the crowd.

"You shouldn't expect too much of this evening, Jordan," Emma responded as the warmth of his hand and his words seeped into her body.

"This is a magical evening. I have high hopes," Jordan commented as his gaze penetrated hers.

"We'll see," Emma stated softly as she took a few more steps forward. She stood only a few people away from the president.

"I'll be waiting for you at the end of the line. I'm willing to accept anything you can offer. I just hope you'll be generous," Jordan replied as he gently squeezed her arm and slipped into the crowd.

Watching him walk away, Emma suddenly felt alone and cold in a room that had only a few seconds ago seemed overly warm. She almost called him back to stand with her, but she knew that everyone would be shocked by the outburst. She was alone again and feeling very vulnerable.

"Ms. Jones, it's wonderful to meet you at last. I've heard great things about your culinary feats. My secretary will be in touch with you next week to arrange a time for you to cater one of our family gatherings. The White House staff handles all of our state dinners, but we'd love for you to handle my wife's birthday party next month," the president quipped as he heartily shook Emma's hand.

"It would be an honor, sir," Emma replied, flabbergasted that the president had heard of her and wanted to employ her company.

"Good. We'll be in touch. I hope you'll enjoy your evening," the president replied as he ended his brief conversation with Emma and turned toward the next person in line.

Although Emma was accustomed to being praised for the professionalism of her catering company, she did not feel her feet hit the floor as she walked toward Jordan. She had never felt so special or so singled out. The president, by recognizing the success of her business and suggesting that he would contact her later, had raised EJ's to a higher level of professionalism.

"Well?" Jordan queried as he searched her face.

Seeing his genuine interest, Emma knew that Jordan had encouraged the president to hire her company. He had previously sampled her wares at one of Jordan's parties and knew that she was a capable caterer. Now, however, with his seal of approval, her business would be even busier than ever. She would have to hire the assistant she had been trying to justify.

"He's a very personable man. We didn't say much to each other, but he made me feel comfortable in saying what little he did," Emma replied noncommittally as she slipped her arm through Jordan's.

"Did he say anything in particular?" Jordan asked, obviously fishing for specific information.

"Not really. Just the usual small talk," Emma responded as she accepted a cocktail from the waiter.

"Oh, I would have thought . . ."

Sipping her drink, Emma commented casually, "He did ask me to cater a family dinner."

Barely able to contain his reaction, Jordan said, "I

don't think I'd be so casual about it if I were in your place. It's not every day that a business gets that kind of shot in the arm."

"I know, and I appreciate your support on my behalf. I'm sure your recommendation helped my business tremendously. Why did you do this for me?" Emma asked as she turned to look in Jordan's eyes.

"I want more time alone with you. I don't want to share you with your work. You can hire an assistant and work regular hours," Jordan replied without hesitation.

"I've given that some thought, believe me. But you're as busy as I am. If I remember correctly, it was your job that caused us to leave the beach early," Emma rebutted sweetly.

"I'm in the process of making some changes in my life. As a matter of fact, if all goes well, I'll have more regular hours by the end of this month," Jordan responded as he led Emma into the state dining room and to their table at the sound of the bell.

"Really? How have you managed that?" Emma asked as she sank into the thickly padded seat.

"I can't discuss it as yet. Just know that I'll still be busy—very busy—but not on call as an adviser and consultant any longer," Jordan replied as they watched the other guests take their seats.

"Sounds intriguing," Emma stated, feeling warm from the cocktail and Jordan's nearness. She was impressed that he trusted her sufficiently to share his plans with her.

"We'd have more time for the beach, too," Jordan added with a wicked laugh. "I'm sure that crabbing's something you never get tired of doing."

"Was I that obvious? I hope I didn't spoil your weekend. I'm just not a crab kind of person," Emma replied with a chuckle.

"From the first minute you saw one of them, I knew that you were ready to go home. I'll do better next time," Jordan promised as he placed his hand over hers.

"I can hardly wait," Emma enthused dramatically. "I wonder what you'll plan this time. We could rent a boat and go oyster dredging."

"No, I had chicken plucking in mind. There's a famous poultry farm on the Eastern Shore that might interest." Jordan laughed openly at the image of Emma on a chicken farm.

"Goodness. I suppose I won't have to break in another new pair of tennis shoes for that one. I can image the poop I'll step into," Emma joked merrily.

The others at the table cast furtive glances in their direction as they continued their good-natured banter. Although they were seated with some of the biggest stars in Hollywood, Emma and Jordan were so involved in their conversation that they were not interested in the others. Through their lack of concern, they became the focus for all attention at the table. Even Bonnie and her husband, Steve, who had slipped into the formerly vacant chairs at the table, went unnoticed.

Before Jordan could respond after recovering from the sip of martini that he had swallowed while trying not to laugh, the president rose to signal the beginning of his dinner speech. Holding a glass of champagne in his outstretched hand, he thanked Hollywood, Broadway, and regional theater for their contributions to the performing arts and encouraged the governors from the represented states to allocate more funds to the support of the arts. He praised public television for its efforts to produce quality programming that brought the best of musical and dramatic entertainment to people's homes. He lauded the accomplishments of galleries, symphonies, and opera houses in keeping the spirit of creativity alive through partnerships with schools and universities. To close, he thanked the public for attending performances and exhibitions and for tuning in to quality television.

While the applause rose to fill the room, discreet waiters slipped among the guests, carrying plates containing skillfully arranged portions. Starting with the head table and fanning out to cover everyone, they served the guests with such skill that all received their plates within the same few minutes. Their actions were so swift and yet so subtle that their presence did little to interfere with the animated conversation that filled the room.

The aroma from the exquisite meal wafted through the room. A cream soup of sweet lobster was followed by a crisp salad of endive, tomatoes, and radicchio. A delicate sorbet cleansed the palate between courses and led the diners to the filet mignon topped with lump crab meat and béarnaise sauce. Stalks of tender asparagus rested gently on the plate. White wine accompanied the soup and salad courses while a sumptuous Merlot proved the perfect companion for the beef.

The usual dinner conversation filled the room as the guests ate their fill and waited for the evening's entertainment. Over coffee and the lightest chocolate cake Emma had ever tasted, the occupants of the table shared tidbits about their professions, the latest performance they had either watched or enacted, and their plans for their future contribution to the arts. The self-righteousness was at times spread so thickly that Emma could hardly wait until they could exit the East Room for entertainment.

Slipping her arm through Jordan's, Emma joined Bonnie and Steve as they strolled toward the room in

which an orchestra sat in readiness to accompany the
vocal majesty of the reigning queen of soul who would
share the stage with one of the nation's premier vio-
linists. Their seats in the center of the gathering
would afford them a good view of the makeshift stage.
Although dinner at the White House was old news
for her friends, Emma did not want to miss one minute of the evening's festivities.

"She's wonderful!" Emma whispered as she leaned
toward Jordan.

"Not in comparison to you," Jordan replied, pressing his shoulder against hers.

"You are full of flattery tonight, aren't you," Emma
noted as the room erupted in applause.

"It's well deserved. You're definitely the most appealing woman here," Jordan stated as he looked
deeply into Emma's eyes.

For a few moments, no one else in the room mattered as they studied each other's faces. Emma, for
the first time in years, allowed herself to open to a
man. She saw honesty and true affection in Jordan's
eyes. Despite his affection for crabs, Emma wanted to
know this man better. She wanted him in her life.

Jordan had known from the first time he met
Emma that she was worth waiting for. Now, as he
watched the veil of skepticism slip from her eyes, Jordan knew that he had not waited in vain. He could
tell that Emma had finally dropped her guard against
him.

The applause for the vocalist slowly subsided and
the introduction of the violinist began. Holding hands
tightly, Emma and Jordan reluctantly turned their attention to the stage. The evening suddenly held
promises of more wonder to come.

"You and Jordan seem to be hitting it off tonight,"
Bonnie chirped softly with a happy smile. As the one

who had united the two, she was happy to see that her efforts had finally paid off.

Emma leaned toward her and whispered, "I thought you were watching the show."

"I was. And to think I arranged the whole thing," Bonnie chuckled softly.

"If it works out, I'll thank you. If it doesn't, you'll be to blame," Emma commented as she pretended to listen to the violin virtuoso.

"That's the way it always is. I'm underappreciated," Bonnie replied with the same feigned interest in the music.

"Whatever," Emma responded through her barely parted lips.

As Emma glanced around the room, she discovered that she and Jordan were not the only ones who would rather be somewhere else. Many of the art world's most famous and renowned painters, actors, dramatists, and writers were leaning invitingly against their partners. Even a few of the congressional types were more interested in their date than the violin solo. The combination of the food, the wine, and the lateness of the hour was making everyone either groggy or amorous.

By the time everyone had become tired of sitting, the festivities ended with the president thanking them for coming to his gala, for keeping the arts alive, and for taking time from their busy schedules to share their time with him. The guests gathered their belongings and exited into the flower-scented night air, taking with them memories that would last a lifetime. For Emma, the evening was definitely one that she would share with her children, if she ever had any.

"Would you like to join us for a nightcap?" Steve asked as they waited for their drivers.

Opening the door to Emma's limousine, Jordan replied, "No, thanks. I think we'll call it a night. See you good people another time."

"Sleep well!" Bonnie called with a wicked little grin playing at the corner of her lips.

"Good night," Emma replied with a chuckle and wave.

As the door closed and the limousine eased into the late-night traffic on the Mall, Jordan pulled Emma into this arms and kissed her ever so gently. Teasing her lips and then firmly kissing each corner, he caused sparks of fire to shoot through Emma's body. His strong arms promised that he would never let her go.

"Now, what do you think Bonnie meant by that?" Jordan asked innocently as he smiled into Emma's eyes.

"I couldn't begin to imagine," Emma said, laughing as she snuggled contentedly into Jordan's chest.

The limousine moved quickly though the starry evening. As the car pulled in front of her house, Emma noticed that Jordan had parked his car in her driveway. She looked at him quizzically and waited for his explanation.

As they walked to her front door with their arms wrapped around each other, Jordan explained, "I had counted on being able to see you home tonight. I don't have to stay if you'd rather that I leave."

Throwing the door wide, Emma replied, "You just try to leave. I have an attack cat that will hunt you down and drag you back. Make yourself comfortable. I'll return in just a minute with a favorite Merlot for you to sample."

"I'd rather sample the caterer," Jordan commented as his fingers lingered on hers.

"There'll be time for that later. First, the wine and

then we'll see what develops," Emma said, laughing softly as she slipped from his reach.

Laughing, Jordan closed and locked the door behind them. He did not intend to argue with the glowing eyes at the end of the hall or with the look of love burning in Emma's. He would sip the wine and wait for the evening to progress.

Hoping that the evening would turn out favorably, Jordan had cleared his calendar in anticipation of a wondrously long weekend. Accepting his secretary's meddling and placement of him next to Emma during dinner had been the most strategic move of Jordan's career. He hoped to show a few more later that evening.

Emma slipped into the kitchen for a bottle of Merlot that she had purchased while at a conference. Thinking that she would one day open it for a special occasion, she had added it to the other bottles of chilling wine in the wine cellar that she had had constructed in the back of the basement. Except for when she added other bottles to the chiller, Emma had not thought about the Merlot at all. Now, pouring it into her favorite crystal stemware, she smiled and was glad that she had it.

Placing the glasses on a small silver tray, Emma rejoined Jordan in the living room where she found him looking through a photo album that her mother had prepared for her when Emma had graduated from college. Inside were photographs of Emma in all stages of her childhood and young womanhood. Some of the pictures were so embarrassing that Emma was surprised that she had left the album on the table.

"You were certainly a little charmer," Jordan announced as soon as Emma returned with the wine.

Laughing, Emma replied, "Some would say too charming. My father used to call me his little princess.

He meant it lovingly, but when my ex-husband said it, the word took on an entirely different meaning."

"Some men have no concept of a good thing. They don't appreciate fine wine or gorgeous, intelligent women. Fortunately, I'm not one of them," Jordan said as he slipped onto the sofa next to Emma.

"Well, I hope you'll enjoy this Merlot. I've been saving it for a special occasion. It's a bit sweeter than most, with a blackberry base. I think you'll like it," Emma stated as she ignored the glint in Jordan's eyes.

"Not bad," Jordan conceded as he sipped the tasty blend. "I'm not much of a wine drinker, but I could get used to this one. It's a good way to end the day. A glass of this wine, a good pipe, and a pretty woman. What more could a man want?"

"It's one of my favorite vintners. I purchased this bottle while visiting the vineyards as a side trip during a conference. This has been such a special night that I thought we should end it with a special glass of wine," Emma admitted as she savored the aroma.

"Yes, it has been a very special evening," Jordan said as he pulled Emma into his arms. "However, I had something more intimate in mind for closing out the night."

Jordan's lips were warm and sweet as they lingered on Emma's. His arms gently enfolded her and pulled her against his chest. His hands caressed her hair and the back of her neck, making tingling sensations course through her body.

Emma had not had a man in her life in so long that she had almost forgotten the pleasure of surrendering herself to one. She slowly began to relax and fuse her body to his. The beating of their two hearts thundered in her ears.

Looking deeply into her eyes, Jordan whispered, "I've been attracted to you since the first day I met you. Bonnie's description failed to include the warmth of your eyes, the gentleness of your touch, and the sweetness of your skin. I think I've been in love with you since the Las Vegas trip. I know that tonight I felt myself being drawn to you in a way that I did not know was possible. I love you, Emma, and I want you in my life forever."

"Jordan, I'm a very deliberate person," Emma began as she tried to express her feelings about him and the evening. "I weigh all the odds before I take a step. I enjoy your company, your smile, and your energy, but I have to take it slowly."

"I won't rush you," Jordan replied as he pulled her closer and nuzzled her neck. "I'll simply use all of my powers of persuasion to convince you that you should think the same way that I do. I'll convince you that marriage to me would be far more interesting than anything you've ever known."

"Marriage?" Emma repeated, wide-eyed.

"Yes, marriage," Jordan announced firmly. "I'm old-fashioned and wouldn't think of any other relationship. I want you in my life permanently. I don't want a modern relationship without ties and a legal basis. I want us to be emotionally and legally connected. I want us to share a life with all of its strings and commitment."

With a reluctant smile, Emma replied, "As much as I enjoy your company, I'll have to give this change in my life considerable thought before giving you any kind of response. I'd hate to jeopardize our relationship by hesitating, but I'd kick myself if I jumped into a situation without looking at all the options."

Pulling her closer, Jordan whispered, "You won't jeopardize our relationship by taking your time. As long as you're in my arms, I'm happy."

"Thank you for understanding, Jordan," Emma

managed to say as he pressed his lips on hers again and covered them with kisses.

As they walked up the stairs to her bedroom, Emma switched off the light and cast the downstairs in a soft amber glow from the one night-light in the hall. The cat meowed once and then vanished into the basement. The house was quiet except for the sound of the footsteps on the stairs.

The dim light in Emma's bedroom welcomed them as they entered. As was her habit, she had left a little lamp burning on the dresser. Usually it welcomed her home when she pulled in front of the house and guided her progress to the dressing room. Tonight, its subtle glow guided the lovers' exploration of each other's body.

Before Emma had a chance to suggest that she might slip into a slinky nightgown, Jordan carefully unzipped the zipper that ran from the neckline of Emma's gown to the curve of her spine. His lips trailed warm kisses along the newly exposed flesh of her back and shoulders. His fingers brushed the gown from her body as if it were made of butterfly wings.

Standing before him in only her strapless bra and panties, Emma did not feel in the least embarrassed. In fact, she felt as if her body had been waiting for Jordan to liberate it from the protective wall that she had drawn around her since the divorce. She knew instinctively that his body would release the long pent-up desire that she had not allowed other men to know. She felt totally at ease with him as if they had known each other all their lives.

Jordan drank in the beauty of Emma's flesh as she stood before him. He had made physical love to other women since his divorce, but he had not enjoyed the union of his soul and being with theirs. He was holding back that part of himself until he'd find the perfect woman with whom to share his life. Now, standing in Emma's bedroom, he knew more than ever that she was the woman. He felt vulnerable, strong, weak, and brave at the same time. He must protect her while surrendering to her.

Throwing off his clothes while she turned down the bed, Jordan marveled at the smoothness of her skin and the evenness of her complexion. Her body gently undulated with muscles that spoke of training at the gym. For a woman who was so dedicated to her company, Emma managed to find time to take care of herself, too. Jordan was very pleased with what he saw. He had guessed at her form from the slender physique that filled the bathing suit the day on the Bay, but until now, with the light casting a rosy glow to her skin, he had no idea just how lovely she was. With a smile, Jordan realized that his love for Emma certainly played a part in the way he saw her stunning figure, enjoyed her exhilarating wit, and relished the simple quietness of being with her.

Emma, too, was impressed with the muscular display that Jordan's nudity presented. On the beach with the sun shining brightly on his body, Emma had missed the swell of his muscles and the beauty of his skin color. The sun had dulled the color of his hair and reduced the ripples of his arms and back. Jordan, for a desk-bound physician, displayed a fabulous physique gained by hours of hard work at the gym.

The covers felt cool against their skin as they slipped into each other's arms. Stroking Emma's face and hair, Jordan reveled at the softness of her. He breathed deeply of the fragrance of her perfume mingled with the natural sweetness and allure of Emma's skin. Pulling her closer, Jordan cradled her in his arms protectively.

Emma was overwhelmed by Jordan's gentleness.

Never before, not even with her ex-husband, had she felt such comfort in snuggling against another person. She could only imagine the depths to which their relationship would progress if this were the way the beginning felt. She experienced a complete happiness that she had not known existed.

Gently caressing her arms and shoulders, Jordan kissed Emma deeply. His lips lingered on hers and then gently brushed her cheeks and neck. His tongue teased her erect nipples as his hands explored her inner thighs. She shivered as the waves of passion ran through her. Sighing, she whispered his name.

Jordan moaned as Emma's fingers explored his back and shoulders on their way to his stomach and thighs. His body tingled from her gentle massage of his neck and back muscles. His condom-sheathed erection greeted her eager fingers as she massaged him until he groaned with pleasure.

Easing his body over hers, Jordan moaned as he entered Emma's warmth and pulled her against him. They joined exquisitely as their kisses mingled. Meeting each other's thrusts, they rose to the heights of passions together like lovers experienced with the tide of the other's body.

Cradling Emma in the fold of his arm, Jordan studied her peaceful face. Their lovemaking had been more enjoyable than he had imagined a first union could be. There had been a familiarity in their closeness and a lack of inhibition in their mutual give and take of pleasure that had surprised him. He had known many women, but none had melded with him as Emma had. Jordan knew that Emma was meant to fill the emptiness of his life and bed.

Emma had experienced the same feeling of togetherness and oneness. After having been alone for a few years, she had expected to feel shy or uncomfortable at being with Jordan. Instead, she had felt as if they had always known each other and had been sharing a bed for years. Their lovemaking had been complete and unhurried as it should be for people who are perfectly matched and wonderfully suited for each other.

Lying in the fold of his arms, Emma discovered that she could not stay awake. She dozed peacefully, without worrying if her puttering snore would keep him awake. She felt completely at ease and did not wonder if the morning would bring awkwardness with the bright light of the day. She was completely content in his arms and in her bed with Jordan at her side.

"I love you, Emma," Jordan whispered sleepily as he pulled her closer.

"Me, too," Emma answered as she nuzzled against his chest.

"I've never understood what that means," Jordan quipped without moving an inch away from her. "Does that mean that you love yourself as much as I love you or that you love me, too?"

Chuckling, Emma replied, "Of course, I love myself, but what I mean was that I love you, too."

"Okay. That's better. I'll understand from now on," Jordan muttered, tightening his arms around Emma in preparation for sleep.

Their hands and lips carried on their own conversation as Emma and Jordan lay together. Punctuating their words with little gentle massages and little kisses, they continued to explore each other's body and learn the sensation-causing spots and the responses caused by each. Their lovemaking continued even as their gentle bantering renewed.

"Good. I'm only too happy to clarify your misunderstandings. Now, let's go to sleep. It's been a long day," Emma stated as she pulled the cover over their shoulders.

"I'm already asleep. You keep waking me up," Jordan replied with a yawn.

"I'm not the one who asked the question. You are," Emma countered with a stretch of her legs as she shifted a bit against his body.

"Okay. Discussion over. It's time for sleep. Wake me in time for breakfast," Jordan replied, throwing one leg over hers.

"Wake you to fix it or to eat it?"

"Eat . . . You fix." Jordan sighed.

"Okay, but next time, you fix it," Emma agreed as her eyes fluttered closed for the last time.

To the gentle sound of Emma's soft puttering snore, Jordan asked as he fell asleep, "How do you like your cereal?"

Neither of them responded as the clock in the hall softly chimed the hour. The cat peeked into the room and, finding no space on the bed, stretched and leaped onto the chair beside the closet door. Plopping down with less than his usual grace, the cat settled down for the night and the house grew still.

Nine

The next morning Emma rose early while Jordan still lay asleep. It had been a long time since a man had slept in her bed—not since her marriage, in fact. She had missed the leisurely weekend breakfasts, the shared newspaper, and the closeness. When the marriage ended, so did the treasured moments. Actually, the happiness had left long before they filed for divorce. However, the memory of better times lingered until her ex had moved his things from their house into that of his mistress—her former secretary.

Showering quickly and quietly, Emma had slipped into navy blue shorts and a white-and-blue striped T-shirt. Pulling a comb through her hair, she had hurriedly brushed her teeth and left the bathroom. Emma had carried her sandals down the stairs so that the heels would not snap on the wood floors and risers. She had not wanted to awaken Jordan.

Emma had grown accustomed to eating alone in the morning room or grabbing something quick at the shop. She hardly ever used her "good" china and silver although she promised herself that she would. It was just too much trouble for one person, or so she reasoned. She often turned on the radio or played a CD as company, but she refused to watch television and eat. Emma thought that a good meal deserved more than the local news or a mindless talk show.

Emma was so busy in the kitchen cooking eggs Benedict, Belgium waffles with strawberry sauce, and freshly ground and brewed coffee that she did not hear Jordan enter. She had set the table in the sunny morning room with her favorite Wedgwood china and Waterford crystal. Beside each plate, she had carefully placed sparkling sterling ware. The only music in the kitchen this time was her contented humming. She did not need the sound of the outside world to make her content and drive away the loneliness.

Until Jordan entered her life and house, Emma did not realize that she had been lonely. She had been so busy working, making her business a success, that she had not noticed the empty nights, the cold bed, and the service for one. She usually returned from work and her exercise session so exhausted that she could only think of grabbing a quick meal, reading the newspaper, checking her e-mail and voice-mail messages, and phoning a few friends and family members. After feeding the cat, she would fall into bed and into a deep sleep only to arise early in the morning to begin the day's routine again.

Now, with Jordan upstairs and the smell of breakfast in the house again, Emma realized what she had been missing. Her life had been full of work and friends but empty of the closeness of love and a relationship. She hoped that the new relationship with Jordan would continue to grow. She wanted and needed the closeness that knowing Jordan promised to provide.

"Something certainly smells good," Jordan commented from the doorway where he leaned against the wall watching her movements. He wore his evening clothing minus the bow tie, which cascaded carelessly from his pocket.

"I hope you'll enjoy it. I really didn't have a chance last night to find out how you like your eggs," Emma replied as she spooned the hollandaise over the combination of poached egg, English muffin, and Canadian bacon.

"If I remember correctly, we didn't talk about much of anything in particular," Jordan stated as he slipped his arms around Emma's waist and nuzzled her neck.

"I remember that you promised to make breakfast next time. By the way, are you complaining about our lack of postcoital conversation? I enjoyed our nonverbal communication a great deal," Emma retorted as she put down the spoon and leaned into his chest.

"Not a bit. I can't think of a better way to end a thoroughly pleasant evening or to begin the morning, for that matter," Jordan hinted as he started to draw Emma toward the door.

"Oh, no, you don't. I've spent too much time on this breakfast to let it go to waste. We can return to bed later, but right now I want to feed your body. Last night took care of your soul," Emma stated with a chuckle as she gently pulled away and pushed Jordan toward the elegantly arranged table on which a bowl of fresh fruit beckoned invitingly.

"Well, if you put it that way, I'll just have to wait for dessert." Jordan laughed heartily as he sank into the chair.

"You mean that you'll have to wait until after we go biking in Great Falls along the Potomac. You promised. Remember?" Emma retorted, adding the last of the serving plates heaped with steaming waffles to the table.

"I remember, but I didn't think you'd hold me to it. I agreed under duress. Your feminine wiles had me bewitched," Jordan whined as he accepted the heavily laden plate.

"That's not the way I remember it at all," Emma replied as she ate her eggs. "You suggested the biking and insisted that I prepare a picnic supper. I've done my part. The grilled chicken, spinach salad, rolls, and tarts are ready. All we have to do is load your car. Now it's your turn."

"I guess I'm stuck. I can't refuse a woman who can make such fabulous eggs Benedict. We'll load your bike and the food, then go to my place. From now on, I'll have to be more careful about making promises around you." Jordan tried to speak through the fruit salad.

"I really like a man who gives in so graciously," Emma said, chuckling as she sipped her coffee. She had not been so happy since the good days of her marriage. Being with Jordan certainly showed promise of enjoyable times to come.

Putting aside his fork and wiping his lips, Jordan said, "Let's clean up and get on the road. The sooner we leave, the sooner we can return. I can hardly wait until dessert."

"You like blueberry tarts that much?" Emma asked as she began stacking the dishes in the washer.

"I'm very fond of them, but that's not the dessert I had in mind," Jordan replied with a quick kiss to her cheek. "I'll start loading the car."

"I'm right behind you," Emma said as she picked up the cooler of tea and her house keys. She was eager to sample a day with Jordan that did not include crabs.

They drove to Great Falls engaging in light-hearted banter along the way. The weather was wonderful, with a clear blue sky and mild breeze on a day that the weather service had predicted would become very hot. Everyone in the Washington area must have thought the same thing because the roads were

packed. Traffic jams greeted them everywhere until
they finally pulled into the parking lot.

Unloading the bikes and the picnic basket took
only minutes, and it was time spent laughing and joking. Emma felt so totally relaxed with Jordan that she
could no longer remember the reservations she had
once felt against forming a relationship with him. The
more time she spent with him, the more Emma knew
that Jordan was a perfect match for her.

Pedaling along the path, Emma and Jordan marveled at the speed of the river and the crowd of people enjoying themselves at Great Falls that day. The
rains of recent weeks had replenished the forests and
the streams. The tributaries that fed the Potomac
rushed with millions of gallons of water. Rather than
having their pick of picnic spots, they had to search
for one that was not heavily populated. They wanted
to be alone for their picnic, with only the ants and
bees as company.

Finally, miles from where they had thought to stop,
they found the ideal spot in a small clearing. They
had pedaled for more than three hours, stopping only
for sips of water, and they were very hungry. Spreading a blanket over the soft grass, they opened the
hamper and dove into the delicious meal with great
gusto.

"You're a great cook. I think I'll marry you so that
I can eat well for the rest of my life," Jordan announced between bites.

"You have a pretty good appetite. I suppose I'll say
yes so that I'll have someone to appreciate my cooking when I'm old and gray," Emma replied with a
chuckle.

"Would you say yes if I asked you?" Jordan asked,
suddenly serious as his heart pounded in his chest.
The half-eaten tart rested on the plate.

"I don't know. You haven't asked me yet. It's rather presumptuous of me to think about the response to an unasked question," Emma answered as she took a small bite of her tart. Her throat had suddenly gone dry and become very tight.

"It's a question that's been on my mind since I first met you. I thought I'd been an open book about that subject," Jordan stated as he removed the plate from Emma's hands and placed it on the striped tablecloth that covered the red-and-black plaid blanket.

"I guess I missed reading that page. I have a habit of skimming some topics," Emma replied as she fingered the hem of her shorts. She tried to lighten the air that hung around them, but Jordan's serious expression would not let it change.

"Well, let me give you a summary of the pages you missed. You see, I rearranged my schedule so that I could be with you in Las Vegas. It took some doing and the cooperation of the president of the United States, but I managed to accomplish it. At my suggestion, some of the most influential people in Washington used your services for their dinner parties. They abandoned their usual caterer—your competition, I might add—and turned to you. I tried to impress you with a crab dinner, but I failed miserably. Even the splendor of Chesapeake Bay couldn't make up for the smell. I asked the president to include you in the list of invitees to the arts dinner because you are truly the most talented caterer I've ever known. I finagled a seat next to yours at the table and managed to impress you sufficiently that we enjoyed ourselves long into the wee hours of the morning. And, last but not least, I've allowed you to haul me deep into the woods so that I might have a leisurely lunch among the ants with you. I think that sums up the items that you've missed." Jordan held her hands tightly in his.

"Your efforts on my behalf did not go unnoticed. Even when you introduced me to the joy of crabbing on the Eastern Shore, I could not forget all that you've done for me and my business. EJ's has doubled in revenue since I met you. Now with the president planning to use the company, I'll become almost as rich and powerful as you are," Emma acknowledged as she leaned forward to receive the kiss that trembled on Jordan's lips.

"Then, let me turn the pages forward to my latest question. Would you marry me if I asked you?" Jordan repeated as he nibbled the corners of Emma's mouth.

"It's really very difficult to think when I've become an after-dinner mint," Emma retorted softly as she melted into Jordan's arms.

"Then, let me ask you again without duress," Jordan replied as he sat apart from Emma and studied her face and eyes. "Will you do me the honor of making me an incredibly happy, and probably fat, man? I love you, Emma, and want to spend the rest of my life with you."

Emma could feel her heart pounding wildly in her chest. Her mouth had gone dry. Her lips would not move to form the response. Her old habits hung in the way. She had long ago stopped thinking about personal happiness and found satisfaction in running an acclaimed business. Now that EJ's was successful beyond her dreams, personal happiness was only inches away. All she had to do was reach for him.

"Marry me, Emma," Jordan repeated with a plea that was almost a prayer. Looking down briefly he added with a smile, "Please, say yes before that ant eats any more of my tart."

Emma burst into almost uncontrolled laughter. Tears of joy and relief flowed down her cheeks. Jordan had both relieved the tension and set her free to say the words that would not form. She knew that her answer no longer mattered. He had read her response in her eyes and felt confident in her love.

"Yes, Jordan, I'll marry you. I love you more than that ant loves your tart. You'd better work fast if you want any of that dessert," Emma replied as she wiped her cheeks.

"He can have it. Take some home to the wife. I have everything I want right here," Jordan stated as he pulled Emma into his arms.

The kiss was slow and gentle, like the embrace of old, comfortable lovers. Although the afternoon shadows had lengthened, they felt no need to rush. The rest of the evening and weekend belonged to them.

Finally they released themselves from their embrace and looked at each other. As if on cue, Emma and Jordan started to laugh. It was as if someone had told an inside joke that only they could understand. Their happiness was so intense that they did not care that the family passing their picnic spot stopped and looked at them before pedaling down the rocky road.

"Well, at least you won't have to hire a caterer for our wedding reception," Jordan said as he wiped the last of the tears from the corners of his eyes.

"Won't my competition be green with envy! One of the most eligible bachelors in town marrying one of their rivals, and they won't even be able to prepare the meal. Naturally, Bonnie will handle the flowers and table linens. We won't even have to book a hotel room because we can hold the reception at my house since we really don't have an army of close friends to invite. With luck, it won't rain, and we can use the yard, too. You already own a tux. All we need is my gown and the invitations. We're all set," Emma stated as she ticked off the usual list of prewedding arrangements that she knew so well.

"How long does it take for invitations?" Jordan asked with a frown.

"About two weeks to print and then four weeks' advance notice of the date. That part won't take long. I know a really good printer. I refer all of my clients to him," Emma replied.

"So we need to clear our schedules—especially yours for the catering job—order the invitations, find a gown, and clean your house. That's not much time but if we work fast we can do it. Let's get married Labor Day weekend" Jordan stated, as if he had settled all the details and everything had been finalized.

"Labor Day weekend? No one will be in town. Most of our professional associates will be away that weekend. That's really cutting it close. You're not giving me much time," Emma blurted out in disbelief.

"That's exactly why I suggested it. We won't have to worry about inviting a whole bunch of people. We can keep it small and intimate. Just our best friends and necessary invitees. I don't see the problem," Jordan responded innocently.

Looking at him as if he had totally lost his mind, Emma said, "No one plans a wedding in less than six months. I'm sure my business is booked that weekend anyway."

"I don't see the problem. You have to take on additional staff now anyway because of the latest astute maneuver by your fiancé and the new business caused by the president's party. Add our wedding to the responsibility of that group. That way, you can test them out yourself." Jordan beamed with confidence at having solved the problem that he had created.

"If you were my client, I'd tell you that there's no way to make this happen in so little time. However, you would insist anyway, and I'd make it happen. So we'll do it," Emma conceded with a nod of her head.

"Doesn't this new spontaneity feel good? No more long hesitations, lead time, or planning. No more looking at all the angles. If it feels good, do it," Jordan replied as he pounded one fist into the other.

"You're right. It's a new day. I'm an engaged woman. I'm about to marry one of the foremost authorities in the country . . . a man who's at the service of a president. I'm a successful business-woman. I've been cautious too long. It's time to let go and enjoy life. Grab some of the gusto, as it were," Emma agreed as she repacked the hamper and folded the tablecloth.

"I knew you'd see it my way. Nothing is beyond the scope of possibility. Together, we can do anything, face any problem, overcome any obstacle," Jordan added as he shook the thick blanket and folded it over the hamper on the front of his bike.

"Before you become too cocky, you might want to tackle that little black-and-white striped obstacle. It looks like Flower has decided to befriend us," Emma said as she pointed in the direction of the fat skunk that waddled toward them.

"I've often thought that a hasty retreat was better than confrontation any day. Let's get out of here before she comes any closer. That smell is impossible to wash off," Jordan declared as he grabbed both bikes and started pushing them toward the road with Emma following behind carrying the blanket that she would stuff into the hamper later.

As they sped down the road, they again burst into storms of laughter. Even the appearance of the little skunk could not spoil their fun. The day had started out to be perfect and had not disappointed either of them.

"Just imagine the stories we'll have to tell our grandchildren," Jordan stated as he bumped along the road that was heavily rutted from the last rain and bike traffic.

"They won't believe us," Emma replied. "How many people do you know who are run out of their picnic site by a skunk in the Washington metro area? It's just not an ordinary occurrence. It's something that happens in the country, not the suburbs of the capital of the United States."

"Good. We're off to an auspicious beginning," Jordan announced as they raced toward the park's entrance.

The parking lot had emptied a bit by the time they covered the three miles and finally returned. Tired, achy, but very happy, they loaded the bikes and basket into the car. They had almost finished securing the trunk with rope when a voice called to them from the edge of the woods.

"Jordan? Is that you? It's been a long time." The woman's voice seemed to echo through the stillness.

As Emma turned toward the sound, Jordan groaned audibly. "Oh, no!"

"Who is that? A former patient?" Emma asked as she watched the smiling woman advance toward them.

"No, not exactly. Just someone I haven't seen in a long time and hoped to keep it that way," Jordan replied as he finished tying the rope into a secure knot.

Before Emma could ask any more questions, the woman threw herself into Jordan's arms. Her substantial breasts pressed into his chest. Her arms wrapped around his neck. Her lips planted a firm kiss on his. Jordan stood stiffly as a passive participant in the scene of reunion while the woman made it perfectly clear that she had missed him.

"It's been ages, Jordan. I had heard that you were in town, but when I never saw you at any social functions, I just thought I had bad information. And then the paper started covering your every move. I felt so proud of you, Jordan. So proud to have been your wife," the woman cooed with a thick Southern accent of syrup and honey.

"Your wife?" Emma asked, incredulous that Jordan could have married someone so flashy and apparently insincere.

"Didn't you know, dear, that Jordan had been married? It's an old story but not a very pleasant one. The best part was the divorce, if I remember correctly. But how you've changed, Jordan. You've mellowed wonderfully. It must be all the public acclaim. I'd love to have another go at getting to know you better. Maybe this time it would work," the woman gushed while smiling sweetly at Emma and clinging to Jordan.

"Emma, this is my ex-wife, Gina. You remember that I mentioned the marriage. She's right. It wasn't a very pleasant chapter in my life. I usually put it so far behind me that I forget about it," Jordan replied as he removed Gina's arms from around his neck and pushed her away.

"Wonderful. Another surprise in a day full of them. You're not at all what I had imagined. It's nice to meet you, Gina. I've heard precious little about you. I'll wait for you in the car, Jordan," Emma responded in a voice devoid of emotion.

"I'll be right there," Jordan said to Emma's straight, retreating back. He knew that Gina's appearance had hurt her deeply. Perhaps if he had said more, described Gina more fully, or said that she lived in the area, Emma would have been better prepared for their first meeting.

"No rush," Emma tossed over her shoulder.

Watching her walk away, Jordan realized how much he would lose if he did not remove this obstacle from their lives. This time, he could not take the approach of running from the problem. He had to face Gina head-on and put her out of his life forever.

"Gina, I don't appreciate your behavior just now. It's been over between us for five years, longer than that if you count the eighteen months that we were separated. Our marriage was a mistake from the beginning, a mistake we've both recognized. As a matter of fact, we've been more civil to each other these past five years than we ever were during our six years of marriage. Let's keep it that way. Distance doesn't make our hearts grow fonder. It just makes it so that we can stand each other," Jordan stated firmly to the woman he had once found sexually attractive but now only saw as clinging and suffocating.

"But, Jordan, we've changed over the years. At least I know I have. I'm not the same woman. I have a job that I love and my own life. I know things would be better for us. I could be such a help to you. You need a woman who knows how to entertain with grace and charm," Gina purred as she stepped closer.

"I don't need your kind of help or your father's bank account. Your money can't buy me or our happiness. I'm a free man, and I intend to stay that way. Good-bye, Gina," Jordan rebutted as he stepped back and pulled the keys from his pocket.

"That's what you think, Jordan. I always get what I want. I did once before. Remember?" Gina stated with all the subtlety of a cat waiting to pounce on a mouse.

"Not this time, Gina. I have all the political and social connections I could possibly need. I've made more money than I ever imagined or could ever spend. I continue to be very much in demand. I'm happier than I've been in years. I feel so good about myself that Emma and I are getting married in a few weeks. So, you see, you might as well retract your claws. I'm beyond your reach," Jordan concluded sternly.

"That's what you think," Gina proclaimed sweetly. She turned and walked away with her shoulder-length black hair blowing behind her.

Watching her walk away, Jordan could see what had initially drawn him to Gina. She had a fabulous body and a strong personality, when she wanted to charm someone. She could be sweet and winning, but, just as easily, she could be manipulative and poisonous. Gina always wanted to control the situation and was never happy until she had turned everything to her favor. She had drained him of self-respect and drive. Jordan had left her in time to save his dignity and a hope that life could be better.

"She's beautiful," Emma remarked as soon as Jordan entered the car.

"I should have told you more about her, but I just didn't think that she was important. As a matter of fact, I didn't think that you'd ever meet. It was a painful time, and I try to forget it," Jordan said without a trace of his usual playfulness.

"I can understand that. My marriage was definitely rocky. I just wish you'd said more about her personality and the nature of your marriage. I wasn't prepared for her clinging-vine approach. You knew all about my past and the possible appearance of my ex. I would have liked the same information about yours," Emma replied as the car eased from the lot and began the trip homeward.

"This doesn't change anything between us, does it?" Jordan asked cautiously.

"I don't know. I'm a little concerned that you might

have other skeletons in your closet that you haven't told me about. I want to go into this marriage fully aware of everything. I don't want any surprises beyond the anticipated dirty socks on the floor," Emma responded honestly.

"There aren't any more secrets. All that's left is the books stuffed under the bed and the wet towels on the bathroom floor. I like to change towels daily— can't stand reusing them," Jordan added, trying to lighten the tension in the car.

"I guess you'll just have to learn where we keep the hamper in our new house. I don't pick up after anyone else," Emma said, assuming an attitude that closely matched his.

"Then all's okay with us?" Jordan asked, casting a quick glance in her direction.

"Everything's fine. But I'll let you buy me an ice cream on the way home, if it'll make you feel any better," Emma joked as they glided along the open road.

"How about an engagement ring instead?" Jordan asked with a tilt of his head.

"That's a reasonable substitute. Actually, a diamond's better. It's icy and won't melt," Emma responded with a chuckle. "I didn't have one the first time. It's a nice idea. Will you wear a wedding band?"

"Haven't you heard that real men don't eat broccoli or wear wedding rings?" Jordan asked in mock horror.

"No, I thought real men did everything except change lightbulbs," Emma quipped as they eased into the traffic on the beltway.

"No, lightbulbs are okay. It's fixing faucets that we don't do. I'd like to wear a ring. I want one that matches your band," Jordan stated as he navigated the traffic that always seemed to flow on the Washington beltway regardless of the time of day.

"Good. Then all the ladies, including Gina, can tell that you belong to me and know to keep their hands to themselves," Emma replied with a smile and raised eyebrow.

"I'll be a marked man in no time even without a ring. Your cooking will give me the married man's physique. I'll make my tailor very happy," Jordan said, laughing with relief that Emma could mention his ex-wife without rancor.

"And you'll make me very happy if you remember not to keep secrets between us. I want to know the entire sordid truth about everything," Emma added with a little smile as they walked into the house.

"Trust me. I won't do that again," Jordan replied as he closed the door.

Although it was late when they finally finished unpacking the hamper and putting away the blanket and tablecloth, Emma and Jordan decided that they wanted to go dancing. After quick showers and a call to Bonnie and Steve, inviting their friends to join them, they headed to a popular hotel known for its swing and jazz combo. People loved the hotel's casual elegance and the easy relaxed atmosphere.

Slipping into the booth and ordering drinks, they settled into congenial conversation. The four of them were so compatible that they felt as if they had known each other forever when, in fact, Jordan was the newest member of their little group. By virtue of being Bonnie's husband, Steve had become Emma's good friend, too. Where their group had been a trio, it now quickly became a happy quartet.

The former hotel ballroom had been divided into a much cozier space with tables and a dance floor. Recessed lighting had replaced the chandeliers. Moonlight streamed through the bare windows that in the old days had been covered by heavy drapes. High polished wood tables stood in place of the brocade cloth–covered ones of the days of cotillions and fancy balls.

Emma and Bonnie in slacks and light sweaters were dressed perfectly for the evening as were Jordan and Steve in their trousers and open-neck shirts. Anything more formal would have looked out of place although older gentlemen donned sport coats and some ladies wore pantsuits in deference to the old days. The high school and college crowd appeared in jeans and T-shirts. Some of the girls wore skirts similar to the old poodle skirt of ages past. Several of them had donned saddle oxfords and bobby socks to add the final touches. Regardless of attire, everyone was there for the same purpose: to dance and have a good time.

By the time Emma had arrived with her friends, the teenagers had already been swept up by the music and were happily moving to the beat of swing. Guys twirled girls over their shoulders and around their bodies with incredible skill and speed. Their dance steps had been patterned after those of the forties.

Nudging Emma in the side, Jordan asked, "Wanna give it a try?"

"I think I'll wait for something a little slower. They can't keep going at that pace forever," Emma replied as she studied the rapid turns and moves.

"I'm glad you said no. I would have embarrassed the heck out of myself if I had tried to imitate those kids," Jordan commented as he sipped his soda and tapped his fingers on the table to the music.

"I thought you looked as if you needed bailing out. I could have handled it," Emma added smugly.

"Oh, yeah? Well, why don't I call over one of those young men? I'm sure that tall, thin one over there would be more than happy to dance with a beautiful woman like you," Jordan teased as he indicated the young man with the dreadlocks.

"That's okay. I wouldn't want to show you up. I don't want anyone to think that my fiancé is an old man," Emma stated with a hearty chuckle.

"You don't want me to have to rub liniment into your sore muscles when we get home," Jordan said, laughing as he patted her hand.

"You're right! Body oil, but not that. My grandmother always smelled of that stuff. I'm not ready for that yet," Emma chuckled, pretending to gum her pretzel.

"Enough of that, you two. You sound like old married people already. Listen, they're playing a bop. Surely you can dance to that," Bonnie interrupted when her sides could take the laughter no longer. She was very pleased with herself for introducing these two perfectly compatible people. For once, her matchmaking had proven successful.

"She's right. Let's go," Jordan commanded as he pulled Emma to her feet.

Holding Emma tightly in his arms, Jordan led her around the floor in intricate steps. This time, the kids sat and watched the somewhat more mature crowd as they showed their moves to the bop and the two-step. For once, Emma felt relieved not to be a teenager and subject to peer pressure. She was very happy to be able to enjoy doing her own thing in Jordan's arms. She did not have to worry if their steps did not quite match since they were from different geographic locations and approached the bop differently. She was comfortable in being able to laugh off the missteps and continue to twirl and step about the floor.

"Not bad for an old woman," Jordan whispered as he pulled her toward him from the sweep of a turn.

"You're pretty good yourself. Seems that we've done our share of slow dancing," Emma commented as she melted against him and the music turned mellow.

"That's the best kind. You can keep that fast stuff. Slow's the only way to go. Gives a guy a chance to sneak a little squeeze and, if he's lucky, a kiss," Jordan replied as he lightly touched Emma's lips with his.

"Not so fast! I didn't give you permission to take liberties with me. I'm not that kind of girl. My mother would have a fit if she were to see you kissing me in public," Emma scolded with a laugh as she eased away just a bit.

"I thought the band of gold that I'm planning to put on your finger in a few weeks gave me carte blanche," Jordan continued as he twirled her in a slow circle.

"We'll see. You might be one of those men who promises marriage and then leaves a girl standing at the altar. Exactly how many women have you lured into your trap with promises of matrimony?" Emma teased as they returned to the table.

"Not more than one hundred," Jordan replied easily.

"Really? So few?" Emma retorted as she eased into her seat.

"I'm a late bloomer," Jordan commented with a tone of regret.

"I see. Well, I hope you have it out of your system now. I'm sure you've sown your wild oats with care, considering AIDS and other STDs. Condoms have been around forever. There's no excuse for not practicing safe sex," Emma added as she looked over the rim of her glass at Jordan.

"Just as carefully as we did last night. Safe sex is

the only way to go. I'll stop by the clinic for a blood test on Monday just to be sure," Jordan concluded as he signaled the waitress.

"I'll go with you, although I don't know why I'd need a test. I haven't been with a man in a long time, until last night, that is," Emma commented as she watched the waitress in a 1950's carhop uniform approach.

"I thought Bonnie was your matchmaker. Didn't she introduce you to any interesting men?" Jordan asked as he studied the menu.

"Plenty. Just not that interesting. Are you ordering another drink?" Emma inquired as she accepted one from the waitress.

"No, an ice-cream sundae. I saw a great-looking concoction on that table. Made me hungry," Jordan replied as he pointed to the treat that he would order.

"Make that two. If you're going to get fat before the wedding, so am I," Emma announced as she ordered a sundae without nuts but with whipped cream.

"No way! This is a one-time thing. I won't have Steve and Bonnie rolling us down the aisle." Jordan laughed at the image.

"What was that about us?" Bonnie asked as they returned to the table.

"I'm ordering sundaes. Do you want one?" Jordan asked as he pointed to the menu.

"Go ahead. Feed them, too. That way we'll look like pool balls rolling down the aisle together," Emma said as she broke into gales of laughter at the picture of them that played through her mind.

Bonnie and Steve looked at them and then at each other. They had obviously missed an inside joke. Although they had been left out of the conversation, they were glad to see their friends so happy together.

They were especially thrilled to see that Emma had found someone with whom to share her life.

While the foursome was talking, they barely noticed the approach of a woman dressed in all black. It was not until her voice penetrated the cocoon of their little group that they looked up. From the expressions on Emma and Jordan's faces, Bonnie and Steve could tell that she was not a welcome visitor to their table.

"Jordan . . . and Emma? How nice to see you again! It's such a small world, isn't it? To think that we hadn't seen each other in ages and now we've run into each other twice in the same day," Gina gushed as she pulled a chair to their table.

Emma and Jordan exchanged glances and then looked at their friends with shrugs of helplessness. They had no choice but to include the intruder in their conversation, at least for a while. The small town of Washington had just become even smaller.

Slipping her chair between Emma and Jordan, Gina turned her full attention to Jordan. It was obvious that she considered Emma to be of little consequence. Gina had looked her over and decided that Emma's presence would do nothing to stop her planned activity.

"Jordan, I've followed your progress from a simple but respectable physician to a presidential adviser. You've really done yourself and your loved ones proud," Gina purred as she placed her hand on Jordan's.

"Thanks, Gina," Jordan replied shortly as he extracted his hand and finished the last of his sundae.

"I've been so proud to be able to tell people that I'm your wife," Gina gushed as she exuded sweetness.

"Ex-wife," Jordan corrected without looking up from his water glass.

"I stand corrected, dear," she conceded with a

broad smile. Then, extending her hand to Bonnie and Steve, she said, "I've forgotten my manners. I'm Gina Fulton Everett, Jordan's first wife."

Looking first at Jordan and then at the waiting hand, Bonnie and Steve introduced themselves. They had not known about Gina since none of the rumor mill had mentioned her name. If they had known of a previous marriage, they would not have expected the former wife to look or act like this one. Gina was dramatic from the tip of her head to the rhinestone buckle on her black flats.

As if reading their minds, Jordan commented listlessly, "We met at a concert to benefit black children with AIDS. Her family is very influential in fund-raising for black charities. I was one of the special guests, mostly because I was single. Gina's job was to keep me entertained. She did her job. We were married two months later and divorced six years after that."

"Oh, well, some things just aren't meant to last." Gina sighed loudly. "I'm a totally different person now."

"So am I. That experience taught me lessons that I'll never forget," Jordan commented more to himself than to the others.

"I've learned that I simply can't bring happiness to the community if my home life is in turmoil. I was so busy volunteering here and there that I just didn't put enough time into us. I've cut back on my community service so that I might devote myself to my home life. I'm looking for a new husband at this very moment. Until I find one, I'm putting my energy in public television and educational films," Gina added. She looked like a merry little black widow spider waiting for its prey.

"Really? Just remember that you can't go home again. Jordan is already taken," Bonnie commented when she noticed that Gina seemed to be looking in Jordan's direction.

"I wouldn't think of breaking up Jordan's happiness. I know he's planning on tying the knot again, and I wish them all the happiness we never had," Gina replied as she patted Jordan's arm.

"On that note, let's dance," Jordan said as he turned toward Emma who had been watching the interplay between former spouses. Actually, from where she stood, the relationship between Jordan and Gina looked like the preliminary rounds of combat rather than the remains of a relationship.

Pushing Emma aside, Gina grabbed Jordan and dragged him to the dance floor. Pressing herself against him, she steered him through a seductive slow dance that caught the attention of everyone in the room. Emma, Bonnie, and Steve could only watch in wonder as Gina made a spectacle of herself.

Breaking free and leaving her on the dance floor, Jordan made it back to his friends. His face was a thundercloud of emotions as he tossed enough money onto the table to cover their tab and a generous tip.

Jordan announced with barely concealed fury, "I've had enough of this public display. Are you ready to go home?"

Jordan barely waited for their reply before he walked toward the door with as much calm and dignity as he could muster. He was furious with Gina for putting him in the spotlight. He detested that level of attention and always tried to keep a low profile.

Climbing into the car beside him, Bonnie said nothing. She could sense that questions about Gina might cause this angry man to erupt. However, she was very curious about the woman who had caused such steam to gush from Jordan's ears. His jaws worked constantly as he ground his teeth in fury. The silence from the backseat of the car was thick with curiosity.

They had reached Bonnie and Steve's house before anyone spoke. Breaking the silence, they wished Emma and Jordan a pleasant weekend. Bonnie raised her eyebrows in one of those confidential expressions between friends that asked for a phone call in the morning. Emma inclined her head imperceptibly but said nothing. Jordan's short good night lay heavy in the air.

As the car pulled into Emma's driveway, Jordan said without preamble, "I didn't know that Gina would be at the hotel tonight. I certainly wouldn't have gone if I had known. She's hardly my favorite person. Our marriage ended because she can be overbearing and manipulative. I think you got a firsthand view of that this evening. Actually, as horrible as she was, I've known her to be even worse."

Walking into the house, Emma stated calmly, "I know you didn't plan it, Jordan, but I think you have a problem that needs solving. It's obvious that Gina has personal, unresolved issues about your former relationship. I think you need to sit down with her and solve them before they surface at the wrong time and in the wrong company."

"She's not an easy woman to speak with calmly," Jordan replied as he poured them tall glasses of beer.

"I could see that, but, if you don't, she'll play this little game of hers in a setting that'll hurt you professionally. Tonight didn't matter. It was embarrassing, but that's all. The next time she does this, she might pick an important social event. I'm surprised that she hasn't done anything before now," Emma said as she sipped her beer.

"She probably would have except that I only attend business-related social functions. Except for the few dinners that I've hosted at my house, I really don't socialize often. I guess it's a good thing that I don't," Jordan conceded, draining his glass and heading toward the kitchen.

Emma could hear him putting the glasses in the dishwasher as she sat in the living room trying to think of something to say that would make him feel better. Yet she knew there was nothing short of action that would solve this problem. Jordan was the one who had to take the initiative in this matter. Gina would only construe anything that she did as jealousy.

"Well, what will you do?" Emma asked as she snuggled against Jordan's warm body. She loved the way he smelled when he slept, when he first woke up in the morning, and anytime that he stood near her.

"I'll give her a call next week. If she's spending her time working for public television, it won't be difficult to find her," Jordan said as he pulled Emma closer.

"You'll be careful around her, won't you?" Emma inquired as she turned her face up to look into his.

"Don't worry. I won't let anything or anyone come between us. I'll step very carefully around Gina. For all I know, she's directly wired to the newspaper's gossip column," Jordan replied, placing a kiss on Emma's lips.

"Good. I'll start making wedding plans early next week. I wasn't sure of the head count for a while there. It looked as if we'd have to invite Gina," Emma joked now that Jordan's mood had lightened.

"We'd elope first!" Jordan boomed.

"Hey, that's not a bad idea. Why don't we simply get married somewhere? A lot of people are getting married in Las Vegas these days. The islands are a popular place and so are cruise ships. We could go alone or hint to Bonnie and Steve that it's time for a little vacation," Emma suggested as the idea of retreating from the city in favor of a private ceremony began to take root.

"No, I want everyone to know that I've found the perfect woman this time. I had a big wedding the first time. It felt like a circus show. I don't want anything that large, but I want everyone to see us taking our vows," Jordan replied firmly.

"Fine. We'll have a small, intimate affair with the feel of a big wedding. I've catered that kind numerous times. I only wanted to offer a suggestion. Aruba is glorious this time of year and so is Cancún," Emma concluded without lifting her head from his chest.

"Since we don't have to give the caterer a deposit on the food or put one on the room, I'll try to be flexible. However, I'd still prefer a traditional, almost formal, wedding here," Jordan said in an effort to keep the lines of communication open. He knew how important it was for both members of a marriage to feel like equal contributors.

"It really doesn't matter one way or the other to me. Big, small, it's of no consequence. I simply want to spend the rest of my life with you," Emma said as she hugged Jordan tight.

"Then it's settled. We'll live together and forget the 'I do' step altogether. We're grown and in love. We don't really need the other stuff anyway. Since the means doesn't really matter to either of us, let's just jump to the end, cut to the chase as they say," Jordan declared enthusiastically.

Sitting up and looking at him with disbelief, Emma replied, "I don't think so. We'll get married before God and company either in a church, a house, or a magistrate's chambers. I don't care if we're wearing shorts or evening wear, but we're saying the 'I do' part loud and clear. I'm an old-fashioned kind of girl, and I want that part of it more than the clothes and the food."

Laughing, Jordan pulled Emma back into his arms and said, "I was only kidding. I just wanted to see if you were a truly liberated woman. We'll get married as we decided . . . Labor Day weekend."

"That's better." Emma sighed as she snuggled against him again. "Now, back to the more urgent problem. How should we react toward Gina? It's clear that she intends a replay of your marriage to her."

"That problem will take care of itself next week. I'll remind her that our marriage is not something that I ever want to repeat," Jordan replied as he snapped his fingers.

"I'll leave it in your capable hands," Emma said, confident that Jordan would solve the problem of Gina.

"I'm getting sleepy. Let's go to bed before I can't move from this sofa. I'm a bit heavy for you to carry, and I'd rather not be dragged up the stairs," Jordan announced as he kissed Emma on the forehead and stretched.

"Don't worry. I'd throw a blanket over you if you decided to sleep down here," Emma replied as she reached out to help him from the sofa.

"I would have to be a major fool to be willing to sleep on this purgatorial sofa with your nice warm bed and body upstairs. My mother didn't raise no fool," Jordan pronounced as he slipped his feet into his shoes in preparation for standing.

Rising, he slipped his arm around Emma's shoulders and led her into the hall. With only the glow of the night-light to guide them, they made their way up the stairs and into Emma's bedroom. In only a matter of minutes, they had undressed and climbed into bed. Both of them were so tired from the long day that they fell asleep immediately. Even the reality of Gina looming on the horizon could not keep them awake.

Ten

Despite Gina's presence looming over them, Emma and Jordan passed the next weeks in relative peace and harmony. Jordan's talk with Gina seemed to have convinced her that he was in a committed relationship and far from her grasp. She listened and shrugged but stayed away, giving Emma and Jordan plenty of time to learn more about each other when the opportunity for conversation arose.

Emma was so busy with EJ's that she really had little time to think about her own wedding. The president had kept his word and hired her company to cater his wife's birthday party. He and the First Lady met with her once and then Emma was on her own to coordinate the most important job of her career.

Naturally, everyone in Washington who had not already contracted with her now rushed to her door as soon as the word circulated through town that EJ's was the president's private caterer. Emma hired the assistant that she had long wanted but could not justify. Further, she lured one of the most cherished chefs from a landmark restaurant. Overnight, her establishment had become the place to work and Emma the caterer to hire.

Word of mouth and phone lines all over Washington and its suburbs burned with details of her success.

Even newspapers in Richmond and Baltimore carried stories about the local girl who made her little business into the mouse that roared in the face of larger, established catering firms. The local television stations aired a special on her success, complete with a reporter who followed her around for a week gathering the news for his five-minute special.

And Bonnie complained the entire time. Her business had increased beyond the point of comfort in her mind. She'd enjoyed her anonymity and the ability to sleep late. Now, with EJ's a success, she had to hustle, too.

Jordan, too, was busy in his advisory role to the president. He was out of town at least two days each week giving speeches and hosting meetings. His long-distance bill, noting his calls to her office and home, reflected his devotion to Emma. When forced to miss a weekend with her, Jordan sent a dozen of the most beautiful red roses that Emma had ever seen.

Jordan was one of the guests to the president's party and, of course, Emma was his date. The evening was special not only because Emma's company had catered it, but because it marked their first formal appearance as an engaged couple. Jordan's connection with political Washington was his reason for being in town. Now, that relationship had united them and brought Emma to celebrity status. It seemed fitting that they should mark their first official appearance at the White House.

Although the evening was informal by White House standards, Jordan knew from past experience as a guest at the First Lady's birthday party that casual elegance would be the attire for the evening. He carefully selected a pair of summer-weight gray slacks, a white shirt with gray and pale yellow pinstripes, black loafers, and a stunning blazer that pulled together the outfit perfectly.

Emma greeted him at the door wearing a mauve silk suit with a subtle floral print blouse and taupe pumps. At her ears sparkled pearl-and-diamond earrings that were outdone by the joy in her eyes at seeing him. She hardly waited for Jordan to cross the threshold before she pulled him into her arms and smothered him with happy kisses.

"I'll stay away longer next time. If this is the way you greet me after four days, what'll happen after a week?" Jordan said, laughing between kisses. He had never been so happy or felt so loved.

"I'd call you on your cell phone every day. That's what would happen. Even though I've been so busy with this job, I haven't been able to keep you out of my mind. I'm so glad you're home," Emma gushed as she studied his face for any sign of change during their short absence.

"I thought I did that this time. I certainly spoke with your secretary often enough. You were always on the other line," Jordan quipped in his defense as he locked the door and propelled Emma toward his waiting car.

"I know you did, dear. I have stacks of callback slips that I'm keeping to remind you of the time when you adored me, if you ever stop showing your affection," Emma stated as she settled into the car with care not to crush her suit.

"You might as well put those pink slips in the bottom drawer of your dresser with all the other forgotten treasures because you'll never need to remind me. I'll never stop showing you that I love you and need you in my life to feel complete," Jordan remarked as he pulled into the silent street and headed toward the White House and the most important dinner of Emma's career.

"I might as well throw them away as soon as we get home. There's no point in keeping excess clutter. I like keeping my life simple and uncomplicated. You know, a good man to love, a cat for company, and a box of chocolates on my birthday," Emma commented as they drove through the now-quiet streets so unlike those of the rush-hour madness.

"That's all you want? I guess I should exchange that ring for a few million pieces of candy, then," Jordan teased as he pulled into the White House gate and showed their invitations and passes.

"What ring?" Emma demanded as they pulled to the curb.

"The one in the glove box. I thought you might like to wear it tonight to show everyone that we're officially engaged, but I can always take it back," Jordan said with a wicked grin as he exited the car.

Opening the glove box, Emma found a small velvet box. Opening it quickly, she discovered a huge sparkling center diamond with a large stone on each side. Without hesitation, Emma slipped it onto the third finger of her left hand. The diamonds glittered dazzlingly in the streetlights.

Allowing the Marine to help her exit the car, Emma joined Jordan on the sidewalk. The magnificent portico welcomed her to step up to the front door of the peoples' house. Vines cascaded from impressive vases that stood under the windows. A red carpet lined the stairs and greeted the arriving guests.

Slipping her arm through Jordan's, Emma asked in a soft voice, "Did you really buy this gorgeous ring at Tiffany while you were in New York?"

"No, only the box. I wanted to impress you. The ring came in a Cracker Jack box that I ate in the airport. I almost broke my tooth on that thing," Jordan teased as they entered the White House and followed the others to the family dining room.

Ascending the stairs, Emma laughed and said, "It's worth the dental bill to me. It's gorgeous. Look at the way it sparkles in this light."

"Put your hand down. We don't want to be arrested for smuggling in the crown jewels," Jordan commented proudly. He was thrilled that Emma liked his selection. "You can exchange it if you'd like."

"Not on your life. You can take me to New York to see a play but not to return this ring. Your taste is exquisite. After all, you had the good sense to love me," Emma retorted as they entered the family quarters.

"I thought you picked me," Jordan retorted.

"I did not . . ." Emma began with ruffled feathers.

Joining them quickly, Bonnie asked, "What are you two squabbling about this time?"

"This," Emma replied as she stuck out her hand.

"Emma, it's gorgeous! Jordan, you have wonderful taste. First, you fall in love with Emma and then you buy this ring," Bonnie enthused as she pretended to be blinded by the glow of the stone.

"See!" Emma teased, and wrinkled her nose at Jordan.

"I'm glad you approve. I'd like you to know that I selected it without any help," Jordan replied as Steve gave him a thumbs-up of approval.

"You're just a man of astounding talents," Bonnie teased as she pecked Jordan lightly on the cheek.

"People, this is hardly the place," Steve counseled in a quiet tone as he motioned around the elegant surroundings.

The room had begun to fill with guests attired in their best casual finery. They were all trying to appear unimpressed about being invited to the White House for an informal gathering. However, each was fairly bursting with a sense of self-importance at having made the president's short list.

Looking around the room, Emma commented, "The president doesn't have too many 'intimate friends,' does he? I wondered who he had invited."

Jordan replied, "Just some of the most influential people in Washington and a few lesser folk like us."

"I recognize a fairly famous black publisher over there and a senator in that corner. Not a shabby turnout exactly," Bonnie stated as she ticked off the celebrities in the room.

"If the meal isn't any good, let's stop for a hamburger on the way home," Jordan teased without looking at Emma.

"Very funny. As a matter of fact, we held a rehearsal of all the dishes this afternoon. You'll love every mouthful," Emma retorted with a forced smile and wildly twinkling eyes. She loved the banter that passed between them and the feeling of familiarity that allowed them to be playful.

"Shush! Here he comes now," Bonnie hissed as she nodded toward the door from which the president entered.

Even dressed in slacks and a blazer, he was an impressive figure. Emma could not say that she found him handsome, but he was definitely an imposing man. The mantel of authority rested well on his broad shoulders. His large smile embraced everyone and immediately made them feel at home.

Franklin Grant shone that smile on the invited guests to his informal little dinner. He wore the gray hair of his sixty years with dignity. The smile lines around his mouth added to his charm. He was tall and still straight although affairs of state could have worn him down. However, as a second-term president, he had life in the White House under control.

At President Grant's side stood his wife, the First Lady. Evelyn Grant was of average build with salt-and-pepper hair that curled charmingly around her ears. Her speech contained the remnants of a Southern accent acquired from her home in Tennessee but modified after long years in Washington where her father had served as a senator. She had been born to the wealth and privilege of the family textile business unlike her husband whose family had been teachers and ministers.

Passing among them with their traditional glasses of club soda in their hands, the president and his wife greeted their guests. Although they knew that Emma and Bonnie were there both as employees and guests, they did not treat them any differently and greeted Jordan as if he were their best friend. It was truly an egalitarian evening with the very rich and very powerful mixing with the middle class.

Emma sat somewhat nervously beside Jordan as her employees mingled with White House staff and served dinner. The meal opened with canapés à l'Amiral, a tasty shrimp butter on toasted French bread, served with oysters à la Russe followed by cream of barley soup. For a third course, Emma had suggested the poached salmon with mousseline sauce. The entrée consisted of chicken lyonnaise with potatoes anna, creamed carrots, and asparagus with champagne-saffron vinaigrette. The waiters carefully served an elaborately decorated birthday cake and vanilla ice cream for dessert. At every course, the guests exclaimed over the food.

Of course, Bonnie's floral arrangements and linens accompanied the meal perfectly. The richness of the soft shell-pink brocade echoed the splendor of the selections from the last dinner of the *Titanic,* which

Emma had modified to fit the current fat-conscious palate. Bonnie had selected a mixture of orchids and roses with splashes of baby's breath that rested in short crystal vases. Coordinating with the entertainment had been more of a challenge since they had wanted to create a theme dinner around the ill-fated luxury liner. However, when the famous singer and composer learned of their plans, he selected songs with lingering, almost melancholy, melodies.

"Isn't this the most fabulous meal you ever tasted? I don't think the White House staff prepared this one. They're good but this is exquisite," Patricia Frost, a journalist, on Emma's right commented as she savored the gentle hint of garlic that lightly kissed the palate before vanishing.

"It's delicious," Emma replied without adding that her company had catered the affair.

"I'll have to ask for the name of the caterer they used. The flowers and table linens blend perfectly. The caterer must have her own contacts. It's obvious that nothing was left to chance here," Patricia Frost continued, enjoying the last of the flavorful sauce.

"I'm sure that the caterer would be very pleased to hear your comments," Emma responded quietly.

Glaring at Emma from across the table, Bonnie raised her eyebrows meaningfully. She had overheard the conversation and wondered why Emma had not disclosed her identity. They could both use the business.

Emma only smiled. She was not as outgoing as Bonnie in accepting praise. She would wait and let the First Lady handle the situation in time. For now, Emma was content to hear that a guest had been impressed with her menu and her staff's culinary ability.

"What's wrong with Bonnie? Is she having a

stroke?" Jordan asked after seeing the antics across the table.

"No, she calls it communicating with me in a subtle manner. She wants me to identify myself as the caterer that prepared the dinner," Emma replied with a chuckle at Jordan's accurate description of Bonnie's raised brows and wild eyes.

"I hate to say it, but I agree with her this time. Everyone should know that EJ's prepared this feast for the palate. I've eaten in a lot of five-star restaurants and enjoyed many privately catered affairs, but this food is the best I've ever eaten. You're an artist as well as a businesswoman," Jordan stated proudly.

"All it takes is a sense of style, a good chef, knowledge of foods, and the time to experiment. But I'll take the compliment anyway," Emma answered with a proud smile. This had been her night. She had become engaged to a perfect man and her business had earned acclaim. She was very happy.

As the guests joined the president and First Lady for the evening's entertainment, the First Lady slipped a note into Emma's hand. Emma had noticed that Mrs. Grant had left the room for a few minutes toward the end of the dinner, but Emma had assumed that she had gone to check on the entertainment arrangements. Now Emma knew that Mrs. Grant had composed the note to her during her absence.

Taking her seat beside Jordan and Bonnie, Emma carefully opened the flap of the oyster-white envelope and extracted the single slip of note paper. In carefully controlled black ink, Mrs. Grant had written of her appreciation for Emma's culinary expertise and ability to turn a humble gathering of friends into a grand gala.

Jordan lightly patted her hand as he read the note. His heart fairly burst with pride for Emma's accomplishments and recognition. He did not want to lose her to increased catering opportunities for her business, yet he could not conceal the pride that he felt for his future wife's accomplishments.

Bonnie passed to Emma a similar note in which the First Lady had expressed her delight with Bonnie's choice of floral arrangements. According to Mrs. Grant, the expertise and skill of the two women had contributed immensely to make the evening a success. Slipping the note into her purse, Bonnie decided to purchase frames for both her and Emma's note as soon as she could.

The evening continued with entertainment from the composer and his most famous colleague. The two had recently agreed to team after a long separation. Separately they made lovely music. Together they made musical history. With him at the piano and her standing at his side, they entertained the other guests with ageless selections that fit the haunting elegance of the meal.

However, for an encore, they performed a rendition of their hits that had everyone in the room either dancing in their seats or tapping their feet. When they sang the greatest of their numbers, the audience grew completely silent. No one moved as she lofted sweet notes and trilled melancholy words of love and desertion. His fingers lingered lovingly over the keyboard as he accompanied her to music that he had written with her in mind.

As soon as they finished, the room erupted in wild applause. The president was the first person on his feet. He rushed the stage to shake first the singer's hand and then the composer's. With a broad smile on his now-handsome face, President Grant thanked everyone who had attended his wife's birthday party, saying that everyone had made the evening special.

Then, to Emma's surprise, he gave special thanks to the proprietor of EJ's and her associate for the outstanding culinary fare and its presentation.

Emma floated from the White House on Jordan's arm with Bonnie and Steve close behind. The evening had been perfect in every way. From her personal joy to her professional success, Emma could not have asked for a better day. Looking at Jordan, she knew that having him to share her success and add to her life had made all the difference. She had experienced professional success before that night but never had it tasted so sweet.

As she approached the car, Patricia Frost called to her. "You should have told me or at least given me your card. I'll call next week. I've gotten your number from Mrs. Grant. You're wonderful," she gushed as she patted Emma on the arm and vanished into the night.

"Well, you've certainly set your star in the sky tonight. I can't imagine that there's a caterer in Washington that will outshine you after this. The competition's purple and gold trucks will be for sale soon," Jordan commented proudly.

"Thanks, but there's plenty of work to go around. I've only made my mark in a small portion of it," Emma replied as they left the White House standing in the spotlights on Pennsylvania Avenue.

"Pretty impressive portion if you'd ask me. I wonder if you'll have time for me after this?" Jordan quipped, pulling into her driveway.

"You'll just have to get in line with everyone else— that's all. I can probably work you into my schedule for the Labor Day weekend. I'm booked until then," Emma said, laughing as they entered her house.

The phone was already ringing off the hook when they entered. Rushing to answer it, Emma almost fell over the cat who had come downstairs to greet her. Swooping him into her arms, she rushed across the room. Quickly she motioned to Jordan that she needed a pad of paper and a pen. Barely able to juggle the cat, phone, and pad, she took down the details of the conversation.

Promising to call the next business day, Emma turned to Jordan and smiled. "News certainly travels fast in this town," she said happily. "That was Mrs. Barrett, of the hotel Barretts. Her sister attended tonight's dinner and raved about me. Not to be outdone, she wants me to cater an affair for her next month. Mrs. Barrett also said that her sister will probably call."

"Great! But when will you have time for me?" Jordan asked with a pout.

"Now," Emma replied as she turned on the answering machine and turned off the light.

She took a quick detour to the kitchen to feed the cat his nighttime snack and then joined Jordan at the steps. Taking off her heels, Emma grabbed Jordan's hand and led him upstairs. As the answering machine clicked on, she closed the bedroom door so that business and Kitty would not disturb them.

With the glow of the many candles that lined Emma's dresser flickering in the night, they caressed each other slowly and carefully. As they savored the feel of each other's skin and the taste of each other's lips, Emma and Jordan forgot about the successful evening, their work, and the outside world. They did not hear the cat thumping impatiently at the door as they tugged at the buttons that kept their fingers from brushing the flesh hidden behind the clothing.

As the clock chimed the hour, Jordan swooped Emma into his arms and carried her to the bed. With nothing between them except her engagement ring,

Jordan covered her naked body with hot kisses from her lips to her toes and everywhere in between. He lingered on the soft flesh of her neck and breasts until Emma thought that she could not endure the delight of his kisses any longer. His fingers drew agonizing circles of fire around her nipples and then trailed downward to her belly.

Emma's fingers were no strangers to the terrain of Jordan's body. She explored the muscles of his arms and back and caressed the silkiness of the skin on the back of his neck. She nibbled playfully at his ears and teased the little hairs with her tongue. Her arms wrapped tightly around him and pulled him toward her. Her fingers linked in his hair and held firmly as her lips kissed the corners of his mouth.

Pulling gently, Emma guided Jordan's face to hers. Their eyes met for a long moment before Jordan covered her lips with his. His hands caressed the warmth of Emma's body in a way that made her moan with pleasure.

As her fingers probed his manhood, Emma gently eased the condom over the shaft. Jordan sighed deeply when she stroked the sheathed warmth. He squirmed with pleasure as she ran her finger around the still-sensitive tip.

Jordan's muscles strained as he rose above Emma and gently entered her womanliness. Their bodies locked in a lovers' embrace and began to move in unison. Each thrust brought them closer to their release and surrender.

Arching their bodies and matching their pace to the flow of their energy, Emma and Jordan kissed and caressed each other as the tension in their bodies increased. They muttered each other's name and tightened their hold as the pace quickened. Feeling their passion peak, they groaned in unison as the waves of pleasure flowed over them and carried them to un-explored depths of enjoyment.

Even as the passion waned and their desire for each other decreased, Emma and Jordan remained en-folded in each other's arms. They did not move for fear of breaking the spell that bound them together. They were happy in a way that neither had ever ex-perienced. For the first time in their lives, they knew the meaning of unconditional love and surrender.

"Do you think lovemaking will always be like this?" Emma asked as she settled her head on Jordan's shoulder.

"No, it'll probably get better," Jordan replied softly, his voice still husky with love. "We're still learning about each other. We haven't discovered all the hot buttons yet."

"I don't know about that," Emma responded with a sleepy chuckle. "You've found buttons that I didn't even know I had. I've never known that love could feel this good."

Looking intently into Emma's eyes, Jordan asked, "Your ex never explored your body?"

"His idea of lovemaking was more the slam, bam, thank you ma'am approach," Emma confided. "He usually finished before I got warmed up. His tech-nique wasn't much, at least not with me. I overheard a conversation in the ladies' room, however, that my secretary thought that he was great."

"She told you?" Jordan asked incredulously, leaning on one elbow so that he could gaze into Emma's eyes.

"No. I heard her talking to the woman in the stall next to hers," Emma replied. "She didn't even know that I was in the rest room. I was supposed to be on a business trip. You see, we had just divorced and he had made the first settlement payment. My business was in its infancy, and I was always at one meeting or the other. The catering business isn't only about food, you know. Anyway, I had suspected that the other woman was my new secretary, but I wasn't sure. My ex had many affairs during our troubled marriage. My new secretary just happened to have worked in his law firm. She hadn't been his secretary, but she had worked for the man in the office next door. I guess Marvin thought it was safe to have an affair with her since she didn't work directly for him."

"How did this woman happen to work for you?" Jordan inquired as he smoothed Emma's eyebrows and traced the outline of her lips with his fingers.

"That's the strangest thing," Emma replied, musing over the set of circumstances that brought Joyce to her new business. "I advertised with an agency for a secretary, and she arrived. I didn't think anything out of the ordinary when I saw his firm listed as her most recent reference. Actually, I was glad to hire someone who was so well trained and professional. It wasn't until later that I discovered that she was the same woman I had found in bed with my husband. I didn't recognize her since he had thrown the covers over her head to protect her when I burst into the room."

"How long did she work for you?" Jordan asked as he pulled Emma into his arms again.

"Not long," Emma replied with a big yawn. "After I overheard the bathroom conversation, I started dropping hints about my past. I don't make it a practice to discuss my life with my employees, but, this time, I needed some information from her. As soon as I mentioned Marvin's name and the fact that I had returned to my maiden name, she recognized me as the wronged wife and quit. It's a shame, too, because she was a terrific secretary."

"I hope she's happy now that she has your ex all to herself," Jordan said with a chuckle.

"But she doesn't." Emma laughed. "He started cheating on her as soon as the ink dried on their marriage license. I heard that she's in the process of divorcing him."

"That's something that won't happen again. Fidelity is a big thing with me. I don't run around," Jordan announced as he eased Emma's head onto his shoulder.

Laughing, Emma replied, "Good thing, too. I'd hate to have to hurt you."

Jordan pulled her closer. "Not to worry. I intend to go out of this world with all of my equipment intact."

"Smart man," Emma replied, nestling into his arms.

Slipping into sleep, Emma and Jordan snuggled together with Jordan's arms around her and her back pressed into his chest. From their hold on each other, they made it obvious that no one and nothing could separate them.

Eleven

The next morning when Emma entered the kitchen to prepare breakfast, she found ten messages on the answering machine. Quickly noting the names and numbers into her planner, she slipped into her apron. She would return the calls later. Right now, domestic duties were far more important than business. Chuckling at her new success and fame, she prepared blueberry muffins and squeezed fresh orange juice. Humming, she set the table and allowed the aroma of freshly brewed coffee to summon Jordan to join her.

The telephone rang again, disturbing the tranquillity of the domestic scene. Grabbing the phone so that the ringing would not disturb Jordan, Emma answered on the second ring. The familiar voice greeted her as she returned to spooning batter into the muffin tin.

"Good morning, Emma! I'm sorry to bother you, but I didn't get an answer at Jordan's house. I thought I'd try you. Is he there?" Gina asked gleefully.

"Hi, Gina. He's still sleeping. I can wake him if you'd like," Emma replied with a slight irritation in her voice that this woman would track down her fiancé in her house.

"No, have him call me. By the way, it's only fair to tell you that I'm back in the picture. Jordan has done quite well in the last few years, and I want a piece of that action," Gina announced with a nasty edge to her voice.

"I don't understand, Gina. You've been divorced from him for a long time. You have your own life. What makes you think that you can simply walk back into his life?" Emma demanded, closing the oven door with an angry shove and giving her full attention to the conversation.

"I've realized my mistake. I never should have agreed to divorce him and never would if I'd known that things would turn out like this. Anyway, I'm back," Gina replied with an annoying level of confidence.

"You mean you've returned now that Jordan has gained national acclaim, has a high-profile position, and is engaged. Sorry, you're too late. There's no room here for you," Emma stated firmly.

"I'll let Jordan answer that one. You're right about his position being a major attraction. However, I could care less about his engagement to you. That's totally insignificant as far as I'm concerned," Gina responded with an even heavier helping of nastiness.

"I don't intend to continue this conversation with you. Your plans are hardly worth my time. I'll tell Jordan that you called. Good-bye, Gina," Emma said as she hung up the phone without waiting for the other woman's response.

Emma leaned against the kitchen wall as the strength flowed from her legs. She had never been so angry. The woman obviously did not understand the depths of Emma's relationship with Jordan and felt that she could have him back in her life. Jordan would have to set her straight on that issue.

The fragrance of baking blueberry muffins had filled the house, reminding Emma of their presence. As she checked them, she heard footsteps overhead. Smiling, she knew that Jordan was awake and would soon be ready for breakfast.

"I'm hungry!" he called down the stairs.

"Breakfast will be ready in ten minutes," Emma replied as she scrambled the eggs.

As she decided how to handle telling Jordan about the call, Emma heard the water running in the shower. In a few minutes, he would appear smelling freshly washed and very sexy. She would have only a few more minutes to decide her approach to this delicate situation.

Jordan came into the room, pulled Emma into his arms, encircling her in a big hug. Kissing her playfully on the back of her neck, he demanded, "Feed me, woman. I'm starving."

Laughing, and freeing herself from his grip, Emma replied, "You'll be hungrier still if you don't let me go. You don't want overcooked eggs, do you?"

"Never let me be the one who causes the celebrated caterer and businesswoman to overcook eggs." Jordan laughed as he carried the pitcher of juice to the table.

As they munched hungrily, Emma said casually, "Gina called while you were still sleeping. She wants you to call her back. The number's on the pad."

"Gina? Why would she call me?" Jordan replied with a touch of irritation already creeping into his voice.

"According to her, she's still interested in you and determined to retie the knot. Another muffin?" Emma asked as her heart pounded in her chest. She hoped that her calm exterior belied her inner turmoil.

"What? She's nuts. Anything between us ended

years ago. I don't think I'll return her call. I have nothing to say to her," Jordan replied with real anger.

"She needs to hear that from you. If you don't tell her, she'll call again. Sure you don't want another muffin?" Emma repeated as she extended the plate in shaking hands.

"You certainly are taking this calmly. I don't think I'd act this way if your ex suddenly tried to ease back into your life," Jordan announced while munching on a second buttery hot muffin.

"I'm not calm, Jordan. I'm furious. But there's nothing I can do about it. Any reaction from me would look like the reaction of a jealous woman. You're the only one who can stop this before it gets worse," Emma replied, pushing her plate aside.

"You're right. I'll make the call after I help you clean up. I have to put a stop to this before Gina becomes an irritant. She can be very persistent," Jordan pointed out as he began to clear the table.

"I'll take care of the dishes while you make the call," Emma replied as she shooed him from the kitchen and closed the door. She did not want to overhear his conversation from the den.

Jordan returned almost immediately with a disappointed expression on his face. "She wasn't there. I left a message for her to call me back," he said, sipping the last of his coffee and placing the cup in the dishwasher.

"We're not waiting here for the call, are we?"

"No way. There's a new art exhibit downtown that I'd like to see. Impressionist work," Jordan said as they gathered their car and house keys.

"Let's stop at the shop first. I need to check in with Jason, my new assistant. I'd like to thank him personally for the success of last night. He said he'd stop by for a few minutes," Emma said as they climbed into the car.

To Emma's delight, a long line wrapped from the front door around the corner. People streamed from the little café adjacent to EJ's carrying bags and boxes of goodies. Many of them munched muffins and cakes. No one seemed too concerned about waistline bulge.

Squeezing past them, Emma entered the office where Jason waved happily while taking copious notes with one hand and cradling the phone against his shoulder. Although the office was officially closed on the weekend, he had reported to work to finish any last cleanup from the White House affair. From the number of sheets of paper strewn across the desk, he had spent most of his time on the phone.

"This is crazy!" Jason announced as soon as he hung up. "I only planned to be here for a few minutes, but the phone wouldn't stop ringing. The message bank was full. I transcribed all of the old messages to make room for new ones. You were certainly a hit last night."

"Not just me. I'd say you and the chef had quite a bit to do with it. I only adapted the recipe. If it hadn't been for you, I wouldn't have been able to enjoy the evening. You took all the responsibility from my shoulders and gave me a chance to have a great evening. Thank you," Emma said softly as she gently placed her hand on his arm.

"Don't mention it. I'll see you later," Jason commented as he headed toward the sunshine.

Fingering the stack of messages, Emma saw names of people who were devoted clients of her most famous and esteemed competition, people she had longed to entice to her business. Now, her peach and mauve trucks would roll through the most famous neighborhoods in Washington and its suburbs.

"Give me a few minutes to see if there's anything here that needs immediate attention," Emma said as she read the copious notes that filled the pages of the yellow legal pad.

"Wow! My fiancée is the proprietor of the famous EJ's. I guess I didn't really understand the impact of landing a client like the White House. I knew you'd gain a reputation and additional business, but I never dreamed that you'd become this popular. Will one assistant be enough?" Jordan asked as he read the names on the pink callback sheets.

"These can wait. You're right. I might have to hire still another person. Don't forget that Bonnie's business will improve, too. I'll have to put her on alert. She's my sole supplier of linens and china. I hope she can keep up," Emma stated as she turned off the light in her office and locked the door.

Slipping through the line as they exited the building, Jordan said, "It's a good thing that your admiring public doesn't recognize your face. We'd never have any privacy."

"Are you complaining already?" Emma retorted as they linked arms and strolled toward the gallery. "I remember when I first met you that, as the new man in town, you had a pretty good following."

"Yes, but the ladies never formed a line that reached around the block for my favors," Jordan replied as he dodged a woman carrying two pastry boxes.

"I'm a fad, the new kid on the block, the instant success. This excitement will subside soon, and I'll become like a pair of old slippers to them. They love saying that they used the same caterer as the president. They'll get over it. Now, let's push the business out of our minds for the rest of the day. This time belongs to us," Emma announced as they entered the exhibit of Impressionist art.

They rounded the corner into a room with cream walls adorned with priceless paintings and mahogany benches for contemplation. Each work of art reflected the artist's talent and voice. People from all walks of life, from students to retirees, stood or sat in silence as the majesty of the work washed over them.

Emma and Jordan did not notice one of the art fans until it was too late to retreat. Gina slipped between them with a beguiling smile and a soft voice that belied her aggressive side. To the others, it looked as if Gina had joined old friends for a day at the gallery. Not fooled, Emma knew that Gina was on a hunting expedition.

"Isn't this the most fabulous collection?" Gina oozed enthusiasm as she began a diatribe on Impressionism.

"Lovely," Jordan replied as he disengaged his arm from hers.

"Fabulous," Emma commented as she allowed Jordan to propel her to the opposite side of the room.

Not taking the less-than-subtle hint, Gina followed them. Continuing to expound on the technique and motivation behind the art, she tried to impress them with her knowledge. Looking at each other, Emma and Jordan slipped away from her and into a crowd of art students led by a woman with a raised folded umbrella.

As the woman led her group around the room, Emma and Jordan eased into the hall. Thinking they had escaped Gina, they quickly walked to the gallery's café and ordered the house wine. As they sipped, they congratulated themselves on their quick thinking.

"There you are! I thought I'd lost you," Gina chimed as she pulled up a chair and joined them.

Emma could feel the irritation rising as Gina lay her hand intimately on Jordan's. She wanted to tell her that her presence was not welcome, but she did not want to sound like a jealous, possessive woman. Besides, she felt that Jordan should be the one to make that statement, and as yet he had not. Instead, he immediately excused himself and escaped to the men's room, leaving the women alone at the table.

"Small world, isn't it, Emma? I had no idea that you and Jordan would be here today. I'm certainly happy to see you. You're quite a celebrity these days. I had to get out of the house to escape the phone calls about the hot new caterer that everyone is just dying to try. Absolutely every one of my friends is talking about you. I've told all of them that you're not that new, just recently discovered. Anyway, hearing them gush about you had upset my stomach. I needed a change of environment, and just think, I ran into you here," Gina stated with a sweet but controlled smile.

"Sorry to ruin your day, but you can always leave. You don't have to stay with us. We're capable of navigating the world of Impressionist art without your help," Emma replied with an equally forced smile.

"I'm not leaving without Jordan," Gina announced confidently.

"That's rather bold of you. Don't you become tired of chasing a man who's to be married in a few weeks?" Emma asked as she continued to maintain a controlled, pleasant facial expression.

"Not when it's Jordan. Remember, he was mine before he became yours. Besides, he's not married yet. A lot can happen between now and then," Gina responded with a false mirth.

"Have you ladies finished talking about me yet?" Jordan asked as he rejoined them. It was clear from his pained expression that he had been hoping that only Emma would be waiting for him.

Taking his hand, Emma replied, "Gina says that she won't leave without you. She has this idea that she has an unsatisfied prior claim to you."

"Certainly not one that I can remember," Jordan commented as he remained standing beside the table. "Actually, Gina, I was of the impression that the court ended that. It's time you left us alone, Gina. There's nothing more for us to say to each other."

Rising to stand beside him as she totally ignored Emma's presence, Gina said, "I don't believe that it's over, Jordan. You get flustered every time I come near you. That wouldn't happen if you didn't find me attractive."

"Gina, there's nothing between us any longer. You're frustrating and irritating, and intrusive—that's the reason for my reaction," Jordan replied as he took a step back. Despite his words, his face had colored slightly.

Emma watched the sparring match continue between the former partners. The more Gina persisted, the more often Jordan's complexion changed and the more his eyes flashed. As the observer, Emma wondered if Gina were speaking the truth about sparks still remaining from their marriage. It might be possible that Jordan really did still have feelings for her.

"Gina, this is final. It's over. I'm getting remarried. Leave me alone," Jordan stated firmly.

Grabbing him by the shoulders and pulling his face to hers, Gina announced, "No, it's not over as long as I want you in my life."

Locking her arms around his neck, Gina planted her lips firmly on Jordan's. Pressing her body tightly against his, she made it perfectly clear that she intended to possess him body and soul. Emma, caught by surprise by the display, could only sit and stare.

Jordan's initial reaction was to shove Gina away hard, but he was afraid of the scene that she might make. Deciding that he did not want to draw further attention, he decided against it and did nothing. His arms lung limply at his side. Yet he could not stop the involuntary reaction of his body to the closeness of her. His mind remembered the nights together when their love was still young and untainted by her demands.

Looking into his face, Gina declared, "Deny that you don't feel something for me. I know that you do, and everyone with eyes can see your reaction. Goodbye, Jordan. You haven't seen or felt the last of me."

Gina exited the room with majesty as all eyes shifted from her to Jordan. She had been right about the visibility of his reaction to her. Emma had been the first to notice that he had not been totally unmoved physically by Gina's show of affection. From her seat at the table, she could tell that Jordan had experienced an impressive reaction to Gina.

"She means nothing to me. Let's put her out of our minds and enjoy the rest of our day," Jordan suggested, looking embarrassed as he took his seat across from Emma.

"I wouldn't say that, Jordan. She affected you physically at least, even if you don't want to admit it. I think we'd better wait until you've had time to sort out your feelings before we get married. I don't want this to be a threesome—you, me, and Gina," Emma stated as she gathered her purse and the exhibit flyer.

"I couldn't help the physical reaction. I'm human. But there's no emotional connection to her. I don't feel anything. My memory of the years with her consists of only a few good pictures, most of them taken before we were married. I love you, Emma, and want to begin our life together. I don't need time out, not from you," Jordan explained slowly and carefully.

"I'm not convinced. I think we should take a little time out—maybe a couple of weeks. Things have been moving quickly these last few days. You'll be able to settle this business with her, and I'll be able to focus my attention on the changes to EJ's. Both of us have too many outside distractions that keep us from giving our full attention to our relationship. A marriage shouldn't start that way. We've both been burned before. Let's give this marriage the chance it deserves," Emma stated with resolution.

"But, Gina, I—" Jordan blurted.

"Gina? I'm Emma. That settles it. You need to work out this problem. I can't have you confusing us like that. I'm going home. I'm not angry with you. I'm just not playing this game. I've been on my own for a while now, and I don't need this extra frustration in my life. Call me in a couple of weeks after you've settled this matter," Emma said as she stood beside the table.

"I—I'm sorry. . . ." Jordan began.

"See you later, Jordan," Emma replied with a wave of her open hand.

Jordan sat for what felt like hours as people walked past his table. He did not look up as their eyes burned into him. He felt embarrassed, used, humiliated, and very much alone.

Finally unable to sit any longer, Jordan left the café and walked through the teeming exhibit to the door. Several people pointed to him, but he did not notice. They must have recognized him from Gina's scene in the café. His mind was locked on his problem. He knew that the physical reaction to Gina's kiss had meant nothing; however, Emma and Gina had thought otherwise. He had to redirect Gina's amorous energy and convince Emma that he loved only her. He could tell from the expressions on the faces of both ladies that the task would not be easy.

Emma's return home had been long and complicated by the need to transfer from the subway to a bus before reaching her house. She was hot and miserable by the time she arrived. While riding the crowded public transportation, she had used the time to think. Now, her mind was reeling from the confusion of thoughts.

"What a day not to have my own car," Emma muttered as she opened the door and slipped into the cool house. "I should have insisted that Jordan give me the keys to his car and made him take the subway."

The cat meowed a friendly greeting that Emma almost ignored in her frustration and anger. Reaching down, she picked up her old friend and hurried to the kitchen for a cool drink of water. The cat snuggled against her hot shirt and purred happily along the way.

"If only men were as loyal as you are, women wouldn't be in this mess," Emma said as she stroked the soft fur.

Pouring herself a glass of water over ice and adding a cube to the cat's bowl, Emma stood where she could look out the window while she drank. The flowers bloomed in profusion in her backyard from all the rain of the last few months. The meteorologist claimed that this summer had been the wettest on record. Even the birds that usually sat with open beaks seemed to be thriving in the summer heat.

The jangling of the telephone broke into the silence, startling Emma and the cat. Both of them jumped at the intrusive sound. Waiting for the answering machine to answer, Emma held her breath. She would not answer although she usually did when at home in case the caller had a concern about her business. She did not want to speak with anyone at the moment, especially not Jordan.

"Emma," the voice said, "I'm sorry. I'll make it up to you if you'll just give me the chance. Call me."

Jordan . . . To his credit, he had tried to make amends. However, it would take more than a phone call to undo the events of the afternoon. Jordan needed to take control of the situation and remove the irritant from their lives. Until he did, Emma had nothing to say to him.

Emma listened as the sound of silence returned to the kitchen. Returning her glass to the sink, she decided to take a shower. Maybe she could wash off the happenings of the afternoon.

As the water pelted her skin, Emma realized that nothing except Jordan's prompt action could put an end to this situation. There was nothing she could do. Any attempt at solving the problem would only make things worse. Jordan was the only one who could put a stop to Gina's interference in their lives.

Twelve

Emma spent the next few weeks trying not to think about Jordan. She threw herself into EJ's and the growing list of clients. She planned menus for weddings, bar and bat mitzvahs, christenings, anniversaries, late graduations, and every other possible reason for a party. Some were small affairs of twenty guests. Others were grand and required additional staff. Emma's celebrity had spread throughout the Washington metropolitan area and required careful coordination of manpower and vehicles.

Bonnie's business was booming, too. She not only teamed with Emma on every job, but she also managed accounts of her own. People often called her when they wanted to dress up a small dinner party but did not want the hassle of cleaning up after it ended. They would rent the china, silver, and crystal with coordinated linen from her. At the end of the dinner, the client would return everything to the oversize hamper for pickup the next day or arrange for a member of Emma's staff to serve the meal and clear the tables.

"Have you heard from Jordan?" Bonnie asked as they coordinated the next week's affairs.

"No. I doubt that I will, either. I suspect that he isn't having an easy job of convincing Gina that he means business," Emma replied as she compared their calendars one last time. There was no room for error with reputation on the line and people waiting to be fed.

"Oh. I guess you haven't seen today's paper," Bonnie said hesitantly. She did not want to be the one to break the news to Emma.

"No. I haven't had the time," Emma replied, returning Bonnie's calendar. "I thought I'd read it leisurely after work. Why?"

"Here. Take a look at the style section. There's an article on the first page that might interest you," Bonnie replied as she pushed Emma's unopened paper toward her.

"Style section? Okay. Which one?" Emma asked reluctantly. She had so much to do and really could not spend the time reading about the society bunch.

"Bottom left. It's rather insignificant actually," Bonnie commented as she waited for Emma to scan the announcement.

"Gina and Jordan are remarrying? I can't believe it. I knew he still had unresolved feelings for her, but I didn't suspect that he still loved her. I'll have to phone them with my best wishes for years of happiness. I certainly hope this marriage lasts longer than the first one," Emma said bravely, fighting the tears that played behind her eyes.

"Are you okay?" Bonnie asked as she studied her friend's face.

"I'm fine—just surprised, that's all. I guess I should return the ring. Jordan can have the stone reset. I wonder if they'll need a caterer," Emma replied as her voice broke and the tears began to flow.

"No way! You keep that ring. Make him ask for it if he wants it back," Bonnie exclaimed with indignation.

Bonnie gently cradled Emma in her arms as her friend's shoulders shook from the flow of emotion. She hated to see Emma so torn up by this unappreciative man. Also, she felt responsible for Emma's unhappiness since she had been the one who had introduced them.

"I'm okay. Don't worry about me. Thanks for caring. It was just the surprise of finding out that he preferred Gina to me. I guess the old ties still bound him, to paraphrase a song. Well, it was fun while it lasted. Just look at all the new clients and the fame I've gained from knowing him. At least I can say that this relationship was profitable even in its end," Emma said as she patted Bonnie's hand.

"I shouldn't have introduced you to that creep. If I had known, I wouldn't have. I'm so sorry," Bonnie apologized, accepting her responsibility for Emma's heartbreak.

"It's not your fault. Things like this happen. At least, this time, I came out on top without having to go to court," Emma replied as she slipped her arm though Bonnie's.

"Hungry?" Bonnie asked, knowing her own reaction to bad news.

"Of course. A good cry always makes me hungry. Any suggestions?" Emma chuckled as she wiped the last of the tears and blew her nose.

Emma had always proven to be very resilient. Bonnie was glad to see that she had not lost the ability to spring back this time.

"Yeah, there's a place next door that I'd like to try. I understand that the best caterer in the Washington area runs it," Bonnie said as she hugged Emma and led her toward the door.

The little café was packed with people even at two in the afternoon. The clerk recognized Emma and

Bonnie and immediately wrapped up their usual selection of roast lamb studded with garlic and lightly flavored with mint jelly in a sandwich of thick, freshly baked light rye bread. Adding bottles of ginger ale to the bags, the women walked across the street to the little park in which they hoped to enjoy their meal without interruption from the telephone or anyone other than a curious squirrel.

But it was not to be.

The park was full of people who recognized her from the article in the style section of the *Washington Post* the night after the party at the White House. When the press discovered that she had covered the intimate dinner in the president's private quarters, a reporter had arranged to interview her about the experience, the menu, and the preparation. Emma had been reluctant to give the interview but had agreed when Bonnie suggested that it would attract even more publicity.

To Emma's surprise, the news channels had picked up the story of her success. Reporters and cameramen swarmed around EJ's, recording her every move and listening to her conversations. By the end of the week, anyone who had missed the article had probably seen the television report. Overnight, she had gone from being the best-kept secret in D.C. to being on the tip of every tongue.

In many ways, Emma wished that she had retained her anonymity. She relished the increased business but longed for the quiet days of operating a little catering shop. Rather than complain, Emma remembered the early days when she wondered if she would be able to make ends meet. However, she reminded herself to be careful what she wished for in the future.

Smiling sweetly at all the people who wished her well, Emma tried to enjoy her sandwich. It was not

easy with everyone watching her. Several of the pass-
ersby asked where she had purchased it and ran
across the street to the shop as soon as they found
out. Even on her lunch break, EJ's benefited from
her celebrity.

"How does it feel to be so popular?" Bonnie asked
with just a tinge of envy.

"Like a bug under a microscope," Emma replied
as she pasted on yet another smile.

"You're holding up well," Bonnie commented behind her napkin.

"My face is killing me. I haven't smiled this much
since my wedding reception," Emma responded
through lips that barely parted.

"Don't make me laugh. I'm trying to be suppor-
tive." Bonnie chuckled as still another person asked
Emma for her signature.

"Whoever heard of asking a caterer for an auto-
graph? People want anything that might connect anyone to a person who's supposed to be great," Emma
quipped while finally having a chance to eat her
lunch.

"You should sign autographs only on bags from
EJ's. Don't give it away. Your signature's another mon-
eymaker," Bonnie commented as she drained the last
of her ginger ale.

"Speaking of giving things away, here comes Jordan
with Gina. Don't let on that I was upset. The last
thing I want to do is to give him the upper hand,"
Emma directed as she watched them approach.

"My lips are sealed. Besides, I'd have to be speaking
to him, which I'm not, in order to tell him anything,
which I won't," Bonnie replied with a grimace. From
the expression on her face, Emma could see that Bonnie's reception of Jordan would be anything but
warm.

"Well, hello, ladies," Gina chirped like a happy little bird as she held Jordan's hand possessively in hers. "Just finishing lunch, I see. We dined at Le Bistro across the street. They serve exquisite ratatouille. You should try it sometime. Oh, that's right. Le Bistro is your competition."

Resisting the urge to smack Gina for her rude comment, Emma replied coldly, "Oh, no, Le Bistro is much too small and has a terribly limited menu. As a matter of fact, they're closing next week. You'll have to find another place that serves ratatouille or make it yourself. It's really very simple and terribly overpriced for stewed eggplant, onions, and tomatoes. It must be the French name that draws people to it."

"Oh!" Gina exclaimed before turning to Jordan and adding, "I guess we'll just have to find another favorite place, darling."

Emma studied Jordan's face for any signs of affection and found nothing. In fact, he looked especially uncomfortable with the rudeness that Gina had shown in greeting her. Emma could not understand what drew him to her. Gina was attractive but not a knockout. She was well proportioned but not foxy. She had good skin, but it was not perfect. Her personality definitely needed repair and her roots could use a touch-up. All in all, Gina was rather unremarkable.

Yet Gina had Jordan . . . again.

"We certainly will," Jordan replied. Turning to Emma he said, "You're looking well. I see celebrity life becomes you."

"Thanks. You're not exactly suffering from the lack of newspaper coverage yourself," Emma responded. Then looking from one to the other, she added, "I understand that congratulations and best wishes are in order for your pending remarriage."

"Yes. Isn't it wonderful? I told you that we'd make a go of it this time," Gina gushed as she clung to Jordan.

Looking less than enthusiastic, Jordan added, "It'll be a rather lengthy engagement. I have quite a bit of traveling to do."

"But, Jordan, I've told you that I'm perfectly comfortable with your travel schedule. I have plenty to do to keep me busy while you're away. I'll miss you, of course, but I'd rather be lonely as your wife than as your fiancée," Gina stated, as if rehashing an old argument. Her tone had changed a bit from sugary sweet to bitter apple.

"No, we'll get married when I return. I might be away a few weeks. I have appointments to keep before Labor Day, a big day for me," Jordan replied, gazing in Emma's direction.

The reminder of the significance of Labor Day stung, but Emma did not allow it to show. She would not give Gina the satisfaction of feeling triumphant or Jordan the pleasure of seeing that she missed him and loved him terribly. She would keep her emotions to herself.

"Jordan always makes this vague reference to Labor Day. I suppose it has something hush-hush to do with work. Well, we'll leave now. I have all kinds of shopping to do. I have to find a dress, rent a hall, and locate a . . . caterer," Gina stated with a big smile and a well-delivered jab at Emma.

Rising to Emma's defense, Bonnie replied, "You shouldn't have any trouble finding a caterer even on such short notice. Anyone who is anyone is using EJ's this season, the president's choice in caterers."

"Bonnie!" Emma whispered under her breath.

Gina's head jerked up as if struck hard. Stiffly she slipped her arm through Jordan's and prepared to leave. It was clear from the rigid set of her shoulders that Bonnie had injured her with the last jab.

Turning toward Jordan, Gina retorted, "I think our presence is plucking Bonnie's last nerve. We'll just see you later. Be sure to check your mailboxes for an invitation to the wedding."

"I'm sure we won't want to miss it," Bonnie snapped through closed teeth.

"I'm sure it'll be a lovely affair," Emma stated cordially although her heart ached from the effort.

"Just as lovely as yours would have been," Gina said with a combination of venom and sugar.

"Gina, that's enough!" Jordan ordered as he pulled her toward him. "I'm sorry, Emma. Sometimes she gets carried away."

"You two should leave before I forget that I'm a lady and someone has to carry *her* away," Bonnie snarled angrily. Emma's hand on her arm was the only thing that kept her from flying at Gina.

"Yes, we're going. Good-bye," Jordan said with a great deal of effort and embarrassment.

"The nerve of that woman!" Bonnie sputtered. "First, she steals Jordan and then she throws it in your face. She's crazy."

Collecting their trash and heading back to the shop, Emma replied, "You can't steal a man. He's not a purse or a piece of jewelry. Whatever she did to get him, Jordan liked it. I guess he found out that it wasn't over between them."

"You're so calm about this," Bonnie said, still smarting from the encounter with Gina.

"One of us has to be," Emma responded as she closed the office door so that the employees would not see this side of Bonnie.

"She just rubs me the wrong way," Bonnie exclaimed as she stood stiffly in the room.

"Me, too, but Jordan's a grown man. It was his choice. I just wish he had told me how he felt," Emma said as she eased into a chair. She looked very tired and not at all the proprietor of a famously successful business.

"If you ask me, he's a coward and a jerk," Bonnie flared angrily.

"I don't think so. There's something else. I can't put my finger on it, but I have a feeling that there's another reason," Emma argued gently.

"You're just too kind. You want to give the creep the benefit of the doubt. I don't," Bonnie replied stubbornly.

"I wonder what he meant by appointments before Labor Day. Why do you think he needed to stress that particular weekend?" Emma asked, trying to put some logic in the turn of events.

"Just one more dig at you, I guess. They deserve each other. Wicked to the core, both of them," Bonnie insisted, staunchly loyal as always.

"Maybe, but I think there's more to it than that. I think Jordan was trying to tell me something. I'll have to think about it," Emma said as she tried to tie up this major loose end in her life.

The telephone rang, ending any further conversation on the subject. For the moment, Emma put Jordan and Gina and their upcoming marriage out of her mind. She had EJ's to run, employees to keep busy, appointments to arrange, and a very busy calendar to juggle. Strangely, she did not feel bitter. Angry, betrayed and hurt, yes, but not bitter. Bitterness would have been self-directed. The other emotions allowed her to name the source of her problem: Jordan.

As soon as she could find the time in her busy schedule, Emma knew that she would sift through her feelings and determine her reactions. He must have had a good reason for going to Gina without warning or a good-bye. To leave her thinking that all was well between them was not at all like him.

However, for the moment, the demands of EJ's kept her too busy to think about her hurt feelings. She only had time to remind herself of her reasons for not allowing herself to become involved earlier in her life. She knew that EJ's had become the source of her survival before, and it would again. Jordan and any message he was trying to send her would have to wait.

Thirteen

While Emma poured herself into her work for solace, Jordan and Gina faced the changes in their lives differently. Each had retired to work or plan with differing degrees of success. Regardless of the distance between them, each was not far from the other's mind.

Jordan was miserably unhappy. He sat in his office trying unsuccessfully to concentrate on the special report that was due to the president by the end of the day. So far he had written only three pages. With Gina torturing his mind, he could not produce the work that he needed to do.

Gina had reentered his life at a time when everything was going right. His professional life had reached its pinnacle. He had a wonderful woman to love and who loved him in return. To complete his life, he had planned to marry Emma, until Gina and her plans and secrets had returned.

Jordan stretched his tired shoulders and turned from the task of trying to capture his thoughts on teenage drinking when his mind was engaged in sorting out issues that were far more pressing at the moment. He could not think of a way to thwart Gina's plans and still keep Emma from being corrupt by association. Until he could, Jordan was helpless to do anything. Gina had the upper hand.

Gina had been lovely as well as beautiful when they first married. She had been horribly spoiled by her parents, but she'd still contained a sweetness that Jordan felt only needed cultivating. He'd thought that, when they'd marry, he would be able to show her the benefits of caring and of giving to someone else selflessly.

Jordan had been wrong. Gina took but never gave. The years of being pampered without reserve and without discipline had marred her for life. She had quickly proven to Jordan that he had made a terrible mistake. Gina was not a nice person. She was self-centered and selfish to the core, possessing little if any regard for anyone else. She was beyond redemption. At last, Jordan had finally given up and faced the facts that nothing he did and no amount of love he showed would stop her from demanding more and giving less.

Jordan had not seen Gina often since the divorce. They traveled in different social circles that only intersected. He preferred to stay with friends and associates in the medical and political professions, whereas she enjoyed the fast-money set. He was grateful for their differences and only too happy to see his ex-wife infrequently.

However, despite the separation, he had always heard talk about her. Even after moving to Washington and staying mostly to himself when not at work or attending a political function, he heard gossip. People were always happy to keep him informed of her antics. Much of what he had heard was just rumor. Since he was no longer married to her, Jordan only shrugged whenever someone brought news of

her to him. He did not care what Gina did as long
as she was out of his life.

Gina, however, had had other plans. She had followed Jordan's meteoric career after their divorce.
She had always known that he would make something
of himself one day and not remain an uncelebrated
physician. She knew that he was capable of greatness
and being the adviser to people with power. Now that
Jordan sat at the right hand of the most powerful
man in the world, she wanted a piece of the celebrity
pie.

Unknown to Jordan, Gina had planned her return
with more deliberation than she had arranged their
first meeting and marriage. She had expanded her
social circle until hers not only overlapped, but included his. She had attended functions, volunteered
for fund-raisers, and hosted parties in order to be
near him or hear about him. She had seen him from
a distance and been content to listen and circulate
on the outskirts of the crowd while she formulated
her plans.

Gina would have waited longer, but Jordan had
fallen in love. As soon as she observed his reaction
to Emma, Gina knew that she had to move faster than
she had originally planned. She would have liked to
have finessed her way back into his life while quietly
and carefully but permanently pushing Emma away.
However, the situation took an unexpected turn, and
she had needed to act fast.

Cornering him at Great Falls had been a stroke of
luck. Gina had spent hours trying to figure out how
to stage the perfect unplanned meeting, only to have
him fall into her lap. She had been just as surprised
to find him in the park as he had been to see her
there. They had never ridden bikes together while
they had been married. Gina had hated doing any-

thing physical and had turned her back on anything that could not be played at a leisurely pace. She played tennis the way women had in the 1930's. She hardly ever broke a sweat.

However, she had learned to ride a bike while dating a corporate giant. He preferred it for exercise since he could be outside, engage in his thoughts, and still burn calories. He hated sweating in public gyms populated by the muscled young men showing off their already perfect physiques. Grant had been the one to introduce Gina to leisurely rides in the country. Because he had insisted on riding through Great Falls, Gina had run into Jordan and Emma.

Finding herself within arm's length of causing trouble, she followed the route that fate had set out for her. She had embraced him meaningfully in front of Emma in order to strike the spark of suspicion. Later, she had gotten lucky again and seen them out dancing. Again, she'd seized the opportunity. Dancing suggestively close to him, she had made it clear to all in the room exactly what she had on her mind. Grant had been furious, but Gina had not cared. Her goal was to land Jordan at all costs. There would always be other Grants in her life, but not another man like Jordan.

Gina knew that she had to strike quickly. She had to break up his marriage plans and secure her future with him in one motion. Reaching into her bag of tricks, she'd taken the only action open to her that would guarantee immediate success. While dancing suggestively close, Gina had whispered the one thing that she knew would bind Jordan to her immediately.

And it worked. He had returned to the table with a perplexed expression on his face, which Emma had misinterpreted to be unresolved feelings toward Gina. Without realizing that she was sending him straight into trouble, Emma had sent Jordan out to solve his problem with Gina prior to their marriage. Gina and her web were waiting for him. Thinking that going to her offered the best solution to the potential publicity, Jordan had fallen into her arms. He was hers now. She just had to keep him. And she knew that she would do just that.

Rather than writing the report, Jordan was at that moment thinking about a solution to the problem of Gina. He had reached for the phone and started to dial Emma's number many times in the course of the day but had stopped short of doing it. He did not know what he would say. He did not know how to explain to the woman that he loved that he was not the man she thought he was. He was flawed beyond repair, and he could not ask her to love the terribly imperfect man. Some imperfections were deadly. This one had just killed their future and made their present a lovely memory.

Reaching for the phone for the last time, Jordan dialed Emma's number. Her secretary immediately transferred the call to her office as she always did whenever he called. He was grateful that the word of his relationship with Gina had not spread throughout all of Washington.

"It's me. Meet me for dinner?" Jordan asked as soon as he heard Emma's voice.

"I can't. I make it a habit of not dating married or engaged men. I don't plan to change now to accommodate you," Emma replied firmly and with a touch of sadness in her voice.

"Then let's have a drink after work. Our usual place. I have to talk with you. I need for you to understand what's happened between us," Jordan insisted as he pushed aside the work that covered his desk.

"There is no 'us,' Jordan. There's only a you and Gina. There's no reason for me to put myself to the inconvenience of meeting you. I'm always tired after work and want to go home," Emma said as she held firm.

"Then I'll stop by your house this evening. I only want a half hour of your time. I'll leave as soon as I tell you about the predicament in which I find myself," Jordan replied softly. He had to win her over. Emma just had to agree to speak with him. His happiness depended on it.

"I don't know, Jordan. What would Gina say? Sounds like the lyrics from an old Johnny Mathis song, but it's true. You're engaged to her. You're not a free man, although that thought didn't seem to cross your mind while we were planning our marriage," Emma replied coldly.

"All of that is what I want to explain to you. Please, Emma," Jordan pleaded.

"Call me later. I can't think about this anymore now. I have clients waiting to see me and a business to run," Emma replied as she hung up.

The urgency in Jordan's voice had almost moved Emma to agree to see him, but she knew that she would regret it if she did. She needed time to think. This moment with Jordan sounding so helpless was not the time to commit to meeting him. She had to step back and give her emotions time to gel. The sound of his voice only confused her and weakened her resolve.

Picking up the phone, Emma dialed a very familiar number. Without introduction, she launched into a discussion of the conversation with Jordan. She felt confident entrusting Bonnie with all of the details, knowing that her friend would listen, and offer advice if requested.

"Well, what would you do?" Emma asked as she tapped her pencil on the cherry desk.

"I'd see him," Bonnie replied without hesitation. "You need to know what caused his change of heart. One minute Jordan was helping you plan the wedding and the next, he was back with Gina. He even insisted on a short engagement and speedy marriage. He couldn't wait to marry you and bought you that fabulous ring. Now he's engaged to someone else. It just doesn't make any sense to me."

"We didn't even have a fight. That's what gets me. I can't understand it. Something must have happened in his former marriage to Gina that prevents him from marrying me," Emma stated as she tried to consider all the angles.

"Maybe they're not really divorced. Maybe they only have a separation. I know a lot of people who have legal separations and never bothered with getting a divorce. They didn't plan to remarry, so they didn't see the reason to go to the expense of the divorce. They were living apart and had divided all of the assets. In their minds, they were divorced and totally free," Bonnie commented, remembering friends of her husband who waited ten years before divorcing.

"I suppose I can understand that. It wouldn't have worked in my case since I was anxious to end it, but I guess it could work for other people. But that still doesn't explain this apparent reunion and remarriage. If they're not divorced, why remarry?" Emma queried as she struggled to put the pieces of this puzzle together.

"Well, maybe it's really a reaffirmation of their vows more than a wedding. Gina's probably just calling it a wedding because people wouldn't understand what they're doing if she referred to it as anything else,"

Bonnie offered as she tried to work through the apparent lack of logic in Gina's statement.

"I don't know. I just can't figure it out. None of this really makes any sense to me. If they were never divorced, then why publicly wed? Why not simply live together? And then, why would Jordan say that he loved me, plan to marry me, only to return to her? This is just too confusing."

"What if she's using force to get him to the altar?"

"Force? She's tiny compared to him." Bonnie chuckled.

"Not that kind of force. I mean blackmail. What if she's holding something over him that she'll reveal if he won't marry her. What if she killed someone or robbed a bank and he knows and is protecting her and his name? What if she's an art thief and committed a heist since their divorce and is threatening to ruin his name?" Emma offered as she continued to search for an explanation of Jordan's actions.

"What if she's just your basic nasty person, and she simply won him the old way. Not all women are liberated. It's possible, I guess, that some still exist who use feminine wiles to trap a guy. He's rich. She's rich. They're from the same social circle and they're former spouses. Maybe that's what happened. Maybe Jordan is simply a gutless louse who didn't have enough spine to tell you that he had fallen for someone else," Bonnie suggested, trying to find an explanation that was more plausible and not as far-fetched as the others.

"True, they are in many ways the same although Jordan didn't start out with much more than a plastic spoon in his mouth. Being associated with me won't benefit his career. To the contrary, I'm the one who gained from the association. Maybe he simply returned to his own kind. Still, that doesn't explain the quick change. I don't understand, but you could be right. He made this switch without even a call. No matter the reason, he should have phoned. That's why I think that the reason is too embarrassing for him to admit willingly," Emma continued, not in defense of Jordan but certainly in the quest for truth and understanding.

"Then I guess you've decided to meet with him tonight. Do you want me to come over?" Bonnie offered, although she had so much to do that she really could not afford to give the time. The increase in clients at EJ's meant the same for her business. "Kinda like a chaperone? You don't know what Gina might try next or what they might have cooked up together. I don't trust Jordan any more than I can spit."

"No, but thanks. I can handle this myself. I'll call you as soon as he leaves," Emma promised as she ended the call and returned to her work. She had much to do and too many distractions in her life at the moment. She used all of her reserve strength to refocus her attention on the appointment calendar and the financial records that lay on her desk.

For the remainder of the afternoon, Emma put Jordan out of her mind. She pored over the books, contacted new clients, called established ones to determine satisfaction, and consulted with her assistants. The chefs had their list of supplies that she needed to order. The wait staff manager needed more dinner jackets and trousers for the new staff. The wedding hostess and her assistant had found a new florist to add to their list and wanted Emma to make the appropriate introductory contact. With all that they had planned for her added to what she had already placed on her to-do list, Emma would have to work late to accomplish everything. At least she was so busy that she did not have time to fret about Jordan.

At eight o'clock, Emma entered her house, threw her things into the hall closet, and walked to the library. On the way, she read through the bills. Depositing them into the hummingbird box on the bowfront chest, she lingered, thinking, and then she phoned Jordan.

Jordan answered on the first ring. "I've been hoping to hear from you. May I come over?"

"Give me an hour to get myself together. I'll see you then," Emma replied as she hung up without further conversation.

Emma had been thinking more or less about Jordan since his phone call. Between meetings and appointments, she had discovered that she really had nothing to say to Jordan until he explained the recent change in events—and maybe not even then. Depending on his explanation for his deplorable behavior, they might spend a very short evening together.

Not that she was hungry, but Emma decided to eat the shrimp salad that she had brought home from the shop. Now that the business was so prosperous and she was so busy, Emma found herself often eating food from EJ's rather than cooking a solitary meal. Besides, a quick meal from EJ's was preferable to defrosting something to cook when she returned home late and tired.

Emma used to enjoy developing new recipes for her own use, but lately none of her old activities had interested her. When she and Jordan had been together, he had relished the little treats that she prepared. Now that she was alone again and had an excuse for not cooking, she had all but forgotten the feel of the omelet pan in her hand.

Even now as she munched the splendid salad made

from one of her own special shop recipes, Emma was
too preoccupied to enjoy the blend of spices and the
creaminess of the homemade mayonnaise. At any
other time, the salad would have tickled her palate,
but that night was different. Finding herself satisfied
after only four bites, Emma covered the rest with plastic wrap and stashed it in the refrigerator, thinking
that perhaps she would finish it for breakfast the next
morning.

Without feeling the need to rush, Emma walked up
the curving staircase to her bedroom. Slipping out of
her suit and into the shower, she scrubbed her skin
until it glowed a healthy rosy hue. Toweling dry, she
oiled herself and then lightly conditioned her hair.
Easing into beige slacks and a white shirt with turned-
up sleeves, she padded downstairs barefoot just as Jordan rang the doorbell.

"Hi," Jordan said sheepishly as he stepped into the
slate foyer.

"You look tired. Is Gina keeping you up all hours?"
Emma asked as she ushered him into the living room.
Only a few weeks ago, they would have sat together
on the very comfortable leather sofa in the great
room.

Indicating the blue floral tapestry sofa, Emma sank
into the soft green tub chair. The shape of the chair
seemed to embrace her as she watched Jordan to see
his first move. She never entertained close friends in
this room, preferring the great room. She saved the
formal living room for company and fancy dinners.
Somehow, sitting there with Jordan seemed appropriate. They were no longer lovers and certainly were
not friends. The formality of the room, with its up-
right piano and posed family portraits on the walls,
coordinated well with the tension in the room.

Emma waited for him to speak. She remembered

learning in a management class that the person who spoke first in a negotiating situation was the one who lost the upper hand. Therefore, Emma decided that she would wait as long as it took for Jordan to state the purpose of his visit. She had nothing pressing to do. The music that always played from the stereo in the den was very relaxing. Emma found that she could zone out on the gentle sound of classical music.

Jordan did not appear in a hurry to break the silence, either. The music was relaxing, the company pleasant although unusually silent, and the surroundings comfortable. Actually, not speaking was at that moment more appealing than facing the situation that brought him to Emma's house at this hour of the night.

As the clock in the hall struck the half-hour, Jordan stirred as if released from a trance. Clearing his voice, he began, "I owe you an apology. Regardless of the reason for my renewed relationship with Gina, I should have phoned you to explain. I have no excuse for my behavior other than to say that the situation was beyond my control at the time."

"And now? Are you in charge of the situation again?" Emma asked with only modest interest. She surprised herself at her ability to keep her voice calm and her emotions detached.

"It's still very sticky. I shouldn't even be here. We shouldn't be having this conversation. I shouldn't tell you any of the details. It's not that I didn't want you to know everything, it's just that the situation is hopeless," Jordan replied grimly.

"Jordan, I find it hard to believe that a man who's as well positioned and respected politically as you are could be incapable of handling the situation with an ex-wife. You'll have to do better than that," Emma quipped as the bitterness and anger crept into her voice at the absurdity of his statement.

Jordan studied the floor for a very long time. His fingers worked constantly as he thought about what he would say, how he would explain the chain of events that had brought him to his knees, and what he would do to restore Emma's confidence in him. Finally, he looked into Emma's eyes and began to tell her his story. The lines at the corners of his mouth and eyes seemed to deepen with each word as the clock ticked away the minutes that lengthened into hours.

"My marriage to Gina was largely of convenience. I needed her money and position in the community, and she needed my innocence to cover her somewhat checkered past. You see, Gina's college escapades had left a trail that her family's money had not been able to cover. She had experimented not only with pot but with stronger drugs. She had hung out with the fast bunch that took weekends on Nantucket, Martha's Vineyard, and the south of France. Wherever there was a party, Gina always appeared. She was everyone's party girl. Beautiful, talented, intelligent, and fun . . . she was probably the first on the list for a good time.

"I knew that she had far more life and sexual experience than I, but I didn't care. She knew the people that I needed to meet. I was from the country, at least compared to her. The first time I even saw a big city was for college, but even then my mom kept an eagle eye on my behavior. Grad school was a real eye-opener. I suddenly found myself alone, unsupervised, grown up, and lonely. I traveled only in the small circle of other medical students. I saw no one socially because I simply didn't have the time.

"Then one day I met Gina. Her father had made a huge contribution to the medical school and wanted a tour of the facility. The dean appointed me his official guide. While touring, we hit it off and he told me about his daughter, his business, and his hopes for the future. He also mentioned that he wanted Gina to meet a nice guy and settle down when she graduated from college. He thought that marriage would give her a focus.

"When he asked me to take on the job and promised an introduction to all the right families, I jumped at the chance. After all, I had decided that I'd never return to the country life. I wanted to shine, to make a difference in a big way, to show the old hometown folks that I had arrived. I needed a woman with the right connections and the social sense that I lacked. Gina was that woman. With her father's confidence that everything would work out for both of us, I married her.

"He was wrong. Gina continued to be wild. She ran through my salary and her allowance. Yes, he paid her an allowance. Technically, she was a member of the board and an officer in the company, but she never went to the office or attended a board meeting. She wasn't in the least interested in the business. All she wanted was the check.

"I'm not being sexist in saying this, either, Emma. Gina isn't like you. She doesn't have the desire to be independent, to make a name for herself. She's cut from the old cloth and believes that a man should support his wife totally and that the wife's job is to stay home and spend money. She would never understand that we couldn't do that on my salary.

"I wouldn't have minded living the way she wanted if she had also taken care of me and the house, but she didn't. Money would have been tight, but other young couples made a go of it. Gina couldn't accept the strict budget. She refused to save her money and live only on mine. She just wouldn't adapt to the new way of life. Gina was always out of town with her old friends.

"Even after I opened my practice and gained a bit of a reputation, Gina wouldn't change her ways. Here I was, a successful professional with a wife, home, and social obligations, but I could never find my wife. She wouldn't call. If she'd appear at social functions at all, she'd arrive high on something, often dirty and vulgar. She missed parties and plays and never offered an excuse for her absence. When I asked for an explanation, she'd become angry and refuse to tell me. Finally I stopped asking.

"When her name was linked with a well-known celebrity and womanizer in the style section of all the papers and on television, I wrote her a note demanding that she act with more discretion. I sent it to her office at her father's company, knowing that she'd eventually return there for her check. I told her that she owed it to her father and to me. We shouldn't have to endure the snide comments and the chuckles because of her behavior. She should be more considerate. I left a second copy on the pillow in her bedroom just in case she came home first. Her response consisted of three words, 'Go to hell.'

"That's when I filed for divorce. I figured I'd already suffered enough embarrassment. Her father understood although he asked that I try to stick it out a little longer. He was very sick and wanted to know that Gina would have someone with her when he died. I told him that I couldn't stay any longer. Someone else would have to pick up her pieces if she fell apart. Knowing Gina, I didn't think she'd notice that he was gone unless her checks stopped.

"He died six months after the divorce became final. She didn't even come to the funeral. She was on vacation in the Swiss Alps and didn't want to leave the good skiing. Being a good and overly indulgent father, he set up a trust fund that will keep Gina in the style to which she has become accustomed for the rest of her life.

"Anyway, I put my life back together, parlayed my contacts into even bigger ones, gained fame and reputation. I thought I had everything until I met you. That's when I realized that the time with Gina hadn't completely stopped me from caring and needing someone in my life. I realized that I could love and that someone could love me in return."

Jordan stopped speaking and waited for Emma's reaction. She studied his face and saw that he was being honest. However, he had not told her the reason for his actions. The history was interesting but not enough.

"You still haven't said why you went back to her or why you broke off our engagement without even a phone call. I had to find out from Bonnie that our marriage was off. Knowing the truth about Gina, how could you return to her?" Emma asked as she shifted in the chair.

Returning to his protracted explanation, Jordan replied as if talking in his sleep. "I don't have an excuse for the way I've acted except to say that I was in shock. I should have called. I can only beg you to forgive me for not doing the right thing by you. I was caught unaware. I guess I had so much trouble believing what was happening to me that I didn't think that anyone else would, either.

"I hadn't seen Gina until that day in the park when she came up to us. I knew that she was in the area but my position with the president kept me very busy. I no longer moved in her circle and hadn't seen any of that fast crowd since the divorce. After seeing her in the park and then later that night, I hoped I wouldn't see her again. For a small town, D.C. has a way of providing plenty of hiding places. I didn't expect her to call me, but she did.

"Gina asked me to meet her for lunch, and I did. I didn't tell you because I didn't see any harm in seeing her just that once. I feel nothing for her. I couldn't imagine that she'd have anything to say to me that would make a difference in our lives.

"I was so busy at work that I almost missed the lunch date. I would have called her to cancel, but I didn't have her number. So I put aside my project and met her as arranged.

"Between the salad and the entrée, Gina told me that she wanted me back. She had used the years since our divorce to do a lot of thinking, she said. She had decided that it was time to grow up and face her responsibilities. She wanted a family life rather than the chaotic one she had lived for so long.

"I didn't believe her since I had seen her name in the paper more than once. I knew that she had lived high among the celebrities and the rich and famous, but I listened anyway. I didn't think that she really meant it or that she was even sober. Gina had spent the majority of our marriage high and incoherent. I could hardly believe that she had changed now.

"But there was something strangely honest and real about her. For the first time, I could tell that Gina actually cared about something. That's when she told me that she wanted the three of us to be together again.

"I was confused. I knew that both of her parents had died and that she was an only child. I couldn't imagine who the members of our trio might be. My first thought was that this was simply another one of her tricks, one of her vicious games.

"That's when she told me about our son. She had given birth to him in Europe and left him there with nannies while she continued to enjoy her carefree life. As she spoke, Gina seemed almost sorry for her behavior and her reckless past. I found myself believing her and hating her at the same time. She hadn't told me about him. If I had known that she was pregnant, I never would have divorced her. I felt cheated and skeptical. I couldn't help but think that the chance was great that he wasn't really mine.

"Gina said that she had brought him to the States and that he was living in a boarding school in the North. She showed me the photograph of a kid who looks like me. As if expecting me to demand a blood test, she produced the results of one. The test showed that he could be mine.

"She took me to see him a few days later. He's a handsome kid. Very quiet and reserved. His teachers say that he's a good student.

"We didn't tell him that he was my son. He thought that I was a doctor friend of his mother who wanted him to have a blood test. If the blood test confirmed my hesitation, I didn't want the boy's hopes built up for nothing. I didn't want him to think that his days in a lonely boarding school without his parents were about to end. I wanted to be able to walk away from Gina without having him on my conscience in any way.

"I received the results yesterday. According to the tests, he's my son, Emma.

"That's why I'm going through with this marriage to Gina. I know it's a farce, but my son deserves a father and a normal home life. I can't pull out on him now that I know about him. I feel nothing but contempt for Gina, but the boy's my son. I'm making arrangements now for him to enroll in a private school down here in the fall. We're buying a house, and we'll make a life for our son. I just hope it's not too late to show him that he's loved.

"I love you and want to be with you, but he has to come first."

Emma and Jordan sat in silence as the clock chimed the hour. Neither of them could speak. Emma was too shocked to form the words, and Jordan was too exhausted from sharing the pain.

When the silence lengthened, Jordan rose and walked toward the door. Without looking back, he walked into the night. He did not notice the rain that pelted him or the darkness of the sky. Driving away from Emma's house, he thought of nothing and felt less.

Emma remained in her seat as the car's headlights faded. She was too numb to move. Jordan had not left her for his ex-wife, but for the good of the son that he had not known he had. She could think of no way to respond and had no plan to take him from Gina. The boy's life meant more than their combined happiness. Feeling the total futility of the situation, Emma covered her face in her hands and cried for the second time since her relationship with Jordan ended.

Fourteen

It was a while before Emma could tell Bonnie about Jordan's visit. She needed time to think about what he had said and how she felt about the information. Emma knew that she would not separate the man from his son, but she wondered if being with Gina was the best thing for either of them. Gina was a wicked woman. Still, the man had chosen the child's mother, knowing that she had been a terrible wife and an even worse mother. Emma could think of no way to counter that decision.

Yet Emma sensed that Jordan still loved her as much as he said. His face had worn the signs of considerable strain as he explained the circumstances under which he felt compelled to live. He had made a sacrifice of his happiness and hers for a child that he did not know. Emma found his devotion to the boy touching and wonderful. Despite the pain that Jordan's decision caused her, Emma knew that he had made the only possible decision.

Emma went about her work as if nothing lay heavily on her mind. She continued to run EJ's as efficiently as ever. No one suspected that her heart ached and her mind constantly puzzled over the future. Despite the apparent finality of her decision, part of her could not accept the fact that Jordan was beyond her reach.

Emma had worked hard all her life for the things she wanted. In putting forth that effort, she had always earned the rewards. She would have to put her considerable resources to this task, also.

"Well, don't you have any suggestions?" Emma asked her main resource as they sipped coffee in her office. She had made the morning contacts and was enjoying a few moments of quiet.

"None that are legal," Bonnie quipped, still angry with Jordan for treating her friend in such a shameful manner.

"They say that two heads are better than one, but in this case the two aren't working any better at all." Emma chuckled as she pointed out the obvious to her friend.

"I'm still too angry. I can't think coherently. I'm amazed at the way you're handling this whole thing," Bonnie replied as she accepted another thick, rich chocolate-chip cookie fresh from the bakery arm of the business.

"We have to think of something. The time's getting away from us. If we don't do something soon, Jordan will remarry Gina. But regardless of the action that we take, we can't in any way interfere with his plans to be with his son," Emma stated as she glanced at the calendar. If she had still been engaged to Jordan, she would be sending out the invitations now.

"How does this sound? I'll throw a party that you'll cater. We'll invite everyone, including Jordan and Gina. He'll see you in comparison to her and realize the poor decision he's made. There's no way that a woman who's as self-centered as Gina could possibly care about the boy. He'll see how cold she is and how distant she can be. He and the boy will come to you. How's that for a suggestion?" Bonnie offered as she licked the melted chocolate from her fingers.

"If there were any possibility that it would work, it would be a good one, but I think there's more that he hasn't told me," Emma replied as she finished the last of her coffee. "Knowing Gina as he does, he could have decided that he wanted to marry me and not her. He still could have brought the child into our home. He knows that I love children. I don't think that's the whole of it. Jordan wouldn't be the only man to have been denied access to this child. He certainly wouldn't be the only one whose wife kept knowledge of a child from him. Neither of these scenarios would ruin him professionally. It's embarrassing to be kept in the dark by a conniving woman, but that's all. No one would hold it against him professionally. There must be something more to this story than he's telling me. After all, embarrassing moments in the lives of political figures always surface. They eat a little humble pie, say a few apologies, and then move on with their lives. Something just doesn't ring true here."

"Well, at least we'll get a chance to see them in public if I have this party," Bonnie declared firmly. "Seeing you and her together will surely have an impact on him. Let's do it. Besides, I've been working so hard on the business that I'm overdue for a party. Let's see what we can pull together for next weekend. We have to work fast. The Labor Day weekend will be here before we know it."

"I guess it's possible that the party idea might work. Even if he doesn't change his plans, seeing Gina in a social setting might help us to formulate other plans. Well, what do you want to serve?" Emma asked, assuming her role as caterer.

"The food and atmosphere must be perfect. What we're creating here is a recipe for love," Bonnie replied thoughtfully as she thumbed Emma's portfolio of tempting combinations.

With a touch of sadness, Emma stated, "Let's serve the alternate menu that I might have used for my wedding reception. It's certainly romantic food."

"No, you'll need it," Bonnie objected, shaking her hand.

"I can always create another," Emma replied as she smiled weakly. "Somehow it seems fitting to use it at this time. I'd like to suggest that you serve asparagus salad with saffron vinaigrette, roasted squab on a bed of spinach, creamed carrots, duchess potatoes, and green peas with caramelized pearl onions. For dessert, let's have strawberry shortcake with whipped cream."

"Stop! I can feel my hips spreading already. Sounds wonderful. If that menu doesn't fill him with longing for the warm, wonderful woman who created it, the man's dead," Bonnie stated loyally as she slipped the last of the chocolate-chip cookies into a baggie for Steve. She always took him a treat from EJ's whenever she paid a visit to Emma.

"I'll leave the table setting to you. You're very creative with table linens and your skill at napkin folding is second to none. Let's pull out all the stops. Only the best wines will do for your party," Emma said as she checked off the wines that matched most perfectly with the meal.

"Great! From menu to entertainment, we'll do it up right." Bonnie gushed as she made note of all the things she had to do. At the top of the list was the purchase of new linens. "I know a little jazz ensemble that might be available. I heard them at the Foster affair that you catered last week. They're young and just breaking into the business. They were a big hit and might be booked, but it's worth a try."

"Okay, the dinner's all set. Between now and your

big night, what should we do? We need to uncover the true source of Jordan's reason for breaking off our engagement without so much as a call," Emma stated, making the last notes in her book.

"Now that it's public knowledge about his remarriage, we shouldn't have too much trouble tracking down all the information," Bonnie concluded as she took up her things and headed toward the door. "I'll see what I can snoop out. In the meantime, I'll make a few contacts. Maybe someone has heard the real skinny on this seemingly sordid affair."

As soon as Bonnie left, the telephone started to ring. Having seen no one at her secretary's desk, Emma answered on the third ring. Grabbing a pen and pad of paper, she eased into her seat and prepared to take her usually careful notes on the conversation.

"EJ's," Emma answered. "Emma Jones speaking."

"I'm surprised that the famous Washington caterer would answer her own phone," taunted the familiar but unwelcome voice on the other end.

"I often do. I believe in giving personal service. What can I do for you, Gina?" Emma replied coldly yet professionally.

"Meet me for a drink or a soda after work. There's something I need to discuss with you. I know about Jordan's visit to you the other night. Unless you want some mighty nasty publicity, you'll agree," Gina threatened in a sticky-sweet voice.

"I have no reason to object to meeting you, contrary to what you infer," Emma stated calmly. "Where shall we meet?"

"There's an ice-cream parlor a few blocks from your shop. I think you know the one. I've seen you there many times. You must have been scouting out the competition. The décor is very open and family oriented, if I remember correctly. It's filled with kids and sticky hands. I just love the little dears. Not at all the location for rivals to meet. I'll meet you there at six," Gina responded with a venomous sneer in her voice.

"You're talking about Rosie's place. We're associates, not competitors. I'll be there," Emma replied with as much cordiality as she could muster when what she really wanted to do was slam down the phone.

Shaking almost violently, Emma wrapped her arms around her body. She had never felt so threatened nor had she encountered anyone who was so cold. She dreaded the meeting, but she knew that she had to attend. Gina had promised dire consequences if she did not. At this time in her life with her business booming, Emma did not want negative publicity of any kind.

The remainder of the day passed very slowly. Despite the pile of work demanding Emma's attention, she found it difficult to keep her mind on business. Finally unable to sit in the office any longer, she went for a walk.

Although the afternoon was warm, people filled the park. Mothers with babies in strollers or toddlers at their sides wandered through the paths. Children ran through the grass, played ball on the field, or splashed in the fountain. Young lovers lingered on the benches and took refuge behind tall hedges. The park was filled with life and happiness.

Emma almost hated to be the source of gloom in such an idyllic setting. However, she needed to walk off her tensions and relieve herself of the feeling of uneasiness that had pervaded her mood since Gina's call. Nothing but sunlight, birdsong, and time would help.

Dodging playing children and dogs, Emma made

her way into the depth of the park. She wanted to
be away from the ball field and the skating path on
the edge of the park that attracted the screaming kids.
She knew that the coolness of the trees and their long
shadows would be comforting.

Walking along the path, Emma at first thought of
nothing. She allowed herself to experience the impact
of the solitude within the noise of the city. She soon
discovered that the gloomy thoughts would not leave
her, and instead forced her to wonder about Gina's
reappearance in Jordan's life and Gina's new demands on her own.

Emma could not imagine what Gina could possibly
want with her. She had not contacted Jordan and had
reluctantly agreed to meet with him. However, the
fault was probably in agreeing at all. Only she and
Jordan knew that nothing had happened between
them. Gina might suspect that Jordan had been un-
faithful with her. Someone with Gina's personality
would only think the worst of others.

Emma felt herself start to relax. Her shoulders began to feel free and her stride lengthened. Walking
through the park proved just the medicine that Emma
needed. She realized that she could never know what
Gina really wanted. Anything she would do would
only result in second-guessing, an often futile effort.
Only the meeting later that evening would disclose
her intent.

Returning to the closeness of people, Emma strolled
the paths and watched the children at play. Mothers
smiled gently as their children tumbled in the grass.
They chatted amongst themselves and swapped stories
of childcare. If they had any real cares, they had left
them at home.

Emma wondered if she would ever be one of these
women. She had not wanted to have children during

her first marriage, knowing that the marriage was doomed from the start. Her first husband had promised her the moon and the stars. In her naïveté, she had believed him. When he delivered only unpaid bills, a philandering heart, and verbal abuse, she was only too happy to end the marriage. She never regretted not having children. They deserved better than the life she had lived.

When Emma fell in love with Jordan, she thought that she had found the right man. He was well respected professionally and was financially comfortable. For the first time in her adult life, she had allowed herself to think of having children. No other relationship had made her feel so comfortable. Despite her initial hesitation toward him, Emma had learned to trust Jordan and looked forward to a long life together.

Now, however, she had to put her romantic future on hold. Emma had learned the benefit of compartmentalizing her life. She had trained herself not to allow one segment to impact the other. Pushing Jordan and Gina into their own little space, Emma squared her shoulders and enjoyed the beautiful day.

Feeling better, Emma walked slowly toward the park exit. As she reached the baseball field and the path leading to the gate, she noticed a tall man walking on a path that ran parallel to hers. He matched each step she took as he maintained the protection of the darkness provided by the overhanging trees. She only slightly wondered what he might want with her. The safety of the park surrounded her and eliminated any fear. With so many mothers and children nearby, Emma doubted that his intentions could be anything other than honorable.

"Emma, I have to speak with you," the man stated as he stepped into the sunshine.

"No, we'd better not. I can't afford to be seen with you. I'm meeting Gina later. She's already angry about our last meeting," Emma replied as she quickened her step.

"I only need a minute," Jordan begged as he matched her pace on the sunny path.

"No. Now leave me alone. You've done enough already," Emma stated as she carefully crossed the street.

"I know about the meeting. Gina told me. I need to speak with you before you see her this afternoon. I haven't told you the whole truth about my relationship with Gina. Give me a few minutes to explain," Jordan continued as he blocked Emma's entry to EJ's.

Jordan's face bore such an earnest expression and the sun made him look so handsome that Emma almost gave in and granted his request. However, the memory of the pain he had caused her still lingered. She pushed past him and opened the door to the business that her own cunning and ability had built.

Turning to him, she stated, "My time is very valuable. I've wasted enough of it on you. Good-bye, Jordan."

Leaving him to stand alone on the sidewalk, Emma gently closed the door. She walked leisurely to her office and sat down. Only then did she begin to tremble. She was grateful that everyone was busy trying to finish the day's work and go home. She did not want to speak with anyone.

Listening to her staff calling their good nights, Emma relished the shelter of her business and the comfort it gave her. She loved the feeling of independence that came from owning her own business. Although she worked harder and put in more hours than most people who were employed by others, she knew that every minute that she gave to the company

went toward making it more profitable. It was her
child, her spouse, and her lover rolled into one mar-
ketable package.

Soon the outer office grew silent. Emma listened
until she was sure that everyone had left and that she
was alone before she opened her office door. She was
not in hiding, but she did not want curious or well-
meaning employees to question her about her plans
for the evening. She wanted to remain focused on
her meeting with Gina.

As Emma locked the door to EJ's offices and began
her walk around the corner, she wondered what she
and Gina could possibly discuss. Other than having
Gina tell her to stay away from Jordan, which she
planned to do anyway, Emma could not think of anything that the two women needed to say. She had no
interest in Jordan and would be more than happy to
inform Gina of that fact if the need arose. Jordan
occupied a chapter in her life that had closed.

The streets of D.C. were quiet. Emma loved this
time of day when the usually busy streets were becoming silent and the crush of people was diminishing.
She could enjoy the shop windows without being
pushed along by the tide of humanity. And some of
the hot air that always hung over the capital had begun to dissipate.

Emma lingered on the sidewalk before opening the
door to Rosie's Candy and Ice Cream Emporium. She
always enjoyed looking at the confections that filled
the windows and the rows of tables at which customers ate hungrily of the sweet treats. Usually, she would
have decided on what to order before entering the
black-and-white tiled establishment. There was always
something enticing on a table near the window that
beckoned to her.

Seeing Gina already occupying a table near the

back of the restaurant, Emma set her mouth in a pleasant expression, squared her shoulders, and entered the crowded room. This time, Emma did not have a sumptuous snack on her mind. She wanted to spend as little time as possible in Gina's company and definitely did not want to spoil her appreciation of the desserts by eating one of them with her. For once, the pleasant surroundings, the music playing on the jukebox, the black-and-white enameled tables, and the freshly starched white aprons did not offer a welcoming atmosphere.

Gina smiled and waved as if she were greeting an old friend. Anyone seeing them together would not have guessed that a confrontation of monumental proportions might erupt between them. They certainly would not have assumed that Gina had threatened Emma in order to arrange the meeting. Gina exuded congeniality mixed with professionalism from every pore.

She looked the part of a businesswoman meeting a colleague. Gina wore an impeccably tailored light green silk suit and a silk blouse of a softer shade. Her shoes were taupe as was the briefcase that doubled as her bag. She looked like a corporate executive waiting to meet a client rather than a predator ready to attack its victim.

Walking toward the back, Emma felt as if she were in the presence of royalty. From the way Gina smiled and oozed authority, she wondered what route the conversation might follow. If Emma had it her way, she would try to turn the discussion toward full disclosure of the details of the doomed relationship between Gina and Jordan. However, Emma could tell by the lights blazing in Gina's eyes that she would have her hands full if she planned to prevail.

"I'm so glad you could join me on such short notice," Gina purred as Emma sank into the chair across from her.

"I found myself compelled to come," Emma replied, remembering the nasty tone in Gina's voice when she phoned.

"There are important aspects of my relationship with Jordan that you and all of his friends should know. I find it amazing that you've accepted him into your circle when, so far, you've known so little about him," Gina stated with something akin to a smile on her carefully composed and made-up face.

"We all have elements from our pasts that we haven't shared with anyone. I'm sure Jordan isn't alone in that regard. It's not always necessary for new friends to know everything about us. Some parts of our lives belong buried in the past. We should all accept each other for who we are. I'm sure that you can understand that. You must have some interesting skeletons in your closet," Emma replied as she ordered a black coffee.

"Yes, I agree in theory, but I'm not a high political advisee with a reputation for straightforward dealings with people. I haven't set myself above others on highly charged matters. However, when those things influence the way we socialize and certainly the way we're perceived by others, then all the sordid little details need to come out into the open," Gina stated as she motioned for a refill on the diet soda she had been sipping while waiting for Emma.

"I suppose that if those things would keep a person from performing his or her job properly, then everyone should know. Otherwise, I don't think that a person's past is anyone's business," Emma replied firmly, making it perfectly clear that she was not concerned about Jordan's past since, as far as she was concerned, it did not impact his present or future.

"Then it looks to me as if I'm justified in disclosing

the nature of Jordan's past," Gina responded with a smug, infuriatingly confident smile. "There's no doubt that it impacts on his successful completion of his professional duties. After all, no one would want a drug abuser as the supposed expert on the negative effects of drug and alcohol addiction. Teens would certainly never listen to anyone who was as hypocritical as Jordan."

Looking incredulously at Gina, Emma replied, "Are you saying that Jordan's a drug addict? That's a terrible accusation to level against anyone but especially a man who works so hard to educate kids against the dangers of drug use. I don't believe you."

"I didn't say that he uses now. It's a part of his past that he didn't decide to share. I doubt that even the president is aware. If I were to phone my contacts at the *Post*, they wouldn't ask if he's still using. They'd simply print that the president's expert on alcohol and drug use in kids is himself a drug addict. I think that would pretty much put a stop to his meteoric climb, don't you?" Gina commented without any sign of hesitation.

"What would you gain from ruining Jordan's career? You'd be the wife of a discredited former government official. You'd lose, too," Emma stated calmly despite the anger she felt toward Gina.

"He'd never know that I had provided the information. With Jordan out of public life, I'd have him all to myself. We'd move to New York and live quite nicely. Jordan, our son, and me. We'd make a terrific little family, don't you think?" Gina cooed as she sipped from the diet soda in front of her.

"You'd do that just to take him away from here?" Emma demanded angrily as she gripped the edge of the table. "Jordan would hate being separated from the work and city he loves. He'd grow bitter and angry. You'd ruin him both professionally and spiritually. What kind of woman are you?"

"I'm the kind of woman who knows what she wants and will not tolerate any interference in getting it," Gina replied coldly. "I want Jordan all to myself and as far away from you as possible. I'll inform the *Post*, ruin his career, and take whatever steps are necessary to accomplish my objective. I made a mistake earlier in our marriage, and I won't do it again. This time, I won't share him with anyone for any reason."

"You'd make him miserable just to have him back? Your marriage would fail again," Emma stated matter-of-factly.

"Maybe, but it wouldn't be because I didn't try this time. The first time, I was too concerned with myself. I considered Jordan and eventually our son to be liabilities to my social life. I've changed, and I want my family back," Gina replied as she pushed away the soda.

"I don't see a change in you," Emma rebutted coldly. "Anyone who would ruin another person's career for personal gain hasn't changed. You're still thinking only of yourself. You definitely don't have either Jordan's or the child's best interest at heart."

"I'm sure you've heard the old saying that when the wife's happy the children and husband are happy. We'll be ecstatic. Besides, you'll be down here and out of Jordan's life forever. You won't have any idea of the things that happen in my happy little home," Gina replied with a smirk.

"I haven't been in Jordan's life since you announced your engagement," Emma stated frankly.

"He's been to your house. For all I know, he's been in your bed, too," Gina said evenly although Emma could see that the woman barely had control of her temper.

"Jordan invited himself to my house. He wanted to explain the sudden change in his affections. Nothing happened. We talked and he left," Emma responded without rancor and with growing fatigue for the trying woman.

"I suppose I'll have to believe you. Anyway, it doesn't matter anymore. As soon as I leak this story to the press, and we leave town, you'll be forgotten history," Gina stated as she dabbed the corners of her outlined lips.

"You don't have to ruin Jordan or leave town on my account. I have no interest in your fiancé," Emma replied as she gathered her purse in preparation of leaving.

"And his interest in you?" Gina asked with a meaningfully arched brow.

"Purely a part of the past. It's over. You've won. I won't participate in the ruination of a wonderful man. He's all yours. Build your family on this very shaky foundation if you like. I'm out of it. You have nothing to fear from me. Now, if you'll excuse me, I have another appointment," Emma said as she stood to leave. She could no longer stand to be in Gina's company. Although the other woman had not signaled an end to their meeting, Emma decided to exercise her rights and quit the discussion and Gina's presence.

"Thank you for seeing me. I trust you'll honor your word. Just remember, if you feel tempted to renege, that mine is as good as yours. I will do as I've said without any reservation. Good-bye," Gina replied as she rose and tossed a ten-dollar bill on the table to cover their refreshments.

Gina brushed past Emma with her shoulders squared and her head high. Following her into the early-evening air, Emma felt incredible relief that their meeting had ended. She had feared that Gina would learn of her meeting with Jordan and was ready to face the consequences of meeting with an engaged man. However, she had not expected Gina to be so vicious or her retaliation to be so swift and complete.

Although she still cared deeply for Jordan, Emma knew that to see him ever again would mean professional ruin for him. She would make sure that she would never be alone with him. If she were very careful, she would never appear in public with him. She would avoid their familiar places as much as possible. Emma would not be the cause of Jordan's disgrace. She would not give Gina a reason to suspect that anything still existed between them. Regardless of the pain, Emma would stay away from the man she had planned to marry.

Fifteen

Emma hardly slept that night and for many nights thereafter. During the day, she was so busy that she hardly had time to think about Jordan and Gina. At night, however, the thoughts flowed freely, keeping her awake. Emma missed Jordan terribly and wanted to speak with him as both a lover and friend. She hated the thought of losing the man she loved to someone as mean and vile as Gina. Defeat in a fair competition would have been preferable to losing due to the threat of scandal.

Jordan phoned Emma's home and office many times since her meeting with Gina. He left long messages on her machine, begging her to go to dinner with him so that he could try to straighten out the mess that had interfered in their lives. She ignored each one of them and instructed her secretary to say that she was always too busy to speak.

To her surprise, Emma had managed to avoid Jordan at all social functions. She suddenly realized that they had few friends in common and really only shared a few political types. She simply declined invitations that did not please her and sent her staff to manage ticklish situations. Emma had quickly learned to protect herself from further embarrassment and heartbreak.

Emma worked every night until she was tired and then exercised until exhausted. She took long walks after dinner and lingered on the phone with Bonnie. Bonnie proved to be an even greater friend as she tried to distract Emma from thinking about her hurt feelings. Still the loneliness filled her heart and almost made her wish that she had never met Jordan.

But she could not regret opening her heart and life to him. Emma had known true happiness with Jordan. Despite the differences or maybe because of them, she had been content to think about spending the rest of her life with him. She knew that Jordan valued her professionalism and her ambition. He listened when she spoke and elicited her opinion out of concern and interest rather than expected behavior or habit. Emma could be her own person while still being a partner in Jordan's life.

Emma missed their long talks and Jordan's frank expression of his opinions. She felt as if she had lost more than just their physical bonding; she had lost their spiritual union. She felt as if she were half, not whole, now that Jordan had left her life. However, Emma knew that she would soon find a way to heal her hurt feelings again.

Emma learned through casual conversation with clients that Jordan and Gina frequented all the social functions and appeared on everyone's guest list. No one ever saw them apart. Many even wondered how Jordan managed to do any work with Gina tagging along everywhere. Most decided that Gina did not trust him to remain faithful and felt that she had to monitor his every move. Her clients said that Jordan looked embarrassed by Gina's constant attention although he appeared incapable of extricating himself from her.

Bonnie phoned more often than usual and appeared without notice in Emma's office more times than Emma could count. They had always held business meetings together, but they had seldom spent all of their time together. Since the breakup of her engagement, Bonnie visited so often that Emma even teased her friend about giving her a desk and an office.

"I just don't want you to feel lonely, that's all," Bonnie explained again as she sipped her coffee.

"I'm not lonely. I'm too busy and you're here too often for me to have any time alone. By the time I return home at night, I'm too tired to be lonely. Tell me the latest gossip and then go away. I have tons of work to do." Emma laughed as she pushed back her chair and gave Bonnie her full attention.

"Well, I heard that Senator Harris and his wife are getting a divorce," Bonnie began with gleeful enjoyment at having news to share. "She's planning to contact you later this week. She wants to host a 'coming out' party, as it were. She caught him 'coming out' and is taking him for every penny her attorney can extract from his wallet."

"That's too bad. They always looked so well matched. They even wore coordinated clothing and looked sort of like Mickey and Minnie Mouse." Emma chuckled at the image of the two joined at the hip who had now severed their ties.

Laughing, Bonnie replied, "They were too well coordinated. From what I hear, she found him wearing one of her outfits one day and assuming the female role in a sexual encounter of a very embarrassing kind. His marriage and career are over."

"That's sad. Don't you have any upbeat news?" Emma asked as she offered Bonnie another little sandwich.

"I heard a juicy tidbit, but I haven't been able to

substantiate the reliability of the information." Bonnie continued, "However, I heard that the Franklins are moving to California in November. He finally decided to relocate his business after much encouragement from her. Their son and his family live out there, I think."

"Good for them," Emma commented. "Gayle had been wanting to move for a long time. She'll be able to open that little boutique she's always wanted, too. Anything else?"

"Yes, one more tidbit. Jordan has accepted a position with a major New York law firm as a medical consultant. He'll leave his White House position at the end of the month, I think. I heard that he's moving to a very impressive condo in Manhattan. I guess Gina had a hand in that," Bonnie added as she studied Emma over the rim of her coffee cup.

"I can't say that I'm surprised," Emma replied calmly and without emotion. "She didn't say that she planned to move, but I'm not surprised that she'd do it. Considering that she wants Jordan all to herself, it seems like a logical move to me and a pretty good idea. They'll start over in a more neutral location and learn to rely on each other."

"Whatever," Bonnie responded at the interruption to her information flow. "They've RSVP'd that they'll attend my party this weekend. It's probably their last social function before the wedding and the return to New York. I feel so honored that she'll make an appearance at my little affair."

"I guess I'll just have to make the best of what could possibly be a very awkward situation. On the other hand, it might be interesting to watch Jordan as he tries to maneuver in a crowd with old eagle-eyed Gina at his side. He's always the diplomat and very good at negotiating his way around people. We'll see who wears the pants in his family. I wonder how long the leash is that she's given him to hang himself."

Laughing, Bonnie instructed, "Wear something especially provocative that night. I want him to know in no uncertain terms exactly what he lost."

"I'll do no such thing. I feel sorry for Jordan. He's trying to protect his career and live a normal life at the same time. It must be really tough on him to balance both. Gina's threats are not idle ones," Emma said sympathetically.

"Maybe not, but they've definitely lowered my opinion of him," Bonnie said as she walked toward the office door.

"Well, that shouldn't have happened," Emma commented as she pulled her chair closer to the desk in preparation for work. "He's trying to save face, reputation, and his son. Gina could ruin his whole life with one phone call. Jordan's paying a high price. I don't know if I could do the same for reputation, but I would do anything to protect a child from painful disclosures. How would you feel if you thought that your parents abandoned you because of your shortcomings? That's just terrible."

Shaking her head Bonnie replied, "My sister always told me that I was adopted although I'm older. I remember how awful that used to make me feel. I see what you're saying. Well, I'd better get going. Believe it or not, I do have a business to run and other clients to see. I'll call you later."

"Not too late. After a soak in a hot tub of water, I plan to turn in early," Emma replied as they waved good-bye.

Emma tried to return her attention to her work. Although she had said the right words about Jordan and Gina, she did not completely believe them. Part of her felt angry and betrayed by Jordan's actions, while at the same time intellectually she understood the reason for Jordan's behavior. Emotionally, Emma thought that he could and should have acted differently even though she could not think of what he could have done. Logically, she hoped that he was plotting a new strategy. In the short term, someone had to get hurt and she was the one. Emma hoped that Jordan was feeling the pain, too.

The last time she had seen him, Jordan had looked as miserably unhappy as she had felt. He had looked as if he had not slept in days. His face had been unshaved and his hair mussed. Fatigue lines had led from under his eyes midway down his cheeks. His clothes had looked as if he had worn them more than once and perhaps slept in them. Jordan had definitely not been the man who had pursued her to Las Vegas and introduced her to Maryland crabs.

Gina, on the other hand, seemed to thrive on the conflict she had caused. She looked more stunningly beautiful at the ice-cream shop than she had on the first day that they had met. Her carefully made-up complexion had glowed with more health than the sun-kissed untouched face that Emma had first seen in the park. Stress and upheaval certainly agreed with Gina.

Looking into the mirror in the office bathroom, Emma wondered if her face belied her careful composure. She did not want anyone to think that Jordan had broken her heart by choosing Gina over her. She wanted to look as if she did not have a care in the world, and as if she and the business were thriving. The reflection told her that the light touch of blush and lipstick had done wonders to camouflage any sign of unhappiness. She looked the part of a prosperous businesswoman.

Returning to her desk, Emma quickly scanned the

morning paper for the article Bonnie had mentioned.
Jordan's name had been featured in a front page article. He was the president's right-hand man and was
busy defending his stand on drugs, AIDS, and teenage
pregnancy. Small wonder Jordan was willing to pay
Gina's price to guarantee her silence. With so much
at stake, Emma might have done the same thing if
the situation had been reversed.

Shelving her emotions, Emma worked steadily as
the afternoon flowed into evening and then night.

One day seemed like the other as the business
flourished and Emma continued to put on a cheerful
face. By the end of the week, she had managed to
fool everyone all of the time and herself most of the
time. Long soaks in the tub, vigorous exercise, and
talks with Bonnie combined to make the incident with
Jordan fit into the overall patchwork of her life.

Dressing for Bonnie' bash, Emma realized that she
was happy. She missed Jordan, but she had her business and social life and her friends. She could think
of nothing else that would make her feel more complete. A husband would have been a nice addition to
her life but not the reason for it. Contrary to her
first thoughts when the relationship with Jordan
ended, Emma realized that she was complete within
herself. She did not need him to make her a whole
person. She had accomplished that by herself.

The evening was hot but not humid as Emma drove
to Bonnie's in her red convertible. On a whim, she
had traded her old car for a new one. She seldom
acted on impulse but a few months ago had felt the
need to make a change in her life. She had always
wanted this particular red convertible sports car, and
it had been the right time to buy it.

Pulling into one of the last parking spaces on the
block, Emma saw that Bonnie had placed lanterns

along the walkway that led to the massive front portico. The crystal chandelier sparkled at the dining room window. The highly polished floors glistened throughout the house. Wait staff from EJ's slipped unnoticed among the guests as they served cocktails, wine, stronger beverages, and tiny sandwiches while a jazz ensemble played on the sun porch. The best Scotch and Kentucky bourbons flowed at the open bar in the living room where Bonnie glistened as brightly as the candles that lined the mantel. She was dressed in a gold lamé, form-fitting evening gown with Steve standing proudly beside her.

Before visiting the kitchen staff, Emma greeted Bonnie and Steve with a kiss and compliments on the glory of their home. She knew that she really did not need to check her chefs, but she always did. Emma liked to let them know that she was available to help if they needed her assistance. After all, Emma possessed a certificate from a noted culinary school, too, and had been known to cover her evening gown with an apron when an assistant did not arrive punctually. She always did whatever she needed to do to make her clients comfortable and their affairs a success.

As always when she had unattached guests, Bonnie had paired Emma with an eligible gentleman for dinner. As Emma entered the dining room, she found herself seated next to a prominent businessman from Richmond. He owned a renowned glass blowing company that produced stained-glass windows and decorative but utilitarian pieces. As an entrepreneur, Frank Masterson understood the importance of giving one hundred percent to the company. He was a confirmed bachelor whose first and only love was his work. He had been chased unmercifully by many women but had managed to escape the long march down the aisle.

However, Emma in her soft pink spaghetti-strap evening gown looked very alluring to him. Frank found himself bewitched immediately by her wit, her business acumen, and her beauty. He hardly noticed anyone else at the table. Emma was the kind of woman that he found fascinating. She was independent, self-employed, career-minded, personable, witty, charming, and beautiful.

Emma would have felt flattered and been overwhelmed by the attention if it had not been for Jordan who sat at the opposite end of the grand table. She could feel his eyes burning into her as he tried to pay attention to his meal and Gina's constant chatter. He was so obviously jealous of the attention from Frank that Emma almost felt as if she were committing a sin by smiling at Frank's jokes.

From her position at the table, Emma could hear Gina's happy laughter and her cute remarks to the gentleman at her side. The poor man did not know whether to be flattered or disgusted by her constant touching of his arm and her rapt attention to his words. Emma watched as he finally resigned himself to Gina's devotion and began to enjoy the treatment. Gina could be most attractive and engaging when she set her mind to the task. That night, the man at her side was her victim.

With Gina occupied with the other guest, Jordan was free to watch Emma. He noted that she looked lovelier than ever. Her hair shone with the reflected radiance of the chandeliers. Her skin glowed a healthy tone from not only the expert application of her makeup but from contentment. Her laughter was free and easy. Emma certainly appeared happy and healthy.

Jordan felt old and quite melancholy at the sight of her. Emma was the embodiment of the life he had thought to lead before Gina had appeared and changed everything. Emma was joy and happiness and laughter; whereas Gina was sadness and threats and blackmail. Watching her, Jordan mourned for the life he could have lived and vowed to free himself from his prison if he could.

Emma saw the look of quiet desperation on Jordan's face and pitied him. He was a man of power and connection, but he was not able to free himself from the bonds that Gina's threats had placed on him. He would never experience happiness until he stopped placing his public face before his private life. Unfortunately, no one could teach him that lesson. Jordan had to learn the source of his happiness for himself. Until he did, Emma knew that he would not be an asset to her life.

As much as she hated to admit it, Jordan's inability to handle the situation Gina created showed a new and unpleasant side of his personality that Emma had not expected to see. She had thought that this man of power who stood on the right hand of the president was as strong and determined in his personal life as in his professional one. However, Emma had been mistaken. Jordan had proven that he was incapable of taking control of the situation and solving the dilemma that Gina's threat had caused. At first Emma had thought that Jordan's desire to protect his reputation was admirable but misdirected. Now, seeing his discomfort, she found his choice a sign of weakness and was relieved no longer to be associated with him.

Although Emma still loved Jordan, she knew that he would not be the man she needed in her life as long as he could not solve the problems in his. She

had read about passive-aggressive personalities and
wondered if Jordan was one of those types. If he was,
eventually he would snap and make a change in his
life. However, the passive side might remain dominant
for years, forcing him to be under Gina's control in-
definitely. The longer he stayed in her power, the less
likely his return to Emma. Emma's interest in having
him return had also dwindled as the days had passed.
If he did not make a move soon, their former relationship would not be salvageable.

That kind of frightened, passive, wishy-washy man
Emma did not want in her life. She was a take-charge
kind of woman, and she wanted a man who was her
equal. She had thought that Jordan was that man.
Now she was not so sure. Whether he stayed with Gina
out of fear for public humiliation or concern for his
son, Jordan had shown his Achilles heel.

Listening to Frank Masterson babbling merrily
about his business, Emma wondered about Jordan's
son and the kind of home life he would have with a
controlling mother and a passive, pliable father. She
understood the need to protect him from the press
and public scrutiny. Many political powerhouses had
kept their children hidden from the probing eye of
the camera. However, Jordan only had to resign his
position to become a private person again. He was
not an elected official. The public would only mar-
ginally care about the tribulations of the former adviser to the president. Many politicians who thought
themselves indispensable had vanished from public
view and memory before the vapor trail from their
cars had filtered through the thick Washington, D.C.,
summer smog.

As Frank continued to probe for the specifics of
Emma's life and to share his own, Emma found that
the evening had lengthened and turned to night. The

chandeliers that had originally added atmosphere to the dining room now provided a golden glow as the guests finished the baked Alaska and sipped liqueur. Needing to refresh her makeup, Emma excused herself as soon as the wait staff began to clear the dessert dishes from the table.

Emma had enjoyed listening to Frank in a detached, safe way. She had learned quite a bit from him about his approach to business management and made arrangements to cater his next social event as well as all of his company functions for the next year. The evening had been profitable professionally and even promised a social element if she could only put Jordan on the back burner of her heart.

Stepping into the now-cool night air, Emma was impressed with the work that Bonnie had done in the garden. A few years ago, Bonnie had hired the top interior decorator in Washington to make her home a showpiece. He had worked wonders by knocking down walls and combining small rooms into large ones. However, saying that she would not entertain in the yard, Bonnie had not made the same effort outside. Although the grass and shrubs were always manicured, until this summer, the yard had possessed a less-than-desirable appearance.

Now, however, lantern lights fluttered along flower-lined walks that led to the center of the yard and the gazebo. Evening-blooming tropical flowers added their sweet perfume to the fragrance of the flickering candles and the roses. Small white lights twinkled in the trees like thousands of fireflies. The grounds as well as the house provided the guests with a magical setting to a perfect evening.

Strolling the walk, Emma did not notice that she was not alone in the night. Unexpectedly, Jordan ap-

peared at her side. The anguish in his face forced
Emma to stop and listen.

"I was hoping to catch you alone. Frank Masterson
had monopolized you at dinner. I was afraid he'd do
the same for the rest of the evening," Jordan began
as he matched his steps to Emma's.

"As a matter of fact, so did I. But I managed to
put a little space between us. The old powder-my-nose
excuse always works. I always have to be sure that I
don't alienate prospective clients," Emma replied with
a chuckle. "Where's Gina? Isn't she joining you for a
stroll through Bonnie's fabulous garden?"

"No, she's inside bending the ear of a senator. I
saw you leave the house and decided to join you. I
need to talk with you for a few minutes," Jordan replied as he guided Emma toward the gazebo.

"What about? We don't really have anything to discuss as far as I'm concerned," Emma stated as she
lingered among the heliotrope.

"I need for you to understand all of this. I still love
you, you know," Jordan blurted in great distress that
the conversation was not following the route he had
planned.

"That's of little consequence to me," Emma replied
sharply. "You're planning to marry another woman
in a few weeks. From where I stand, our book is
closed."

"Not if you let me reopen it," Jordan said as he
stepped closer.

Looking him directly in the eyes, Emma saw all the
pain that Jordan suffered spread out for her inspection. She wanted to help him, but she could not. He
had to tackle this set of problems that Gina had created. He needed to take control of the situation that
he allowed to continue. His problems were outside
the realm of her control.

Summoning her strength, Emma replied firmly, "No."

As she walked into the house, Emma could feel Jordan's eyes burning into her back. She felt anger and pain mixed in an almost intolerable combination. She wanted to be with him, but she knew that she would not. Emma needed for Jordan to free himself before he came to her. Any other arrangement was impossible.

For the remainder of the evening, Emma kept as far away from Jordan as possible. If he entered a room, she left it. If he joined a group in conversation, she excused herself from it. She would not give Gina the opportunity to say that she and Jordan were plotting something behind her back.

Finally, finding comfort in the kitchen, she checked on her staff. The kitchen sparkled as if new. The staff had cleaned up so perfectly that not even a crumb remained of the wonderful meal. Emma thanked them for their hard work as she gave the room the final white-glove check. Not even Bonnie, a woman who kept an immaculate house, would find anything out of place when they left.

Seeing that they had the cleanup effort well in hand, Emma returned to the garden where she was promptly cornered by Frank Masterson. After listening for as long as she could to his stories of fishing on the Bay, Emma excused herself and returned to the house. She was too tired either to force a smile to her lips or pretend interest in his conversation.

Emma drifted from one group to another for a while, but when the grandfather clock in the hall chimed midnight, Emma thanked Bonnie and Steve for the delightful evening and drove home.

The next morning, flowers arrived from both Jordan and Frank. Placing Frank's bouquet of long-stemmed yellow roses in the dining room and Jordan's vase of dendrobium orchids in the living room, Emma slipped into dressy slacks and went shopping. Although she felt quite flattered and wanted to share her news with Bonnie, she did not linger to make the call. The day looked too inviting to spend it on the phone.

As usual, the mall was crowded, but Emma did not mind. She tried on dresses that she had no interest in purchasing, simply to pass the time. All the while, thoughts of Jordan kept creeping into her mind.

Occasionally, she thought about Frank and wondered if she should pursue a relationship with him. He was definitely interested in her and very entertaining company. He was successful and easygoing. However, he was not Jordan. Until she could push Jordan to the recesses of her mind, she could not think seriously of another man.

Although Emma knew that she had made the right decision by not listening to Jordan, she still wanted him in her life. With each dress she tried on, Emma found herself wondering if Jordan would approve. Finally, she gave in to the melancholy that had settled on her spirits and drove home. She could be unhappy in the peace and quiet there. She would spend the remainder of the evening alone with her memories of the days with Jordan.

Sixteen

Jordan wanted closure on every element of his life with Gina. Now that the story would appear in the *Post* and would be on every radio station in the city, he needed to close that chapter with her personally. Even if Emma never forgave him, he needed to put Gina out of his life forever.

He stopped at Gina's condo after his visit with the *Washington Post* reporter. He wanted to tie up all loose ends before asking Emma to forgive him. He had to be rid of all the unpleasant baggage before he could come to her again.

Jordan rang the doorbell for several minutes before Gina finally appeared. Opening the door, she looked the part of a prosperous Washington business-woman in apple-red silk slacks and a matching blouse. A rope of diamond and gold sparkled at her neck. Matching earrings glittered at her ears. On her feet, she wore gold slippers with a multicolored rhinestone buckle.

As she opened the door and motioned toward the living room, Jordan noticed that Gina appeared a little intoxicated. Her speech was a little thick and her step a little halting when she joined him on the sofa. On the coffee table sat an untouched glass of Scotch on the rocks. He wondered at the number that had preceded it.

Turning toward her, Jordan noticed that Gina's eyes sparkled with unusual light. Her lips were tight and drawn. Her hands shook noticeably when she reached for the glass. Her makeup looked freshly touched up. Her carefully coifed hair had the appearance of dishevelment that had been tidied but not redone. Something about the way she looked reminded Jordan of their marriage and the days that he had returned home early to find Gina recovering from a day of drunkenness.

"Drink?" Gina offered as she raised her own to her lips.

"No, thanks. I don't plan to stay long," Jordan replied as he moved a little farther away from Gina.

"I didn't expect to see you until tonight for dinner," Gina pointed out as she pressed the cool glass to her temples. Despite the chilly temperature in the room, her forehead had a light sheen of perspiration. "Why are you here, and why didn't you call first? You know that I'm not always here this time of the afternoon."

"I just came from a visit to the *Washington Post,*" Jordan began as he watched her carefully composed face for any change in expression. "You see, I'm not going through with the marriage. I've resigned my position with the president and told my whole story to the press."

"You're lying," Gina responded calmly behind eyes that blazed despite her composure.

"No, I'm not. I couldn't live with the threat of blackmail hanging over my head all the time. It's over between us. The marriage is over. This sham of a life is over. I'm free of you," Jordan replied with a slight triumphant smile playing at the corners of his lips.

Gina's anger was swift and immediate, causing the huge gold-and-white room to appear too small. The walls seemed to close around her and radiate her fury like the glow of an angry ember. If she had been one to resort to physical violence, Jordan would have been afraid for his life. However, knowing that Gina believed that the power of the press was mightier than the sword, Jordan did not worry about his safety. Instead, he wondered about her reaction and tried to read her raveling composure.

"You can't mean it," Gina sputtered as she returned the drink to the table. She placed it down so hard that Scotch splashed onto a nearby magazine.

"But I do. It's over. You can't do anything to hurt me ever again. I'm going to beg Emma to take me back. That's how over we are," Jordan replied calmly as she continued to glare at him.

"What about your son?" Gina asked as she tried to manipulate Jordan into changing his mind. "You made all that noise about the boy and wanting to do the right thing by him and now you're calling it quits. I can't believe you. You're lying."

"He's a nice kid, but he's not my son," Jordan stated without emotion.

"Yes, he is! The blood test proved it," Gina insisted emphatically.

"The blood test only proved that I might be among the possible candidates for fatherhood. I drew an extra vial and took a hair sample. I didn't tell you, but I had a DNA cross-check done on both. The boy's not my son. We're the same blood type, but that's all. I have no reason to stay with you," Jordan responded. From the tone he used, he could have been instructing a classroom filled with eager students.

"That's a lie. You didn't run a test on the boy.

Don't push me too far, Jordan, or I'll . . ." Gina began with a menacing tone in her voice.

"You'll do what? I've already told the newspaper everything. I told the reporter about your drinking and drug use, the blackmail surrounding a boy who isn't mine, your threats of disclosure, and the facts of my college-age drug experience. It's all public knowledge now. The interview will appear in the paper in a couple of days. I've given him a copy of the test results and here's another for you. I've defeated you, Gina, and I'm a free man," Jordan replied as he rose to leave, waving the envelope.

"I still don't believe you about the boy or the interview." Gina grimaced drunkenly as her anger began to abate only to be replaced by an almost desperate tone of voice. "You'll have to prove both to me."

"Here's your copy," Jordan responded as he tossed an envelope onto her lap. "That's the DNA report. I don't know who that boy is, but he isn't my son. You'll have to wait for part two until tomorrow."

For several long minutes, Gina stared at the enclosed sheet of paper on the letterhead of a well-reputed lab. As Jordan loomed over her, Gina slowly dissolved into a sobbing mass. For the first time, her confidence disappeared as the makeup washed from her face.

Regaining her composure, Gina commented, "Well, I guess you would have found out eventually. I knew that you'd take additional steps, but I thought you'd wait until after the marriage."

Taking the paper from her outstretched hand, Jordan asked, "Whose son is he?"

"Don't worry," Gina replied as she wiped the last tear from her lashes. "You don't know the father. You didn't move in that circle. If I remember correctly, you called all of them 'fast.' "

"Do you plan to leave him in that boarding school even now?" Jordan asked as he inched toward the door. He had had enough of Gina's ways to last a lifetime and had been anxious to leave her apartment.

"The funny thing is that he isn't even mine," Gina confessed with a short laugh. "I borrowed him. The boy's the son of a friend of mine. I paid the school for him to stay there for a week while I carried out this little charade. He had a great time in their camp. He's back home now on his family's estate in McLean. So you see, he isn't a little unloved boy after all. He's actually a rather accomplished little actor, don't you think? I don't like children, Jordan, and always practice safe sex. I've never even had a close call."

"Good. Then no one gets hurt by my leaving and confession. Why did you go to all this trouble, Gina?" Jordan commented as he gazed at Gina's evil face.

"Oh, well, I tried to get you back, Jordan," Gina replied as she made a move to stand but fell back into the seat. "I wanted your position, connections, and power. I've always enjoyed being with influential men. Now that you're a well-recognized man and a bit of a celebrity, I thought it might be nice to have a piece of it. I wanted to dine with the political upper crust. I've always envied power. I have lots of wealth— my father saw to that—but I have no power. I wanted to be among the important people of this country. I guess it just didn't work."

Looking at her with disgust, Jordan said, "You're a sick woman, Gina. You've tried to destroy me and my relationship with a wonderful woman for your own greedy purposes."

"I would have done anything to get what I want," Gina confessed with a shrug. "You should have re-

membered that from our first marriage. I'm actually
surprised that you fell for my little charade. A man
of your accomplishments should have seen through
my game. You always thought that you were so much
above everyone else. I must have touched your male
vanity. Don't all men want to think that they've fa-
thered a son who'll walk in their footsteps one day?
The addition of a child was a touch of genius, I must
admit."

"You're right," Jordan snorted angrily. "I should
have seen through you and not turned my back on
Emma. Maybe you're right. Maybe it was my vanity
that you touched. I don't know. I had to do something for the boy in case he was mine, but I see that
I made a terrible mistake."

"Well, he isn't, and he never could have been."
Gina smiled. "If you remember back to that time in
our lives, I was sleeping with Todd Morgan of the
pharmaceutical Morgans at the time. We weren't ever
together often enough to produce a child. Your vanity
led you to believe me. I fooled the wonderful and
talented Jordan Everett."

Red-faced and tight-lipped, Jordan snarled, "That's
enough, Gina. You got the upper hand for a while,
but I'll recover just fine."

"I don't doubt that you'll recover professionally, but
I'm concerned about your social life. Will Emma forgive you, or have you destroyed all possibility of re-
covery?" Gina asked with feigned concern.

"That's between us, Gina, and isn't any of your business," Jordan replied angrily as he regained his composure. "Actually, you've taught me many valuable
lessons about myself and my dealings with others. I
suppose I should thank you, but I'll leave instead.
This time, Gina, there's nothing you can do or say to
stop me."

Her venom flowing, Gina cried, "You're not worth the effort, Jordan. You're just one of many fish in a very large sea. I'll just have to bait my hook with my inheritance and my looks and catch another. I hope you and Emma will be very happy. That is, if you can heal the wound inflicted by another woman. What I've done to you, you can restore. No great loss. The political and financial worlds like a little intrigue. But what I've done to her, you'll have a difficult time undoing."

"I know," Jordan replied as he stood in the massive foyer, "but I'll spend my lifetime trying."

Jordan left the apartment knowing that he had closed an unfortunate chapter in his life. He had allowed someone to take advantage of him by playing on his weaknesses. Never again would that happen to him.

His main task now lay in convincing Emma to forgive him. As Jordan drove down the street, he thought of all the words he would say and all the actions he would take to win Emma's heart. Regardless of the complexity of the scenarios that played out in his mind, Jordan did not feel his usual confidence. He had won the trust of political and business leaders without giving the process much thought. Now that he wanted to succeed more than anything in this new and more difficult endeavor, Jordan wondered if his negotiating skills would stand him in good stead. He would have to wait and see. His life and happiness lay in Emma's hands.

Seventeen

Jordan called, not just once but repeatedly that evening and into the next day. When Emma would not return his calls, he stopped by EJ's to see her. He waited more than an hour for a few minutes of her time—without getting to see her—before giving up and returning to work.

Thinking that he might be more successful at her house, Jordan rang the doorbell that evening, and for the next few, until he feared that someone would call the police and report him for loitering. In the cover of darkness, he parked in front of her house in the hopes of catching a glimpse of her. He sent her every variety of flower that the most renowned florist in Washington carried in his shop. Finally, he gave up. Rather than being able to talk with Emma personally, he would have to allow the article in the *Washington Post* to speak for him.

The morning that the article appeared on the front page of the paper, Emma slept late. Awakened by the persistent jingling of the phone, she reached across the expanse of the bed. Leaning on her elbow and rubbing the sleep from her eyes, Emma listened as Bonnie excitedly read the report to her.

"I can't believe you're not out of bed yet," Bonnie seemed to blast into Emma's still-sleep-filled ear. "It's a wonderful day and the newspaper contains a must-read article. It's about Jordan. Listen, I'll read it to you, and you can check it out later. No, reading will take too long. I'll just tell you about it. Are you listening?"

"I'm listening. What's so important that you'd disturb the best sleep I've had in weeks?" Emma replied as she yawned and stretched simultaneously.

"Jordan has resigned—that's what's so important. Effective immediately, he's no longer the president's man on teen drug and alcohol abuse." Bonnie paraphrased the article.

"What brought that on? I'll bet that Gina's angry. Now she has nothing to hold over his head. Does it say why he resigned?" Emma asked, suddenly awake and very interested.

Bonnie replied, "It says here that Jordan resigned his position for personal reasons. Let's see."

"He really is cutting his cord with Washington," Emma exclaimed, sitting up and swinging her long, lean legs over the side of the bed.

"Not only that," Bonnie summarized with glee, "but he confessed to having used drugs while an undergraduate and in medical school. He's stepping aside so that someone who can be a true role model for the youth of today can assume this very important advisory position."

"Wow!"

"He's done it, Emma." Bonnie breathed in disbelief. "He's put his personal life ahead of his professional. He finally did it. Even though he took his sweet time doing it, Jordan has risked everything he has worked so hard to acquire."

"Is there any mention of Gina?" Emma asked as she quickly slipped her feet into slippers and eased her arms into her robe.

"Wait a minute. You're suddenly in a hurry to know everything," Bonnie scolded. "Let's see. Yes, here in the last paragraph it says that Jordan has also ended his engagement to Gina so that he might concentrate on a prior relationship. Well, well, well . . . Do you suppose that this is what Jordan wanted to tell you this week? It certainly looks as if he had rather important news to share with you. He probably wanted you to know before his business appeared in the paper."

Conceding the point, Emma replied, "Maybe that's what he had in mind. We'll have to wait and see. If this is what he wanted, he'll contact me pretty soon. If it isn't, oh well. At any rate, now that I'm up, I'm going to the shop to check on the arrangement for Senator Jasper's party tonight."

"You're not going to call him? The man has just thrown off everything and you're not going to make the next move?" Bonnie commented incredulously.

"That's right," Emma stated firmly. "For all I know, that 'prior relationship' could have been with any number of women since he divorced Gina. Until I hear from Jordan, it's business as usual for me."

"All right. If that's the way you want to play it, it's fine with me. However, if my man had made the kind of move that Jordan has, I'd phone him," Bonnie stated with determination.

"No, you don't. Not this time, Bonnie. I won't change my mind on this. I'm following my gut all the way," Emma replied as she ran the water in the shower until the steam filled her bathroom. "This is where I'm glad we're different, and we'll just have to agree to disagree. I'm not calling Jordan now or at any other time. He's the one who made the mess of our lives, and he's the one who has to make the repair. He's knows where to find me. He has left enough phone messages and flowers to show that he has forgotten neither my number nor my address. Jordan has even sent electronic cards begging forgiveness. It's on him to make the next move."

"I certainly hope you're not making a mistake," Bonnie commented firmly.

"Me, too. If I am, it'll be the worst one of my life," Emma answered as she hung up the phone.

The steam penetrated every pore and helped to clear her head of the confusion that lingered from her talk with Bonnie. Emma knew that, right or wrong, she had made the right decision. At least it was the right one for her. Emma had learned long ago that the only person to whom she was accountable was herself. If what she did felt right to her, then she was content. She had given up trying to please people, knowing that she only made herself unhappy in the process.

Listening to the radio while driving to EJ's, Emma heard the newscaster retelling the front-page story about Jordan's separation from the government. Although she had finally read the paper over a hurried meal, the news seemed almost surreal as the calm voice spoke of an event that had shaken the lives of people she knew. She could only imagine the anguish Jordan must be feeling and the struggle he must have endured in order to come to that decision. Although she wished that Jordan had come to this decision sooner, Emma appreciated his courage in having made it.

The phone rang as soon as she entered EJ's. Friends from all over the city called to comment on Jordan's actions and to speculate as to what they might mean to his life with Emma. Not having heard from Jordan, Emma gave the only answer she had.

Finding that all of the preparations for the eve-

ning's festivities were in order, Emma left her staff to
finish their work.

As she entered her office, Emma let out an excla-
mation of surprise when she saw a man standing at
the window with the sun flooding his face. His back
was turned to her, but Emma could tell from the
straight carriage of the shoulders and the slight pro-
trusion of the ears that it was Jordan.

"I hope I didn't startle you too badly," Jordan said
as he turned toward her.

"No, I'm used to finding men in my office even
during nonbusiness hours. Of course you startled me,
but it's still a pleasure to see you," Emma replied as
she flicked on the light and walked toward her desk.

"Have you listened to the news this morning?" Jordan asked as he crossed to sit in the wing chair beside
her desk.

"Yes, I have," Emma responded with a touch of
nervousness at being alone with Jordan again. "Bonnie called early this morning and told me about the
story. I'm sorry to hear about your departure from
the government. You really loved the job with the
president."

"But I love you more," Jordan stated without even
the slightest hesitation.

"I hope you didn't resign your position on my account. That's something that you had to decide without thinking of anyone else. You needed to make that
kind of decision only if it was right for you," Emma
pointed out as she struggled with her feelings about
his declaration of love.

"I decided to resign because I could not live my
life under the microscope any longer," Jordan replied
in a matter-of-fact tone. "I have skeletons in my closet
just like anyone else. Gina threatened to expose them
and make them seem larger than they were. I should

have disclosed them honestly from the start, but I didn't. I couldn't continue to live with the fear of disclosure hanging over my head. Gina would have ruined me if I hadn't spoken out. It took me a while, but I discovered that Gina had reached a new level in ruthlessness that none of my sacrifices could abate. At any rate, I've resigned and cleared the air. Gina can't touch me now."

"I'm happy to hear that you're content with your decision," Emma commented as she leaned back in her chair. She could feel the tension easing from her body as she listened to Jordan's explanation.

"I wouldn't say that I'm content," Jordan responded with a snort and shake of his head. "I would have preferred a different ending to my career in politics, but I didn't have a choice in the matter. Gina's behavior left me no alternative but to resign. By not disclosing my former fairly innocent drug experimentation, I had already jeopardized my standing as an antidrug and alcohol expert. If I had long ago disclosed my use of drugs, I could have built a different platform. As it is, I constructed mine on never having used illicit drugs, which was not true. Experimentation is usage regardless of the short-lived nature of the experience. Anyway, it's done now."

"What will you do now?" Emma inquired with genuine curiosity.

"I've already received calls from several headhunters representing firms in the area and elsewhere," Jordan replied without arrogance and with more than a little surprise. "They've offered fabulous contracts and lucrative partnerships. I only need to stick out my hand and pick the best opportunity."

"That's great. It's good to realize that one's work is appreciated," Emma commented with a smile for her dear friend.

"I think I'll take a little time off before I decide on anything permanent," Jordan declared as he stretched his long legs and relaxed into the chair. Their meeting was going well, and he was feeling comfortable with Emma.

"After all of this, you probably need a break," Emma added as she watched him relax in her office.

"You're right," Jordan replied with a smile as he locked his fingers behind his head. "I haven't had any free time since I started this job. I need some time to relax. I was thinking of maybe traveling a little. Maybe going to exotic countries or visiting cities in this country that I've never seen. There's no limit to the places I could go and the people I could meet."

"I seem to remember that when you did steal a little time off it was interrupted by phone calls from the White House." Emma chuckled at the memory of their dinner at Jordan's house on the Bay. "It would be good for you to get away for a while. Have a little time to yourself."

"I was thinking of asking you to go with me," Jordan stated while looking Emma directly in the eye. "Maybe make it that honeymoon trip that we postponed."

Hesitating, Emma replied, "I don't know, Jordan. A lot has happened since you broke our engagement."

"I know. I'm not asking you to forgive or forget anything that has happened between us," Jordan stated honestly. "I'm only asking that you remember the way we felt about each other . . . the way we still feel. . . . That's all I ask."

"It's hard to put aside the hurt feelings, Jordan," Emma responded without rancor. She wanted to believe that Jordan had only their best interest at heart, but she remembered all too well the impact Gina's conniving had had on their lives.

"I know I was wrong, but I couldn't think of any other way to handle the situation quickly and without publicity. I didn't mean to hurt you. I was only trying to protect us," Jordan pleaded with sincerity.

"You were protecting yourself and your reputation, you mean," Emma stated with sadness. "I would have stood by you through all of this sordid business if you'd only given me the chance. There's nothing you could have disclosed that would have driven me away from you. I wouldn't have turned my back on you, Jordan, but you didn't give me the opportunity to prove it. You took the easy way out by giving in to Gina's demands rather than facing her and them. You copped out rather than confessing your questionable behavior. I would have understood. So would all of your friends, but you didn't give any of us the chance to prove it to you. You judged us with the same swift sword that you expected the press to use against you. That hurt, and it wasn't right, Jordan."

"You're right," Jordan admitted sadly. "I didn't give you or any of my friends a chance to prove their loyalty and love. But if you think that giving in to Gina was easy, you're wrong. It might have looked like the easy route, but it was very painful and marked by constant threats of blackmail and disclosure. I needed to buy some time to think of an escape. That was the only way that looked open to me. I could be with Gina and she wouldn't talk behind my back. The easy and honorable thing for me to have done would have been to come forward when she first threatened to tell all. I would have taken a few knocks from the press and resigned. I wouldn't have hurt us that way."

For a while Jordan only sat and thought. He could see the pain on Emma's face and hear it in her voice.

He had acknowledged his wrongdoing and wanted her at his side, but he knew that the decision lay with Emma. Jordan only hoped that she could find a way to forgive him and welcome him into her life again. He had done the worst thing any man possibly could have done; he had left Emma for another woman. Jordan knew that even his honest intentions could not stop the wounding of her heart. He now hoped that Emma loved him enough to push aside her pain and look to their future.

Emma, too, sat without speaking. It seemed to her that they had said everything that remained to be said between them. Jordan had accepted the responsibility for his past deeds and his present mistakes. He had said that he loved her and wanted her in his life. She needed to sort out her feelings and make a decision.

Taking a calming breath, Emma spoke softly. "I need some time to decide how I feel, Jordan. I know that I still love you, but I don't know if that's enough after all of this. I'm sure you understand."

"I do, and I'm sure that I'd have the same reaction if the tables were turned," Jordan replied as he pulled a long white envelope from his jacket pocket. "Here's where you can reach me at any time, day or night. My bags are in my car. I'm going to my house on the Bay first, and then . . ."

"Thank you," Emma said as he laid the envelope on her desk and walked toward the door.

"Good-bye, Emma. I love you and want you in my life, but I'll understand if you can't see your way clear to welcome me back," Jordan stated as he left the office, taking the warmth with him.

Emma sat in silence for what felt like ages. Slowly, she reached for the envelope and opened it. Inside was not only a carefully typed sheaf of paper containing a detailed itinerary, but also a ticket. Reading the

fine print closely, Emma saw that Jordan had purchased a ticket for her to accompany him on his trip
to Paris, France, and onward to Barcelona, Spain. Jordan had made the arrangements for the honeymoon
trip they had planned to take and Gina had spoiled.

Suddenly, everything came clear. Emma wanted Jordan in her life again as much as he wanted her in
his. She knew that she would never forget the way he
had acted, but somehow it did not matter anymore.
She understood his motives as well as she could and
found that she could comprehend his reactions to the
situations that Gina created.

Emma wanted to be with Jordan more than she had
ever craved the acceptance of her peers. She wanted
him in her life. She had spent all the evenings alone
that she intended to spend. She wanted someone to
share her happiness and success, her sadness and fail-
ures, her joys and frustrations, and her bad and good
moods.

She wanted to feel joy and rapture. Emma needed
to be with a man who could lift her up and make
her sing. She had dated many other men, but none
of them had been able to give her the total happiness
that she had felt with Jordan. The bottom line was
that Jordan made her happy and quiet inside. She
wanted him and that feeling again.

Emma grabbed her purse and stuffed the tickets
inside. Quickly, she phoned Bonnie and left a message on her answering machine. Then, she scribbled
a hasty note on the itinerary and tossed it on her
secretary's desk. As she pulled her door closed, Emma
chuckled at her new sense of power. She was doing
something for herself that felt wonderful and very
right.

Emma waved as she passed the massive kitchen
and the busy chefs. For the first time since opening

EJ's, Emma was doing something that was completely for herself. She was thinking of her own personal well-being rather than the health of her business. Right or wrong, she was putting her life ahead of her business.

COMING IN AUGUST 2001 FROM
ARABESQUE ROMANCES

__SURRENDER
by Brenda Jackson   1-58314-145-6 $5.99US/$7.99CAN

After moving from army base to army base as a child, Nettie Brooms is determined to secure a stable life—and never get involved with a military man. Then she meets Ashton Sinclair, a handsome Colonel in the U.S. Marines, intent on capturing her heart. Now, a man she swore she would avoid is igniting an irresistible passion inside her.

__FLIRTING WITH DANGER
by Kayla Perrin   1-58314-188-X $5.99US/$7.99CAN

Khamil is intrigued by Monique's chilly indifference to him. But when the high-profile attorney discovers the pain that lies beneath her coolness, he's the one who melts. Now he has vowed to help her as she digs into dangerous, long-buried secrets. He knows that once her tragic past is laid to rest, she will give him her heart.

__NOTHING BUT THE TRUTH
by Roberta Gayle   1-58314-209-6 $5.99US/$7.99CAN

Brant has only agreed to work with Kate to stop her from destroying an innocent man. Never has he met a woman so pushy—or sexy. The more time he spends with her, the more he wants to stop their heated arguments with a kiss. Each day, Brant and Kate's trust in each other grows . . .

__SACRED LOVE
by Shelby Lewis   1-58314-210-X $5.99US/$7.99CAN

When Great-uncle Fred invites Bailey Walker and her husband Sam to his beautiful estate in San Francisco, she can't wait to see the sweet old man. But the visit becomes a nightmare when the aging tycoon is found murdered in his bathtub, and Bailey is the prime suspect . . .

Call toll free **1-888-345-BOOK** to order by phone or use this coupon to order by mail. ALL BOOKS AVAILABLE AUGUST 1, 2001.

Name_____

Address _____

City_____ State _____ Zip _____

Please send me the books that I have checked above.

I am enclosing $_____

Plus postage and handling* $_____

Sales tax (in NY, TN, and DC) $_____

Total amount enclosed $_____

*Add $2.50 for the first book and $.50 for each additional book.

Send check or money order (no cash or CODs) to: **Arabesque Romances, Dept. C.O., 850 Third Avenue, 16th Floor, New York, NY 10022**

Prices and numbers subject to change without notice. Valid only in the U.S. All orders subject to availability. **NO ADVANCE ORDERS.**

Visit our website at **www.arabesquebooks.com**.

More Sizzling Romance by
Gwynne Forster

CAPTIVATING ROMANCE
BY *BRENDA JACKSON*

ONE SPECIAL MOMENT
0-7860-0546-7 $4.99US/$6.50CAN

To help her brother's company, Virginia Wingate must convince superstar Sterling Hamilton to endorse their products. Instantly smitten with the beauty, Sterling now must prove his intentions are for real and that he will cherish and love her . . . forever.

TONIGHT AND FOREVER
0-7860-0172-0 $4.99US/$6.50CAN

Returning to her roots in Texas, Loren Jacobs never expected to meet handsome widower Justin Madaris . . . or to succumb to her passion. But they both must fight through painful memories to fulfill all the promises of tomorrow . . .

WHISPERED PROMISES
1-58314-021-2 $5.99US/$7.99CAN

When Dex Madaris is reunited with his ex-wife Caitlin, he not only discovers a daughter he never knew he had but also learns that no heartache, no betrayal, is so strong as to withstand the enduring power of true love.

ETERNALLY YOURS
0-7860-0455-X $4.99US/$6.50CAN

Syneda Walters and Clayton Madaris are just friends—the last two people likely to end up as lovers—but things heat up when Syneda accepts Clayton's invitation to join him for a vacation. He must get her to trust him by convincing her that she will be eternally his.

USE COUPON ON NEXT PAGE TO ORDER THESE BOOKS